A ROSE AMONG THORNS
BELOW THE SALT
BOOK TWO

ELIZABETH ROSE

OLIVERHEBERBOOKS

Published by Oliver-Heber Books

0 9 8 7 6 5 4 3 2 1

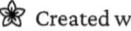 Created with Vellum

CHAPTER I
BLAKE CASTLE, ENGLAND, 1374

Lord Rook Blake awoke and turned over in bed to find the maidservant he'd spent the night with already dressed.

"Leaving so soon?" he asked, his voice deep and groggy.

"I'm late for my kitchen duties, my lord," said the girl, pulling her gown over her head. "I must hurry."

"Don't worry about that. You're with me. Now, come back here." Rook patted the mattress and waited. By rights, the girl was a servant and needed to obey his commands. Still, he could see the worry on her face and knew he needed to lighten the mood. "Just one more kiss," he coaxed her. "Unless my face is too ugly for you to want to get that close to me?"

"Nay, my lord," she answered, giggling softly, tying the strings of her bodice. The wench wasn't half bad in bed. Rook wouldn't mind a repeat of last night before he started his day.

As she leaned in to kiss him, he reached up and yanked at the string, causing her breasts to pop out. He moaned and reached out to touch them, but the girl playfully stepped back, holding his braies in the air.

"Give me my braies," he told her. "I'm going to need those."

"Come get them," she teased, waving the linen braies back and forth. This one was a playful wench. He liked that about her. She knew how to have fun. Rook was all about having a good time. He sprang out from under the covers, totally naked, running after the wench. She giggled and ran away from him, still waving his braies above her head. Damn, why was this exciting him so much? He liked things out of the ordinary. And that included in and out of the bedchamber.

He was in the mood for a little game. "The wolf is hungry, and the little sheep is about to—"

"God's eyes, brother, cover up your bare arse!" a woman's voice from behind startled him. Rook spun around to see his twin sister, Raven, and his Scottish cousin, Lark, standing in the open doorway of his bedchamber.

"Och, nay!" Lark covered her eyes and turned her head. His sister made a face and rolled her eyes, looking up at the ceiling, shaking her head in disgust.

"What the hell are you two doing here?" Rook yanked the braies away from the servant girl, holding them in front of his groin. "And who in the devil's name said you could enter my bedchamber without knocking first?" Rook was more embarrassed that the girls saw him naked than being caught with the serving wench.

"We did knock," spat Raven, crossing her arms over her chest. "I guess you were a little too preoccupied to notice?" Her eyes flashed over to the kitchen maid.

"I'm so sorry, my lady," the servant said, fixing her bodice and curtsying to the women in respect. "I'll leave now." She took a step forward to exit the room, but Rook's arm shot out to block her way.

"Nay," said Rook. "I have not dismissed you yet."

"Aye, my lord," said the wench with downcast eyes, suddenly acting obedient and humble.

"Rook, you've got to stop using all the servants as naught more than your private harem. You are acting like the devil," scolded Raven, making her way across the room and pulling open the shutter. Bright sunshine and a warm spring breeze filled the room. The scent of fresh bread from the bakehouse wafted in, mingling with the stale air inside Rook's chamber.

"I don't do that, and I'm not the devil," said Rook, quickly turning and stepping into his braies.

"Aye, ye do," said Lark, with her eyes still covered. "Can I look yet?"

"At least you, dear cousin, have the decency to cover your eyes," Rook grunted. "That's more than I can say about my sister." He scooped up a tunic and pulled it over his head.

"Well, if there was anything at all to see, I would have covered my eyes too," said Raven with a sarcastic grin. Her long black hair was braided, circling each ear and pinned to the top of her head, now that she was a married woman. "The fact still remains. You think every servant at Blake Castle is naught but your personal plaything. You disgust me."

"Me too," said Lark, peeking out through her fingers.

The servant girl stayed quiet, with her gaze focused on the floor.

"I don't have a harem. I only have a few servants that are my favorites," said Rook. "She happens to be one of them." He nodded at the wench, causing a blush to rise in the girl's cheeks. "So stop making me sound like some kind of lustful cur."

"Stop acting like one, and mayhap I will," retorted Raven. "Making love should be something that is special and sacred."

"Sacred? Are you daft?" Rook shot her a sour expression and continued to dress.

3

"Well, at least it should be done only with the person you love or at least have strong feelings for," Raven continued.

"Oh, I had strong feelings for her, believe me," said Rook under his breath, speaking of physical feelings and not emotional ones, but he didn't care.

"Can I look yet?" asked Lark.

"Yes, drop your hand," Raven told her cousin. Lark slowly let her hand fall to her side.

"Raven," said Rook, running his fingers through his long, tangled hair. "Since you're married now, you seem to think you are an expert on these types of things. Well, you're not. You know nothing." Rook finished dressing and sat on the edge of the bed to don his boots.

"I know nothing?" asked Raven, her hand thumping against her chest. "I know more than you. I'm sure you, dear brother, don't even know the poor girl's name with whom you've spent the night."

"Don't be silly. Of course, I do," he said, honestly having no damned clue of the wench's name, and neither did he really care.

"Prove me wrong, then. What is it?" asked Raven in a challenge, crossing her arms over her chest. Rook's sister wasn't afraid to throw down the gauntlet, and neither was she shy about picking it up. Raven oftentimes acted more like a man than a woman, knowing how to use weapons even better than some of the castle's soldiers. Sometimes she even went as far as to wear trews instead of a gown. Or at least she did before she married the armorer, Jonathon Armstrong. Now, she dressed and acted more like a lady.

Rook looked up at the serving wench, trying hard to remember her name. He'd had her now on several occasions, and honestly, all he could remember was the way she performed in bed.

"Don't try throwing down the gauntlet at my feet, because I'm not picking it up, sister," Rook told Raven, looking for a way not to answer her question.

"Tell me." Raven wouldn't back down. "We want to know."

"Aye, we do," added Lark with a nod, her long blonde tendrils of hair framing her face, bobbing up and down. She was his Scottish cousin visiting here in Devonshire for a spell.

Rook realized Raven would never back down. It wasn't in her nature to do so. She would keep pestering him until he answered. He let out a deep sigh. He had to say something. Vaguely, he remembered that the servant's name was something short, with mayhap five letters, or so he thought. It started with an S, but that was all he could remember.

"We're waitin', cousin," said Lark, getting in on the addled game now as well. She walked over and held on to the bedpost and smiled.

Rook stood up and walked across the room. Picking up his weapon belt, he glanced at the servant girl. He secretly hoped she'd help him out and silently mouth him her name, since she was so good with her mouth.

She didn't.

"Susan," he spat, just needing to say something at this point. "Her name is Susan." His gaze shot over to the servant and he nodded, hoping she would understand to go along with him, even if this wasn't really her name.

"Nay, I'm not Susan," the girl said, disappointment filling her eyes. "My name is Sally, my lord."

Damn. She didn't catch on. Then again, she was known more for her looks than her mind.

"Susan, Sally, what does it matter?" Rook threw his hands in the air. When he looked up, all three girls were glaring at him now. It sent an icy chill up his spine. "You're dismissed, Susan."

5

"Sally," all three girls said to him at once.

"Go," he said with a shake of his head, sending the maid-servant running out the door. He swore to God he thought he heard her crying.

"That wasna very nice," scolded Lark. "Ye upset the lassie."

"Well, you two upset me," Rook answered. "Why the hell do you care what I do? And for that matter, why are you even here?" He strapped his weapon belt around his waist.

"We came to tell you that Father requests your presence in the great hall," said Raven. "He has an announcement to make."

"Really?" Rook's head snapped up. "Curious. I wonder what he wants. By the way, why are you two fetching me, instead of a page? This is an action much below your status. Or was it a job that paid you so well that you couldn't resist?" he asked with a deep chuckle.

"Very funny, Rook," said Raven, her hands going to her hips now. "Honestly, there is no sum of money large enough to make anyone willingly want to come to your bedchamber." She faked a shiver.

"We were lookin' for the kitchen maid since she didna show up for her shift this mornin'," explained Lark in a soft voice. "We figured we'd find her here." His cousin was a single mother with a four-year-old bastard daughter, so it almost amused Rook that she acted so shy or that she even covered her eyes at all when she saw him naked.

"And you couldn't send a page for that? Or did you purposely mean to barge in here and embarrass me?"

"Lark, don't answer that," warned Raven. "My brother doesn't deserve a response, and neither does he need to know a thing that has gone on at the castle already this morning. Let him hear the news from wagging tongues since he seems to think using wenches for his own pleasure and sleeping all day is an accepted act of the nobility."

"Raven, stop it," growled Rook, tired of the women telling him how to act. He walked over and picked up a boar's bristle brush, dragging it through his long black hair. "After all, you're no better, if I must remind you. And Lark, your past is more tarnished than both mine and Raven's put together."

That got a gasp from Lark and a deep sigh from Raven.

"What?" he asked with a shrug, looking at the girls' reflections in the convex round mirror hanging on the wall. Mirrors were only owned by people with status since they were scarce and very expensive. The church once frowned on them, saying the devil was looking back out, but Rook didn't care. He liked to see his own reflection, even if it was distorted. Besides, Raven already referred to him as the devil, so what did it matter? "You both know I'm right. I might seem like the devil to you two, but neither of you is close to being a saint either."

"Rook, you're being unfair," warned Raven, wagging her finger at him before turning and heading to the door. Lark quickly followed after her.

"Nay, I don't believe I am," Rook told them. "After all, Lark never married and has a bastard child. And you, dear sister, married naught but a commoner."

Raven stopped in her tracks and both girls turned around. "Remember, Jonathon is a lord now, so don't call my husband a commoner again."

"Yes, he's a lord, but with a courtesy title only. God's eyes, Raven, the man still works in the smithy."

"I thought ye liked Jonathon," said Lark. "That ye two were friends."

"I do and we are," stated Rook. "I'm just saying that one of the Blake siblings has to put an end to sullying the family name."

Raven scowled at him. "And you think that's going to happen as soon as you marry Lady Adeline Croiset?"

"Who?" asked Rook.

"Yer betrothed. The French lassie," said Lark. "The one yer father decided ye will marry."

"Oh, is that her name?"

Raven and Lark looked at each other and shook their heads. When Rook was sure they were going to start chastising him again, he changed the conversation.

"You know how important it is to Father that we all marry from above the salt and not below it." Rook looked directly at Raven when he said it. "Besides, I've never had a French-woman before. I hear the French are lions in bed." He smiled. "Is that right, Lark?"

Lark frowned. The man who had impregnated her was a Frenchman who never married her and abandoned her to go back home, where his real wife awaited him.

"Lark, the stench filling this room is strong," said Raven, throwing her nose in the air. "Let's go."

"I agree," said Lark, following Raven out of the room.

Rook put the brush down on the coffer, a flat-topped chest, and looked at himself in his mirror once again. "I only hope my betrothed is not a hideous ogre," he said to himself. This was really bothering him, that he was expected to marry a foreign woman whom he'd never met or even seen. He'd heard rumors that the wench was downright arrogant, demanding, and that she used people for her own needs.

"Damn," he said, leaving the room and closing the door. "I never want to have anything to do with someone like that."

~

"Son, where have you been?" asked Rook's father, Corbett Blake, as soon as Rook and the girls stepped foot into the great hall.

"I was... in bed," he answered, seeing Susan or Sally or whatever her name was, coming from the kitchen with a tray of food held over her shoulder. He smiled at her, but she scowled at him and looked the other way.

"I frown upon anyone sleeping this late, and you know it," Corbett reminded him.

"Oh, he wasn't sleeping," Raven interrupted, taking her place at the dais for the meal.

Rook decided he'd better hurry and change the subject again before anyone asked him just what he'd been doing.

"Father, what is this announcement you're going to make?" asked Rook. He walked up the steps to the dais and kissed his mother, Lady Devon, on the cheek. Then he took a seat next to his father. He happened to be sitting next to Raven as well. Her new husband, Jonathon, sat at the dais now too. It wasn't right since he wasn't a noble, but Rook didn't really mind. He liked the man and had known him for years. Jonathon used to be the town's armorer, servicing many nobles as well as those of Blake Castle. Now he had a brand new smithy right inside the castle walls to call his own. With the marriage, he'd also gained a courtesy title, thanks to Rook's father.

Corbett stood behind his chair, lifting his tankard of ale to the rest of the occupants sitting below the salt. "Quiet, please. All of you," he said.

Since it had been Raven's wedding day when Rook found out he was betrothed, no official announcement had been made just yet about his future. Rook had a feeling his father was about to do that now.

"I want to announce that my eldest son, Rook, is now

betrothed to a very important Frenchwoman in a well-needed alliance."

The crowd cheered. Rook wasn't happy about this but decided he'd pretend to be.

"To Adelaide," said Rook, lifting his tankard. That got him an elbow to the ribs from Raven.

"Adeline. Her name is Adeline," Raven whispered.

"Lady Adeline Croiset will marry my son, Rook, in one month's time when she comes from France to live here in England," Corbett continued. More cheering came from the crowd, and this time, even some whistles. "As my wedding present to my son, I've decided to give him his own manor and estate from my holdings. It is actually my newest accommodation that I inherited just recently near the forests of Dartmoor."

"What?" Rook almost choked on his ale. He had hoped to get Torquay Castle, which his uncle held. Then again, that was from his mother's side, so he really had no chance of it happening. Still, Rook wanted a castle on the cliffs of the sea. He always had. His father was giving him a manor house inland and close to a forest, which was less than ideal. The forest gave too much cover for any raiders in the nearby area. Rook knew exactly which manor it was since Corbett said he'd inherited it recently. "Not Horrabridge," groaned Rook.

"Why yes, it is," said Corbett, lifting his tankard again. "Horrabridge Manor and its estate is all yours now, son. Congratulations."

"Rook, the landscape is beautiful there," said Devon. His mother always tried to be positive, even if Rook didn't see a good thing about this situation.

"Aye, Mother," Rook answered, biting his tongue, not wanting to be rude to his parents. The manor had been vacated recently when the old Earl Clive Mannering, an eccentric, crazy man that Rook's late grandfather had ties to, just died. It had always been a standing jest amongst the nobles that the king putting Crazy Clive in the middle of nowhere was the only way to keep him from any rash behavior.

Well, it seemed that didn't stop the earl from doing what he wanted. The man put it in writing that when he died, his manor would go to Lord Ethan Blake or passed down to his firstborn, who was Corbett. That alone was proof of his addled state, since everyone knew Ethan Blake had married the daughter of a vicar and had his title and castle taken away because of it.

Horrabridge Manor was off the beaten-path and more or less forgotten, or so Rook had heard. It was said there was a small village of serfs in Horrabridge, but not enough to really provide a good income for the manor.

Rook had never been there, and neither had he ever held any interest in it. The earl was said to be a recluse who had no friends and very little staff at all.

Rook didn't want to live like a recluse. He liked to be in busier places, not hidden away like a hermit. It was in his nature to always be where things were happening and also to be close to the sea. Feasts and celebrations, tournaments, and even battles were what he lived for. Being sent to Horrabridge was like being condemned, in his opinion. It upset him almost as much as the idea that he'd soon be a married man, tied to a woman he'd never even seen or met.

"Rook, you only have a month to get the manor ready for your new bride." Raven lifted a spoonful of fresh berries with cream, looked at her new husband sitting next to her, and purposely licked her lips before taking the spoon into her mouth. Jonathon gave her a lustful smile. Then, her new husband reached over and kissed her, right there atop the dais. Rook would never act like that. After all, they were kissing and flirting in front of everyone. At least he had the decency to do that behind closed doors.

"That's right, the wedding is approaching quickly," said Rook's mother. "There is much to do before your betrothed arrives. I will go with you to the manor until the wedding day. I can help instruct the servants with the preparations and hire a household staff for you, Rook."

"Thank you, Mother," said Rook, not knowing how else to answer. He was grateful to have his own holdings, but knew someday he'd inherit Blake Castle when his father passed away. Mayhap, he should just make the best of this for now.

"Raven, you and Lark will join your mother," said Corbett, sitting back down and filling his trencher with food.

"What? Me? Why?" That got Raven's attention off doting on her new husband. "I just got married, Father. I need to stay here with my husband."

"I dinna mind goin' to Horrabridge to help ye, Rook," said Lark. "Since Florie is still in Scotland, I dinna have much to do." She spoke of her four-year-old daughter back in the Highlands, being watched over by her parents for now.

"Thank you, cousin," mumbled Rook, shoving a piece of venison into his mouth and chewing forcefully.

"Mayhap Jonathon can accompany us to Horrabridge as well," suggested Raven, sounding hopeful. Rook knew his father well enough to realize he wouldn't agree to that.

"Nay. I need Jonathon here," objected Corbett. "He's our only blacksmith and work is piling up since the smithy is still in the process of being enlarged."

"I agree," Jonathon told his wife. "Raven, I need to be here. This is my new shop now that I'm a master armorer. I need to get the place set up and running, as well as oversee everything. There is so much to do."

"I understand," said Raven with a sigh. "All right, I'll help you Rook. After all, how much work can there be at Horrabridge? I'm sure we'll be able to quickly make it acceptable for your new bride, and I'll be able to return home soon."

"I wouldn't bet on that," mumbled Rook, taking a drink of ale. He had a feeling the manor needed lots of work. And from the rumors he'd heard of Lady Adeline, there was no one or nothing that would ever please the stuffy wench.

CHAPTER 2

"Well, at least it's fortified," said Rook in surprise as he and his traveling party rode through the gatehouse of Horrabridge Manor and into the courtyard.

"It's not strongly fortified, but it's enough to keep raiding parties out," remarked Corbett. "Later on, you might want to think about adding a moat and drawbridge as well, to ward off any potential sieges. Plus, you'll need to find your own soldiers to guard the place. I can spare a few, but this is your responsibility now, Rook."

"I understand," said Rook, perusing his new home. High stone walls surrounded the manor house, much like any castle. There was even a wall walk and guard towers at each corner. The keep itself looked to be a good size, made of stone with slate roofing. It was not one of those tiny manors that could barely house a lord's staff, let alone his family. "How many rooms does it have?" he asked his father, his interest suddenly growing.

"I'm not sure, but I know it has a chapel and a great hall. It also has a sizeable kitchen and plenty of bedchambers."

"Not bad," said Rook with a satisfied nod. His focus left the keep now, and he took in the surroundings. Several outbuildings were scattered about the bailey, but there was a lot of overgrowth in the inner ward.

While the manor looked impressive, the grounds, on the other hand, were abominable. Everything was so unkempt and wild-looking that they'd probably need scythes and axes just to carve a path to the outbuildings. Vines tangled their way up the sides of the manor, and weeds grew everywhere, many almost as tall as he. Ivy and what looked like wild rose vines clung to the manor walls, even covering a window or two completely.

"Oh, my," said Raven, her eyes opening wide as she took in their surroundings. "This might take a little longer to prepare for the wedding than I thought."

"It's frightenin'," said Lark, her mouth hanging open.

"I think your bride might get lost in here," piped up Harold, Rook's blond-haired, eighteen-year-old squire.

"Now, now, you just have to use your imagination. It's not that bad," said Devon, accepting her husband's help to dismount her horse.

There was a small entourage of several guards and about a dozen servants who came with them from Blake Castle, walking on foot or riding in the supply wagons. They all carried bags and boxes filled with food, wine, and household items that would be needed to set up the manor for residency.

"So, Rook. What do you think of Horrabridge?" asked Corbett.

"I...I mean, it's all right," Rook answered. "However, I will need to make some changes. The first one, being the name of the manor."

"What's wrong with callin' it Horrabridge Manor?" asked Lark.

"I don't like it," Rook grumbled.

"Brother, for some reason I thought you'd like anything that had the word whore in it." Raven burst out laughing and even Lark giggled.

"Girls, please," said their mother under her breath. "Rook, I know the grounds need a little work, but underneath all this overgrowth, it is a vision of beauty, I assure you."

"Aye," agreed Corbett. "If I'm not mistaken, there is even a labyrinth of bushes, as well as herb, flower, and vegetable gardens. Somewhere. Oh, and a small orchard out back."

"Out back," repeated Rook, wondering what that looked like since the front was so atrocious.

"I will be away for a while attending a meeting with some of the other lords and barons of the area," Corbett informed him. "However, I've already sent a missive to Oliver Ashdown, and he'll be here in the morning with his workers to attend to things."

"Oliver Ashdown?" asked Rook.

"That name sounds familiar. Isn't he a gardener?" asked Raven.

"Yes, he is," said Devon. "He worked on Blake Castle's garden when your father and I were first married."

"He is a master gardener and the best there is," Corbett told them. "He has even worked on the king's gardens at one time. His work is well renowned."

"Oliver is the one who put in the gardens here at the manor, isn't that right, dear?" Devon asked Corbett.

"Yes, but it was a long time ago and when Oliver was a young man. At one time, this place was a masterpiece, I hear. I'm sure it can be brought back to that state, eventually. With a little work."

"Little work? Hah!" spat Rook, no longer able to stay silent.

"I doubt even a miracle could make this place ready before the wedding."

"How long ago did the previous owner die?" asked Lark.

"Crazy Man Clive, died about a month ago," Raven told her.

"Raven! Have respect for the dead," scolded Devon. "Remember, he was an earl."

"Well, it's what everyone is thinking," said Raven. "Besides, no one would know who we're talking about if we called him anything else."

"Your mother is right. Have respect," said Corbett. "After all, it was the earl who we have to thank for this manor."

"Oh, all right. I meant Earl Clive," said Raven, not sounding happy about it, but giving in to please her parents.

"If he died so recently, why is there all this overgrowth?" Lark's green eyes scanned the tangles and massive weeds and wild bushes.

"I think I can answer that," said Devon. "Earl Mannering, who lived here, was a little... eccentric, should I say?"

"Crazy. Just like I said." Raven waved her arms in the air as she spoke.

Devon continued. "Rumors say he didn't like to go outdoors and that he focused all his attention on the inside of the manor only."

"Why didn't he have servants keep up the grounds?" asked Rook.

"I'm not sure," said Corbett. "He was odd, and by the time he died, he didn't have a very big staff left at all. I heard he didn't trust anyone and fired most of them. Mayhap that's part of it."

"I dinna understand. Why did the earl leave the manor to the Blake family, Uncle Corbett?" asked Lark.

"My grandfather saved the earl's life on the battlefield

once," explained Corbett. "That's when Clive made a contract with him, stating that when Clive died, his manor would go to my father or be passed down to his eldest son someday, which is me. It was his way of saying thank you, I guess. Well, he died, he's buried, and now it is mine. Or Rook's, I should say."

"I want to see the inside," said Rook, handing the reins of his horse to Albert, the thirteen-year-old castle page who'd accompanied them there. "Albert, take the horses to the barn. If you can find it."

"There's the stable," said Corbett, pointing to it. "There is also the mews, a kennel, and even a bakehouse, I believe. However, I've heard they haven't been used in years."

"Is there a smithy, too?" asked Raven, sounding hopeful. It made Rook realize she was still thinking about bringing her husband here.

"Nay," answered Corbett. "I don't believe so, but Rook can always build one later. Let's take a look inside." Corbett instructed the servants to go directly to the kitchen to start setting things up and getting ready for the meal.

Rook made his way to the manor, focused on nothing but the weeds and overgrowth all around him. He was sure the inside of the manor would prove to be just as disappointing. To his surprise, he was wrong.

"God's teeth," he said, stopping in the open doorway, looking up a long flight of winding stairs that led to the upper floor. The place was majestic inside, not unlike a castle, just smaller. The main floor held a great hall with tapestries on the walls, and even weapons displayed that were left behind.

"This doesna look at all like the outside," said Lark, walking over to the stairs.

Rook entered the great hall, the sound of his bootheels echoing off the stone floors. "It looks like it's fully furnished, too," he said, eyeing up the trestle tables inside. To the far end of the great hall was a hearth with wood still stacked nearby.

"He died suddenly," said Corbett. "The agreement also stated that his things would be left behind, since he didn't have a wife or an heir."

"Mayhap this is a better deal than I thought," mumbled Rook with a satisfied nod.

"Och, look up there," said Lark from the hallway, pointing up the stairway. "I see light streamin' in from some stained glass windows. It's a bonnie sight to see!"

"That must be the chapel," said Raven, hurrying over to her cousin. "Let's go explore." Raven was halfway up the stairs before Rook could stop her. "I'm going to choose the bedchamber I'll use while I'm here," she called out.

"Me too," said Lark excitedly, picking up her skirts and following Raven upstairs.

"The main solar is mine, no matter how much the two of you might like it," Rook told the women.

"The kitchen is clean and also a good size," said Harold, coming from the other room. "It's fully stocked with pots and pans. They even left food behind in the larder." He held up a jar of what looked like pickled pig's feet. "I wonder if there is wine and ale here, too."

"Everything seems clean and in good order," agreed Devon. "I guess most of our efforts will be focused on the outside then."

"Most of the servants' efforts, Mother," Rook reminded her since Devon was once his father's servant and was used to doing things for herself. That is before she discovered she was noble.

"Yes, of course. That's what I mean," said Devon. "Harold, show me the kitchen." She hurried into the other room, chatting with the squire.

"Son, this is all yours now," said Corbett. "I know things will get better in time. Just give it a chance." He put his hand on Rook's shoulder.

"I'm grateful," Rook answered. "The manor I can live with, the grounds, I'll tolerate, but I'm afraid I can't say the same about my bride-to-be."

"You don't even know her, Rook. How can you say that?"

"I have ears. I've heard rumors."

"Don't put your faith in wagging tongues," Corbett warned him. "I have never met your betrothed, but I don't think she's homely, if that makes you feel any better. Plus, they are offering a dowry I couldn't refuse. It's all yours, Rook, so you should be happy."

"Why did you betroth me before consulting me?" asked Rook, still feeling very upset about this situation. "I'm not a child, Father. I can find a bride and make an alliance on my own."

"I know that, Rook. But you're a knight and also one and twenty years of age now. Still, you have done nothing to secure a wife. You squander away your evenings with light skirts, and think nothing of your future. Besides, you don't have a castle. It took a lot of convincing, but I finally managed to make the alliance anyway with just a manor house."

"Father, it's fine if you find wives for my brothers, but I am your eldest son." Rook had two younger brothers, Tolin and Daegel, but they were away being fostered by other knights.

"Yes, you are my eldest, Rook. You also put your importance on all the wrong things, I'm sorry to say. I decided I was tired of waiting and this will force you to move on with your life. You'll thank me someday. And you'll do the same for your own children, I am sure."

"Well, couldn't you at least let me choose my own bride? After all, I have a certain type of woman that I like."

"Yes, and I've seen the type," said Corbett with a scowl. "Even more reason that I chose for you."

"Why a Frenchwoman?" asked Rook. "The French are too pompous and demanding."

"Rook, everyone knows about you and how much you like the wenches, so it wasn't easy. I tried to make an alliance with several English lords for you to marry their daughters, but they'd heard the rumors and objected."

"You should have at least talked with me. Given me a chance to choose."

"I'm sorry, son, but I couldn't take the chance that you might fall in love with a commoner."

"Ah, so that's the real reason."

"I tried to secure a proper husband for Raven, and we see how that worked out. You have to see this through," said Corbett. "You know how important it is to me that my children marry someone of their same status or higher. A daughter making this mistake might be overlooked, but not the firstborn son of a noble."

"I would never make that mistake, I assure you."

"At least now I can sleep nights knowing that my son will marry a noblewoman who has much to bring to this marriage."

"I still say I don't want the wench," spat Rook.

"Wench?" Corbett raised an eyebrow. "You might want to choose your words carefully from now on, Rook. Especially around your bride-to-be. I don't know any lady who wants to be referred to as a mere wench."

"I'm sorry. I didn't mean anything by it."

"I know it'll be hard for someone like you to change, but from now on, you will be expected to act like a noble. Understand?"

Even if Rook didn't, saying so would only bring about the ire of his father.

"Of course I do," Rook answered, wondering if his days of pleasure were over.

CHAPTER 3

"Father, come down from there." Primrose Ashdown shaded her eyes from the sun and looked up to the top of the ladder. "The workers have everything packed and are ready to leave for Horrabridge Manor. We need to go now if we want to get there before sundown. Lord Corbett Blake is expecting us and we can't disappoint him."

"Just a few more snips and I'll be finished, Rose." Oliver leaned closer to the tall bush, reaching out with his shears, trying to cut a couple of wild sprigs. He was obsessed with details and perfection, and didn't ever leave a job before he was satisfied that it was totally finished. Sometimes, Rose thought he spent too much time with the small things that didn't matter. However, that same desire for perfection is what earned him the title of Master Gardener with the gardener's guild. It was also how her father got the privilege of working in the king's garden several years ago. He had been hired to plan a pleasure garden for King Edward III that far surpassed anything the royal gardeners could ever do.

Right now, they'd finished a job for Lord Morcant of Somerset.

Rose and her father lived with the peasants on Lord Morcant's land, in the village nearby. Most of the peasants were serfs, but Rose, her father, and a few others were free tenants. Not tied to the lord or land, they were free to come and go as they pleased.

The lord of the castle exited the keep, his hounds running out to chase down a squirrel. The squirrel ran over to the ladder her father used and scampered up it to keep from being caught. The hounds barked and jumped, knocking against the ladder. The squirrel dove into the tall bush, but the ladder wobbled, and this caused her father to lose his balance.

"Nay!" shouted Primrose, or Rose as nearly everyone called her, running to try to help her father, but it was too late. He tumbled from the ladder, hitting the ground hard. When he fell, Rose swore she heard the snapping of a bone. Her father let out a loud groan.

"Master Gardener," called out Lord Morcant. He ran over, followed by his kennel groom, who grabbed the hounds, pulling them away. "Are you hurt?"

"Father!" Rose fell to her knees, cradling her father's head on her lap. Through blurry, tear-filled eyes, she could see by the odd angle of his leg that it was indeed broken. "Your leg," she cried.

"God's eyes, kennel groom take these hounds away from here," shouted Lord Morcant. The kennel groom put leads on the dogs and hauled them away. "Master Gardener, I think your leg might be broken."

"Nay, it can't be," said Oliver, trying to get up, but cringing and shaking his head. "We have a big job to do. I have to go. I can't be hurt. We promised Lord Corbett Blake. This is important."

Servants from the castle, as well as some of Oliver's workers, rushed over to see what had happened.

"Father, nothing is as important as your health and well-being," said Rose, trying to calm him.

"Fetch the healer, fast," Lord Morcant ordered one of his servants.

When the healer returned and checked Oliver's leg, the man shook his head, looking over at the lord of the castle. "I'm sorry, but I'm afraid this man's leg is broken, my lord. I'll have to set the bone, but it looks to be a bad break. This man will need to lie still and stay in bed until it's healed."

"How long will that be?" asked Rose, her heart beating rapidly in her chest. Worry started to set in since they had another important job to get to right away.

"It's hard to say, until I can decipher how bad it is," answered the healer. "It could take anywhere from a month and a half to five months to heal. And afterwards, he'll still need to be careful. No climbing ladders for a long time."

"Nay," said Oliver, shaking his head. "This can't be. I have work to do. I need to go. We have a big job to complete and only a month to do it."

"I'm sorry but you're not going anywhere," said Lord Morcant. "I feel responsible since my dogs did this. I insist that you stay right here at my castle until you're healed. I won't even let you go back to the village. My healer will tend to your wounds."

"Nay, I can't," protested Oliver.

"It is what we'll do, and I'll not hear another word about it." Lord Morcant called to his servants to bring around a cart to carry Rose's father back to the keep.

"Rose, this job for Lord Blake is important," said her father. "He's a respected knight and lord and is very wealthy. You'll have to take charge and go to Horrabridge without me." The servants helped him onto the back of a cart.

"Me? You want me to take your place?" asked Rose, shaking her head. "I can't do that."

"Of course you can. I've taught you everything I know."

"I won't be accepted. I'm a girl!" The thought horrified her. Women were not treated well, and especially not commoners. No one would respect her in this important position.

"Rose, you're the only one I trust to bring Horrabridge Manor back to its former state. You helped me with that job when you were a child. You remember what it looked like, don't you?"

"Why, of course, I do. But please don't ask me to do this for you."

"This isn't for me, Rose. It's for Lord Corbett Blake, who is a good friend of mine. His son is getting married in a month and there is much work to be done before his bride arrives. I've heard the grounds are in disrepair and we need to bring them back to perfection."

"Lord Corbett Blake's son?" she asked. "Are you speaking of Lord Rook?" Rose had never met Lord Rook personally, but she'd heard plenty of gossip about the arrogant man. He had a promiscuous nature and was said to even be heartless at times.

"Yes, his son, Rook," said Oliver as the servants settled him in the cart, ready to bring him back to the castle. "He is a knight as well. Horrabridge Manor is now his, and he is setting up his household."

"Nay, I don't want to go." This sounded horrible to Rose, and she wanted nothing to do with the man.

"You have to, daughter. Please. For me," begged her father with tears in his eyes. Ever since Rose's mother died when she was a child, Rose had become close with her father. They had never been apart, and she didn't want to leave him now, either.

"It doesn't matter, Father. Lord Rook will not listen to me since I am a girl."

26

"Would it help if I wrote and sent a missive saying that your daughter is in charge and capable of doing the job?" asked Lord Morcant.

"You would do that for me?" asked Oliver, hope resounding in his voice.

"Of course." Morcant nodded. "This is an unfortunate accident and since it took place at my castle, I'd be happy to write the missive. Especially since I've seen what Rose can do. I'm extremely pleased by her work and won't hesitate to say so. Even if she is a girl."

"This is perfect!" Her father smiled through his pain. "Then it's agreed. My daughter will go in my stead."

"Nay, Father. I don't think this is a good idea," protested Rose. "Mayhap one of the other men can head this job instead of me. What about Phineas?" she asked, speaking of one of the workers who lived with them.

Her father wouldn't hear of it. "You're the only one I trust to be in charge of such an important job," said Oliver. "You can do it, Rose. Do it for me. Do it for your late mother. Goodbye, daughter," he said with a wave of his hand as the servants wheeled him away with Morcant walking at his side.

Rose got a sick feeling in the pit of her stomach. True, she knew gardening better than anyone, having been taught by her father who was a master at his trade. She had even been part of his team when they'd worked in King Edward's gardens a few years ago. She didn't want to go to Horrabridge Manor, but it wasn't because she didn't think she could do the job. Secretly, she feared being around Lord Rook. He was said to be demanding and also a womanizer. She didn't have a lot of experience with men, and no experience at all with dealing with a nobleman on her own. Especially not one like Lord Rook whom she was about to work for.

Her head told her not to go, but her heart told her she had

to do this for her father. She couldn't let him down after everything he'd done for her through the years. He meant the world to her. The last thing she wanted was to desert him in his time of need. She also didn't want to disappoint him. She was his only child, and he did everything for her. Now it was time for her to give something back to him.

"Wait," she called out, rushing after the cart. "I'll go, Father. I'll do it for you, I promise I will. And for Mother, since I know that is what she would have wanted." She reached out, giving her father a half-hug and kiss on the cheek. "I'll be back soon."

"Not too soon. Make sure you finish the job properly," warned her father. "Horrabridge Manor was one of my first projects and also one that I was most proud of, too. Make it right for Lord Rook and his bride-to-be. Make me proud, Rose."

"I will, Father," she promised, still wishing for a way out. "I'll make you proud, no matter what it takes."

Now, she could only hope Lord Rook didn't give her trouble, because if he did, she wasn't sure what she would do.

Rose rode up to the gatehouse of Horrabridge Manor later that day and stopped, feeling even more nervous than when she'd agreed to come here in the first place. The manor was much like a small castle and very foreboding, not to mention intimidating. Here she was, a simple common girl, marching up to a nobleman's home with her gardening team and a horse-drawn wagon of tools right behind her. She had never gone on a job before without her father. He was a well-known master gardener who was accepted and well respected. She had always been at his side, but honestly, no one had ever paid any attention to the gardener's daughter. Now, all their focus would be on her. She was about to meet with Lord Rook and was sure that was going to be a problem.

"Rose, why did you stop? Is something wrong?" Phineas, one of the workers who was her father's good friend, exited the wagon and ran over to talk with her. Since they were commoners, they didn't have many horses between them. Rose's horse was really her father's, given to him by the king. The other was a plow horse that pulled the wagon full of tools and supplies. There were eight gardeners total, but that included her father. Without him now, they only had three women and four men to complete the job. It wasn't a large number, but it was all they had. Luckily, when they'd worked for the king, he'd provided some of his gardeners to assist them with that job. But now, it was only Rose and six others. Then again, this was only a manor and not a castle, so it should be more than enough people to do the work.

"Nay, nothing is wrong, Phineas. I'm just a little nervous," she admitted to the man who was in a way like a second father to her. "I've never had to be a leader before."

"Sure you have, Rose. You do it all the time, working hand-in-hand with you father," Phineas assured her. He was an older man, about her father's age, but strong and good with a spade. His thinning hair had turned white and hung down to his shoulders even though the top of his head was almost bald. His wife, Thomasina, waited for him on the bench seat of the wagon. She was a large, round woman, but faster than any of the other gardeners when it came to weeding. She grabbed two handfuls of weeds at a time and yanked them out like she was plucking a chicken. Rose hoped she would never get the woman angry. When Thomasina had a pair of gardening shears in her hands, she could be lethal if you rubbed her the wrong way.

"I know, but this is different," said Rose. "Now I'm in charge. And I'm a woman."

"Don't let these nobles look down their noses at you, Rose. Don't allow them to belittle you. You are talented and just as respected as your father. Never forget that," Phineas told her.

"He's right, cousin," said Georgiana, rushing up to join them. "We have faith in you, Rose. Show you're strong. You can do it."

Georgiana was Rose's cousin who had come to work with them only a few years ago after the death of her family. She was like a sister to Rose, and two years younger than Rose's age of twenty. While Rose had wavy long blonde hair down to her bottom end, Georgiana's red hair was cut short and didn't even touch her shoulders.

"Thank you. I'll try," Rose told them and started forward, leading the way into the courtyard. Once inside, two women saw her and hurried over to greet her.

"Hello," said the woman with the black hair. "I'm Lady Raven, and this is my cousin, Lady Lark."

"Aye, hello. How are ye?" asked the blonde lady, sounding Scottish. They both were donned in elegant long gowns as worn by English nobles, with long tippets, sleeves that hung down to the ground. Around their shoulders they wore ermine-trimmed cloaks since it was only late spring and the days were often cool. The noblewomen looked elite, only making Rose more self-conscious about the way she was dressed in naught but a simple tunic and woolen work gown.

"Good day, my ladies." Rose slid off the horse, lowering her head and greeting them with a slight curtsy. "I'm Rose. Primrose Ashdown." When the women looked confused, she realized she'd better explain. "My father, Oliver Ashdown, is the master gardener who was summoned by Sir Corbett Blake."

"Oh, yes. Lord Corbett is my father," said Raven. "Welcome. We're so glad you're here."

"There is so much to do before Lord Rook's weddin'," agreed Lark.

Rose looked around the courtyard, seeing the overgrowth and weeds that choked out whatever plants were supposed to be there. It looked like no one had lifted a finger in the least to tend to the grounds for mayhap a decade or more.

"My, this will be a challenge," Rose commented, remembering this place as a girl. It certainly didn't look like this back then.

"I need the work finished in a month's time. No later, and hopefully earlier." A nobleman with long black hair walked up, his red cloak billowing out behind him. It was a bold choice of color and brought much attention to oneself. Rose didn't think anyone would purposely wear a red cloak, except mayhap a whore. She supposed this man did it to stand out. That told her exactly who he was. "Where is this master gardener?" the man asked. "I need to speak to him anon." He was tall and looked right over Rose's head, acting as if she weren't even there. "You there," he called out to Phineas, who was still sitting on the bench of the wagon. "Come here. Are you the master gardener?"

"Me? Nay," said Phineas, running over and bowing deeply. "I'm Phineas, my lord."

"Excuse my brother's rudeness," said Raven. "This is Lord Rook Blake, and he's not known for his manners." That earned her a scowl from Rook.

"It is Sir Rook, but you may call me lord," the man told her.

"Hello, Lord Rook, I am Primrose Ashdown," said Rose, lowering her eyes and curtsying to the man. "My father, Oliver, is the master gardener."

"Well, where is he? Hurry up and tell me. I don't have time

to waste." Rook's eyes scanned the courtyard, looking for her father.

"He's... he's not here," said Rose, her throat becoming so dry that she found it hard to speak. There was no doubt in her mind that Rook wasn't going to like this. She also knew it was only going to cause trouble when she had to tell him she was in charge of the job.

Rook was losing his patience fast with the girl. He had much to do inside the keep, and didn't have time for this nonsense. He needed to take inventory of what food had been left in the larder when Crazy Clive's household moved out. He also needed to get a count on the wine bottles in the cellar before he ordered more to stock the manor properly. Not to mention, he was in dire need of hiring more servants. All this had to been done quickly since his betrothed was arriving in a month. Rook's father had given him a dozen servants only, but wasn't willing to let loose of his steward, a man Rook needed desperately right now. He'd have to hire the proper help quickly to get the manor in shape and to keep his household running smoothly. His head spun with all that needed to be done in such a short amount of time.

"Well, when will the master gardener arrive?" Rook demanded to know. "There is much to be done, and I won't put up with his tardiness. This job needs to be started right away."

"My father is not coming," the girl told him. "He broke his leg and had to stay behind."

"He what?" Rook's attention finally went to the girl standing before him. She was a comely little thing, but didn't look strong enough to hoe the land, let alone pull weeds. She seemed so tiny and frail.

"My father has sent me in his stead," she announced softly.

"What did you say?" asked Rook, thinking he'd misheard her.

She looked up and took a deep breath and answered louder this time. "I am in charge now. All orders will need to go through me."

"Really." Rook's eyes scanned down the wench's body and he chuckled. Long wavy blonde hair was tied back into a tail that reached past her cute, little rounded rump. She was dressed simply, but clean, in an earthy brown tunic covered by a plain, coarse dark woolen green gown. His eyes traveled to her hand as she reached for something in her pouch and pulled it out.

Her long, thin fingers almost looked more like a noble-woman's than a peasant's who worked the land. He'd expected to see dirt jammed under her nails, but there wasn't any. Her fingers and hands were clean, to his surprise. Her eyes were chestnut brown, and so were her eyebrows, though her hair was blonde like the sun. The girl had a dainty, turned-up nose and a cute little turned-down mouth. Her cheekbones were high and strong. It almost seemed a shame that such beauty was wasted on a mere peasant. "I'm sorry, but this won't work for me."

"What won't work?" asked Raven.

"This," said Rook, holding out his arm toward the girl. "She can't head the workers or be in charge of such a big and important job."

"Why not?" asked Lark. "It seems that she has her workers and all their tools and supplies with her. Let them start workin'."

"Nay. She's not going to be able to do this," spat Rook, irritated to be put in such a position. "I'll find someone else to do the gardening." He turned to go, but stopped in his tracks when he heard the girl speak brashly to him.

"Because I'm a girl? Is that why you're dismissing me as if I was naught but yesterday's spoiled meat?" she said, loud and strong.

He slowly turned around, shocked to hear this coming from her mouth. A minute ago, she spoke so softly that he could barely hear her, and neither could she look him in the eye. Where was this coming from? "I don't believe that is the proper way to speak to a noble," he told her.

"My lord," she added quickly, almost making him laugh, as if that made it all better.

"Rook, what are you doing? You don't have time to find anyone else," Raven pointed out. "Your betrothed will be here in a month's time and there is still so much to do."

"Ye dinna want to disappoint yer betrothed, do ye?" asked Lark. "Let them do the job. We need them."

"But she's a girl," he pointed out, in case his sister and cousin hadn't noticed.

"Yes, we've established that fact," said Rose.

He scowled at her.

"My lord," she said, adding a slight nod that was similar to a half-bow.

"Give her a chance, Rook," said Raven. "Who cares if she's a girl?"

"I do," he answered quickly.

"As long as she has the skills, that is all that matters," said Raven.

"Of course, you'd say that, sister." Rook was ready to yell.

"I have assisted my father since I was a child," said the girl, holding her head high and proud now. The man named Phineas stood next to her, nodding. "I assure you, I can get the job done. You won't be disappointed, my lord. I have brought a recommendation letter from Lord Morcant of Somerset, where we just completed our last job." She handed the missive to him.

Rook opened the parchment and scanned it quickly. Sure enough, it was exactly what she said. How could he turn down a recommendation from another noble?

"I see." Rook held his hand to his chin. The girl was mouthy, but then again, he liked his women spirited. This one was also a real looker. Mayhap if he let her stay, he'd find out what other kind of skills she had as well. After all, he was getting tired of the same old servants warming his bed. "All right. Let's see what you can do." Rook walked a full circle around her. "I'll need the grounds cleaned up and prepared for a very finicky French noblewoman. And I'll need it completed in a month."

"There are only seven of us to do the work," said the girl named Primrose. "I haven't even seen what lies behind the manor yet, so I don't know how much time we'll need to do the job properly."

"Och, it's worse than ye think. A lot worse," said Lark, waving her hand through the air.

"Really?" The girl's eyes opened wide and then narrowed again. "I'm sorry, my lord, but I can't promise it'll be completed in a month, then. I can only say we'll try our best. These things take time and can't be rushed."

Rook didn't like that answer at all. "Well, Prim, you have only a month to complete things, and that's it. If you don't, you won't be paid. At all."

"Brother!" gasped Raven, but Rook held up his hand.

"What do you say, Prim? Is it a deal?"

By the look on her face, Rook was sure she was going to object. No one but mayhap a master gardener could fix up these grounds in that short amount of time. And no one would be stupid enough to risk their neck with workers standing behind her who might possibly not get paid for a month's work in the end. After all, they were just peasants, and he was sure they were all in dire need of money. He stopped and folded his arms over his chest. Then, to his surprise, she walked a circle around him, perusing him the same way he just did to her. What in the name of the devil was she doing?

"All right. I'll agree to the deal," she finally said, stopping in front of him and folding her arms over her chest, mimicking him. "However, my name is Rose, so you'll need to stop calling me Prim."

"You told me your name was Primrose, so what's the difference what I call you?" he asked.

"The difference, my lord, is that I am not one of the prim and proper noblewomen of the castle, but neither am I one of your strumpets. Therefore, I'd appreciate it if you'd please stop looking at me as if you're sizing me up to warm your bed."

Raven and Lark bust out laughing, and this only made Rook explode with anger. The worst part was that it was exactly what he'd been thinking, but felt embarrassed to have the girl call him on it aloud in front of everyone.

"Get to work!" he shouted. "And by God, you'd better pray you can finish in time." He threw his hands in the air for effect and stormed away without looking back. The last thing he needed in his life right now was a commoner—a woman, standing up to him with his sister and cousin laughing at him as well. This was going to have to end right now.

Rose watched the pompous man storm away, and a smile pursed the corners of her mouth. Her heart beat loudly in her ears, but new life flowed through her from standing up for herself. She had been frightened of Lord Rook, but his arrogance and ignorance angered her enough to push her fear aside and speak freely. Now she was glad that she had. It seemed that the noblewomen were on her side, and that alone gave her the courage she needed to say how she felt. Phineas, who was still standing there with his jaw dropped open, leaned over and spoke in a soft voice.

"I think you angered him, Rose."

"Don't worry about that, Phineas," said Raven, overhearing him. "Sometimes my brother can be quite cruel and insensitive. He might be angry now, but he'll get over it in time, I assure you."

"I'm sorry that I spoke out of line, my lady," said Rose, lowering her head and half-bowing to Raven, who she truly respected, even if she couldn't say the same about the woman's brother. "I—I just didn't like the way he was... oh, I'm sorry. My father would scold me for this if he were here right now. I think I got carried away."

"Well, we applaud ye for it," said Lark behind her hand. She peeked over her shoulder to make sure Rook didn't hear her. "Would ye like to see the manor?"

"Me?" asked Rose, shocked to hear that she was being invited inside a noble's home. She was even more shocked that noblewomen were offering to show it to her.

"Of course, you," said Raven. "You and your workers will be sleeping in the great hall, so let me show it to you."

"Oh, no, we couldn't. We usually stay outside." Rose shook her head. "Phineas, set up the tents for us outside the manor walls."

"Nay, that's not safe," said Raven. "You will all sleep inside during your stay. I insist."

"Will Lord Rook agree with that?" asked Rose.

"There is enough room in the manor," said Lark. "I dinna see why he would object."

"I don't want to cause trouble," said Rose. "We can sleep in the tents like we usually do."

"It is too overgrown out here for that," stated Raven.

"Aye," said Lark. "Besides, ye will have to come inside to eat. And we want to get to ken ye better. I'd like to hear all about gardenin'."

"Thank you. But are you sure Lord Rook won't protest?"

"He's always angry about things that don't matter," said Raven. "Besides, I can match my brother in a sword fight if it comes to it." She giggled.

"You can?" Rose's eyes opened wide. "I hope it won't come to that."

"Raven can go up against any man, so I'm no' worried," said Lark. "Now come, and we'll show ye around."

"All right, then," said Rose, feeling accepted by these two women. They were nobles, but they weren't arrogant or demanding and demeaning like Lord Rook. She liked them already. And while Lord Rook was a handsome man, she'd heard enough rumors about him to know to keep her distance. If she didn't, she would most likely fare no better than the other peasants who usually ended up in the man's bed.

CHAPTER 4

"What's this?" asked Rook, entering the great hall that night to find all the gardeners sprawled across his floor, lounging by the hearth in front of the fire.

"They needed somewhere to sleep, so I told them they could stay in here," said his sister.

"What?" asked Rook, not sure he liked the idea. He had only just inherited the manor and hadn't had the time to get things in order yet. "I suppose I'll have to feed them too?"

"Rook," said his mother, who had accompanied him here. "You are lord of a manor now. It's your job to take care of those less fortunate. It is what your father always does. If he was here right now, he'd tell you the same."

"Aye," agreed Lark with a yawn. "Ye have enough bedchambers, Rook. Why dinna ye give Rose one to sleep in?"

His head jerked around and he scowled at his cousin. "Nay," he ground out. "She's a commoner. And a mouthy one, too. Why in the world would I even consider such a thing?"

"Then do as ye please," said Lark. "I'm goin' to bed."

"Aye," agreed Raven. "Me too. We have a lot to do tomorrow. Good night, everyone."

"Lord Rook?"

Rook turned around to find the gardener girl standing there. He hadn't even heard her approach. When he moved so quickly, he accidentally stepped on her toe.

"Ow!" she cried, holding up her foot and hopping up and down.

"Rook, be careful," warned his mother.

"I didn't know she was there," said Rook, not knowing how to respond. He honestly hadn't meant to hurt her.

"My dear, are you injured?" Devon put her hand on Rose's shoulder.

"Nay, I am fine, my lady, but thank you for asking." Rose's eyes roamed back over to Rook. Big reddish-brown orbs drank him in, and he realized she was probably waiting for him to apologize.

"I didn't mean to do that," he said, not wanting to say the word sorry. He didn't feel it was right when talking with peasants. Neither should a noble ever apologize to a commoner, so he wasn't sure why the hell he was. "Did you want something, Prim?" he asked, just wishing the girl would leave him alone. Her presence shook him up for some reason.

Her eyes narrowed, and he realized why.

"I mean, Rose," he corrected himself, not seeing what difference it made what he called her. Obviously, it bothered the wench, so he'd try to remember that from now on.

"Is everything comfortable, Rose?" asked Devon. "Did you perhaps need more blankets? I could bring more from the bedchambers if you'd like."

"More blankets?" complained Rook, wondering what else his mother had given these commoners that she shouldn't have. The blankets were meant for the nobles. The commoners should be happy to be sleeping inside, because he thought they should be staying outside in their tents. He considered making them move outdoors, but before he could say so, the girl spoke.

"Nay, Lady Devon, we're fine, but it is very kind of you to offer. I just wanted to thank Lord Rook for allowing us to sleep inside by the fire."

"Mmmph," he grunted, knowing he could never demand they move outdoors now.

"I also wanted to request an audience with Lord Rook in the morning to discuss the restoring of the grounds."

"With me?" Rook couldn't imagine why he'd have to meet with the girl. Shouldn't she just know or be able to see what needed to be done?

"I have some questions for you. My lord," she added quickly. "Before my workers start, I need to know exactly what you want."

"Anything. Just fix it up," he said with a swish of his hand through the air.

"But it's important that I know what you expect from us. For instance, do you want an herb garden, a vegetable garden, a pleasure garden, or all three?"

"Pleasure garden?" he asked with a chuckle. "Now, that sounds interesting."

"Why... yes, of course it is," said Rose, her eyes roaming over to Rook's mother. The look on her face was as if she thought he was a simpleton for not knowing about this. Rook was a warrior and didn't spend time in gardens, nor did he care about them in the least. He almost told the girl so, but decided not to waste his breath on it.

"I could handle this for you, if you wish, Rook," said Devon.

"Yes, I think Lady Devon would be better for this. I agree," said Rose.

That comment annoyed Rook, and he decided then and

there that he would be the only one giving the girl orders. After all, it was his manor now. Besides, he was slightly intrigued, and wanted to know more about a pleasure garden and why the girl was even suggesting it to him in the first place.

"Nay, I'll handle it, but thank you, Mother," said Rook. "We'll meet out back right after the first meal in the morning," he told Rose.

"Of course. Thank you, my lord," said Rose, bowing her head. "Good night, my lady. My lord." She quickly turned around and walked back to join the others sleeping in front of the fire.

"I like her," said Devon, as soon as the girl had gone. "Rook, I want you to be nice to her."

"Nice? What does that mean?" he asked his mother.

"I mean, don't treat her the way you do all your other servants. Be kind. She's probably not used to being around nobles, so please don't scare her."

"All right. I can do that, I guess," he said, watching the girl lay down on the floor and cover herself with a blanket. Rook liked a challenge, and this girl had already challenged him more in the last few hours than any of his servants ever had. Something about her intrigued him and he wanted to know more about her.

"Not too nice, if you know what I mean," said his mother, dragging him from his thoughts. "She is not one of your trollops, nor is she your adversary, so treat her with respect."

"Mother, she is a commoner. How can you even suggest that I respect her?"

"Her father is also a master gardener and favored by many nobles as well as the king," Devon reminded him.

"Mayhap so, but that is her father, not the girl. She is still only a commoner and nothing else."

"Rook, at one time, when I first met your father, I was considered naught but his servant too, remember."

"Did Father treat you in any special way?" he asked.

"Well, nay. Not at first. Until he got to know me."

"You mean until he discovered you were a noble, even if you didn't know it at the time."

"That's not true. He cared for me long before he knew."

"Well, this is different, Mother. Rose is not a noble, I assure you." He turned and walked out of the great hall, heading for the stairs.

"Rook, you are my eldest son, and I don't like the reputation you seem to have." His mother wouldn't let this go.

He stopped in his tracks and turned back to talk to her. "You mean, you've heard rumors."

"Are they rumors?" she asked in a knowing manner. "It is said people see you as arrogant and that you use girls for your own needs and think nothing of it. In a way, you are a lot like your father used to be when I first met him."

"I am no different than any other nobleman," Rook told her. "Men of my status are expected to act a certain way. It is just accepted."

"Just because most noblemen act a certain way, doesn't make it right," said his mother.

"And what would you have me do? Marry a commoner, like Raven did?"

Devon raised her hand and shook her head. "I am not saying that."

"Good, because Father won't hear of it. Neither will I. You know how important it is that I marry well. Father wants all his children to be wed to someone of their same status."

"I didn't know we were speaking of marriage, Rook. I only asked you to be kind to Rose, that's all."

"I know that," said Rook, feeling confused as to why the conversation even went in this direction.

"Are you happy with the betrothal?" asked his mother.

"I don't know. I suppose. Although, I can't say I'm thrilled to have to marry a noblewoman I've never met and who has such a bad reputation."

"She has a bad reputation?" asked his mother with a smile.

"I know what you're thinking, and you're wrong. My reputation is not bad. I mean, not really."

"Am I wrong? Really?" asked Devon.

"I'll prove it to you. I'll go out of my way to be nice to that gardener girl, just as you ask. I'll show you that all those horrible things that are whispered through the rushes about me are not true in the least."

"I'll believe it when I see it, Rook." His mother reached up and kissed him on the cheek. "I only want the best for you, and I hope you can find a woman who makes you happy. Good night."

As his mother ascended the stairs, Rook turned back and looked into the great hall once more at the girl named Rose. It wouldn't be so hard to be kind to her, he supposed. After all, she was the daughter of a master gardener, like his mother said. She probably had skills to be admired. It also wouldn't be as if he were trying to befriend a rag picker. Yes, he decided. Tomorrow, he would prove to his mother, as well as his sister, his cousin, and everyone else, that all the rumors about him were not true. He had a heart. He wasn't a womanizer. Now that he was lord of a manor, those rumors would stop. Lord Rook Blake was about to change those stories, and when he did, everyone would like him. He would make sure of it.

~

"Are you meeting with Lord Rook today to go over plans for the garden?" Georgiana asked Rose the next morning as the group of gardeners sat at a back trestle table, eating the pottage and brown bread given to them by the household servants.

"Aye," she answered, taking a sip of cider. "I'm to meet him in the back garden right after the meal."

Rose looked up to the raised dais where the nobles sat to eat. Rook, his mother, his sister, and his cousin all sat above the salt.

Salt was expensive and usually only the nobles could use it freely. A big ornate salt cellar graced the dais table, made out of silver and shaped like a ship. Another was constructed in gold and had dragons holding up the bowl that was filled to the top with precious salt.

The nobles were eating what looked like fresh fruit, some kind of egg dish, and white bread. Brown bread was given to those below the salt since the white bread took extra time to grind the flour and was more expensive to make. Rook looked up from his trencher and their eyes met. Then, to her surprise, he smiled and nodded.

She almost smiled back at him. That was, until she saw him wink at her next.

Rose quickly dropped her gaze to the table, her heart beating so quickly that she felt it in her throat.

"Did Lord Rook just smile at you and wink?" asked her cousin, taking a bite of brown bread.

"Nay," Rose answered, feeling embarrassed by the lord's action. She had a feeling he might be trying to get her into his bed.

"Yes, he did. I saw him do it." Georgiana grabbed Rose's arm, her fingers gripping tightly. She leaned over and whispered into her ear. "I think he wants to couple with you."

"What?" Rose jerked backward, spilling her cider. She

quickly picked up the goblet and used her sleeve to sop up the liquid, since she had nothing else to use.

"Does that upset you?" asked Georgiana. "I hear it is an honor to be invited to Lord Rook's bed. One of the kitchen maids told me that sleeping with him is exciting and something she'll never forget."

"That's nice," said Rose, still trying to wipe up the cider.

"Look, here is that same kitchen maid now."

Rose looked up to see a voluptuous kitchen wench with a very low bodice meeting with Lord Rook as he walked down from the dais. The girl gazed up at him and batted her eyelashes. Then she leaned in really close. Rose swore she saw the girl quickly run her hand up Rook's leg.

"I'd better go out back for our meeting," said Rose, hurrying away, not stopping until she was outside of the castle. Her heart still beat rapidly in her chest, and she wasn't sure why. Mayhap it was just the thought of the lord of the manor possibly laying with her that upset her. The last thing she wanted was to fall prey to Rook's games with women.

She felt something on her shoulder and spun around, using her hand to swipe it away.

"Whoa! Don't attack," said Rook, standing there with a smile on his face and his hands raised in surrender. "I'm unarmed."

He wasn't exactly unarmed. He still wore his weapon belt with a dagger, even though he didn't have his sword with him right now.

"I'm sorry, my lord. I didn't know it was you." Rose let her gaze drop to the ground once again.

"Rose," he said, as if testing out her name on his tongue. "That is what you wished to be called?"

"Aye. It is my name," she told him.

"I see," he said, as if he debating the fact. Thankfully, he hadn't called her Prim again, because she didn't like that. "Walk with me," he commanded, turning and going without even waiting for her.

She followed right behind him, having trouble keeping up since he had long legs and his strides were wide. They walked out into the bramble and tangled vines of the garden, and then he stopped suddenly.

She stopped as well, taking in a deep breath of the fresh late spring air, and slowly releasing it, trying to calm herself.

"I get the feeling you don't care for me much. Is that true?" He looked at her from the sides of his eyes, not bothering to turn his head and talk to her directly. Of course, Rose didn't care for the man, but he was a noble and she couldn't admit it.

"Nay, that's not true." Rose avoided eye contact when she answered. Not that he was actually looking at her anyway.

"So... you like me, then? Is that what you're saying?"

Her gaze slowly lifted to meet his now. He had turned and was staring straight at her. How was she supposed to answer a question like that? If she said she liked him, which she didn't, he might take that as an offer to join him in bed. And if she admitted she didn't care for him at all, he might turn her away and give this job to someone else. She couldn't have that either. This job meant too much to her father. She promised him she'd make him proud, and that was exactly what she intended to do.

"I think it would be best for us to stick to business. We came out here to talk about your garden, not to determine my interest in you, or my lack of it."

"Oh," he said, looking at her as if he was about to chastise her for being so blunt.

"My lord," she added quickly, hoping this meeting wasn't going to take a wrong turn.

"All right, then. Talk," he said, looking out at the tangled vines and weeds. "Tell me what you think we should do with this mess."

Rose walked down the path, looking in one direction and then the other. "I remember how this used to look when my father first constructed the gardens here many years ago. I was just a child then, but I assisted him."

"Really?" he said, actually sounding interested, if she wasn't mistaken. "So tell me, what did it look like back then?"

"Well, if I remember correctly, there is a labyrinth made from the bushes... over there." She pointed to where tall bushes that stretched up way over her head were wrapped with climbing vines. "And there used to be an herb garden up there, near the kitchen." He looked to where she pointed. "A nice sized vegetable garden filled the other side."

"What about this pleasure garden you mentioned? I'd like to hear more about that," he said, his voice suddenly sounding low and sexy. Or was she just imagining it?

"A pleasure garden is for–"

"Pleasure?" He chuckled softly, and she figured he was thinking of all the illicit things he could do in there with his voluptuous servants.

"I'm not sure what you mean by pleasure, but yes, the garden's only purpose is for enjoyment," she explained, trying not to react to his insinuations. She was here for business only. "It is filled with colorful flowers, benches and statues, and serves no real purpose at all. It is a luxury for the nobles."

"No purpose?" he asked. "At all?"

"Well, I mean, you can't eat any of the plants, and neither are any of them used for medicinal purposes. It is a garden to please nobles in frivolous ways."

"Hmmm," he said. "I like to be frivolous. It sounds like exactly what I want."

It figured. She released a breath, realizing it was going to be impossible to talk about anything seriously with this man.

"What about the other gardens?" she asked.

"I want you to restore the herb and vegetable garden too, of course," he told her.

"You do?" She looked up into his bright blue orbs, surprised he'd even care about this at all.

"Yes, I do. I am lord of a manor now, and there will be many expenses. If I can grow my own food and herbs to use as medicine, it'll help to tamp down expenses and keep my coffers filled."

"Yes, of course. Good idea," she told him.

"I heard there was an orchard here? I see trees over there," he said, pointing to the far side of the grounds.

"Aye. There are a few cherry trees and several apple trees, but not a lot of them," she told him. "Or, at least, that is what used to be there. Did you want more? I'm not sure if there is enough room for more. That is, unless you planted an orchard outside the walls of the manor, of course. There is plenty of room there."

"Excuse me, my lord," said a kitchen maid, approaching them. It was the same girl that Georgiana had said slept with Rook.

"Susan, what is it?" asked Rook.

"It's Sally, my lord," said the girl, seeming upset that Rook couldn't remember her name. It almost made Rose laugh aloud. She was sure Rook didn't know or even care about the actual names of all his strumpets.

"Did you have a message for me?" he asked, doing nothing to correct himself.

"Lady Devon asked me to inform you that your cousin, Sir Robin, has arrived. He awaits you in the great hall."

49

"Robin is here?" asked Rook. "I haven't seen him in some time. You're dismissed," he told the maidservant.

The girl named Sally glared at Rose and then stomped off, seeming as if she didn't want to leave Rose there alone with Rook. As if it truly mattered. Rose would never do anything with this man other than talk. He was much too pompous for her liking. She was attracted to men who had a softer side to them. Ones who had a heart and cared about people, not just used them for their own needs.

She froze when she felt Rook's hand on her. Her eyes slowly traveled downward, seeing his long fingers wrapped around her upper arm.

"Come," he said, pulling her gently along with him as he started back toward the manor. "I want to speak more to you about this pleasure garden, as well as look at the front of the castle. But first I must greet my cousin."

"Aye. My lord," she said, walking with him. He slowly let his hand slip from her arm. With it went the feel of the warmth of his hot skin. Still, she somehow felt burned by his touch.

What was the matter with her? Her cheeks felt flushed and her heart pounded loudly again. She didn't like that she couldn't control these feelings around such a cur of a man.

"Robin, you scoundrel, how the hell are you?" Rook walked into the great hall with Rose quietly following behind him. "I haven't seen you in some time now." He grasped his cousin's hand and shook it. With his other hand, he slapped Robin on his back in a manly form of a half-hug.

"Nice place you have here, Rook," said Robin, looking around. Robin was a knight, like Lord Rook. He had dark blond hair and a short beard and mustache. He wore a weapon belt with an array of blades attached.

"It has a lot to be desired, and is a work in progress," Rook answered. "However, I have high hopes of what it can become in time."

"Cousin? There is a girl standing behind you," said Robin in a low voice.

"Aye, this is my master gardener, Primrose," he introduced her.

"Master gardener?" Robin raised a brow. "Is that right, Primrose?" he asked Rose.

"Nay, not exactly," she answered. "My father is the master gardener, but he broke his leg and sent me in his stead." Rose stepped forward to greet Robin with a curtsy. "And you can just call me Rose, instead of Primrose, my lord."

"I see." Robin looked over at Rook and chuckled. "Well, I am Sir Robin Blake, but you can just call me Lord Robin. We're very informal in my family and usually just use Lord instead of Sir, along with our Christian names."

"Of course. Lord Robin," she said with a nod.

"She is going to build me a pleasure garden," Rook told his cousin.

"She is?" asked Robin, seeming amused for some reason.

"She and her garden workers, that is," Rook continued. "I hear her skills are unmatched."

"Really, now," said Robin, giving Rook an odd look. "And you are... all right with a woman in charge of your ground work?"

Rook took two tankards of ale from a servant carrying a tray and handed one to his cousin. "It's all right," he whispered back. "I told my mother I'm trying to change my ways. I'm being nice. To everyone," said Rook, taking a drink.

Robin almost split a gut on that one. "Rook, you are like a leopard who can't change its spots and you know it," he told him. "Who the hell do you think you're fooling?"

"That's not true," said Rook, a scowl washing over his face. "Now that I'm about to become a married man, I plan on changing."

"Changing what? Your clothes?" Robin laughed at his own jest. "I see you are still wearing that obnoxious red cloak, so mayhap that is the first thing you can change out of." He continued to chuckle.

"I like the color red," Rook told him, shooting daggers from his eyes at his cousin. "And I'm serious about changing my ways. When my betrothed arrives, you'll see."

"Yes, I heard about your betrothed." Robin sat down atop a trestle table, leaving one foot on the floor. He was a tall man like Rook. His blond hair was tied back with a leather band. His attire was that of a fighting man. "You'll change all right. You'll have to, if you're to survive being married to that French shrew."

Rose cleared her throat, subtly reminding the men that she was still standing there listening to them talk about Rook's betrothed in an inappropriate manner.

Rook's gaze shot over to Rose and then back to his cousin. "We'll talk about this later," he said. "Tell me, how are Uncle Madoc and Aunt Abbey and your sisters?"

"Fine, fine," said Robin with a nod. "Martine and Regina are proper ladies now and want to get married, but my parents told them I had to wed first since I'm the eldest."

"What about little Dorothy?" asked Rook. "Is she still singing like meadowlark, everywhere she goes?"

"Little Dorothy isn't so little anymore," Robin told him. "She's not only singing, but starting to have a mind of her own. She insists on everyone calling her Dot."

Rook chuckled. "I guess stubborn women run in our family line."

"Cousin!" Raven ran down the stairs with Lark right behind her.

"Robin!" shouted Lark, sounding excited to see him.

Both of the girls threw themselves at Robin in a hug. Robin chuckled, the force of the girls in his arms making him spill his ale.

"Cousins, I'm happy to see you, too." Robin put down the tankard and stood up, one arm around each of the women.

"How long will you be staying?" Rook asked Robin.

"I'm on my way to Hermitage Castle on the border. I thought it was time I visited Uncle Storm and Aunt Wren. However, I'm in no real hurry, and thought I'd stay here with you until the wedding," said Robin.

"Good. I could use you here," stated Rook. "I need to choose my staff, filling the empty positions. Plus, having another sword around for protection would put my mind at ease."

"I'm at your disposal," said Robin, looking back at Rose standing there silently, not saying a word. "Rose," he called out to her.

"Yes, my lord?" She answered with a slight bow of her head.

"I want to warn you about my cousin and his horrid reputation."

"God's eyes, Robin, not you too," Rook ground out, trying to shut him up, but Robin kept on talking.

"If you don't watch your step, he'll lure you into his bed."

"Thank you for the warning, but I am quite aware of Lord Rook's reputation," said Rose in a steady voice, not sounding nearly amused as Robin did at the moment.

"You are?" mumbled Rook, wondering what the girl had been told about him. It seemed word traveled fast around these parts.

"I assure you, I am here for business only, and have no desire to warm anyone's bed," Rose answered with a sniff. "Now, if you'll excuse me, I need to give instructions to my workers. There is a lot to be done and I cannot be wasting precious moments with idle chatter." Rose left before Rook could even dismiss her. Actually, she left him speechless, as he'd never expected her to say anything like that!

"Lark, let's make sure the gardeners have everything they need to do their job," suggested Raven.

"Excuse us," said Lark to the men before the women followed Rose across the room.

"My, my, cousin, it seems you have a feisty one there." Robin lifted his tankard to his mouth, watching Rose walk away.

"Yes, she is a rather outspoken wench. For a commoner, that is." Rook picked up his tankard and downed it all at one time. His eyes roamed back over to Rose who was standing beside the trestle table, instructing her workers.

"Egads, Rook, I'd know that look anywhere," said Robin in surprise. "You're attracted to the wench, aren't you?"

"Nay." Rook's eyes flashed back the other way. "I mean, she is comely and all, but she's only here to do a job."

"And what job is that?"

"She's restoring the grounds. And building me a pleasure garden," he tried to explain.

"Pleasure garden? Now, that sounds about right where you're concerned."

"Robin, please. That's not what I meant." Rook's eyes flitted back toward Rose again. Damn, the woman was intriguing.

"Just watch yourself around her, Rook," said Robin, finishing off his ale.

"What do you mean? I can keep my hands off of her. I'm only being nice to her because I promised mother I would."

"Uh huh," he said, not sounding at all as if he believed him. "That's how it always starts. Next thing you know, you'll be just like Raven, marrying a commoner."

"Bite your tongue, you bastard," spat Rook. "It'll never happen to me. I am a noble and will only marry someone of my own status."

"Let's hope not. After all, Uncle Corbett made sure that all his siblings knew we were all to marry nobles only. He'll have it no other way."

"Yes, that's true," said Rook, his stomach clenching thinking about who he was to marry. Even if he didn't want to, it was the right thing to do. "If you'll excuse me, I need to give the gardener more instructions. Then I need your help in getting my staff together and my manor in order."

"I'd be happy to help however I can," said Robin, looking over at Rose. "And since you're not interested, I'll even take that attractive garden girl off your hands too."

"You do that, and I'll break your arm," spat Rook.

"What?" Robin shrugged. "I thought you said you had no interest in the wench, so what does it matter?"

"She is here to work and not to be distracted by the likes of you or anyone else. So digging in the garden is all she will do. Do you understand? Keep your hands to yourself."

"I thought so," said Robin, brushing invisible lint off his clothes. "I'll be sure to leave before your father finds out your true feelings for the wench, because I don't want to be here when he explodes."

CHAPTER 5

Three days later, Rook and Robin practiced their sword fighting in the courtyard. The gardeners had been busy weeding the area, and it already looked so much better.

"Filling the positions of your household isn't going very quick, is it?" asked Robin, blocking a blow from Rook.

"Nay. It's not as easy as I thought." Rook's sword clashed with his cousin's. "I've got my mother seeing to the kitchen servants, and Raven and Lark are interviewing peasants to hire as chambermaids, but I still need to find a steward. Not to mention, a bailiff, groomsman, and eventually when I have birds, a falconer too."

Robin stopped fighting, and both men lowered their swords. "You're lucky, Rook."

"How do you figure that?"

"I mean, look at you and what you have here." Robin held out his arm at the manor and courtyard that was much like a small castle. Half the gardeners were up front loading the pulled weeds and debris into a cart. Rose and the others were out back. "It has so much potential. You'll inherit your father's castle someday, but this isn't a bad place to wait it out."

"Aye," said Rook. "It'll get better, and the money will increase once I attain my betrothed's dowry."

"You're marrying a noble, and that is all that is important."

"Yes. I want more than anything to please my father. Since Raven married a commoner, it is even more crucial that I marry a noble to make things right for my family."

"You have two brothers for that as well," Robin reminded him.

"True, but Daegel and Tolin won't be married off before me. This all falls on my shoulders. I have to make certain that the Blake family name will be respected and honored by all. I am the eldest son and it will be my heir who receives the inheritance someday."

"Doesn't it bother you to be marrying a shrew?" Robin raised one eyebrow. "I hear the Frenchwoman is no prize."

"Aye, it does." Rook slipped his sword into his scabbard. "But then again, I've been told I'm no prize either. Who even knows if my betrothed will even want me after she meets me."

That made Robin laugh. "Rook, you do seem to worry a little too much for being a man."

"I'm just trying to do the right thing—what's expected of me."

"Oh, stop it. Uncle Corbett adores you, and you can do no wrong in his eyes."

"Not yet, mayhap, but who knows how long that will last," mumbled Rook, thinking about the gardener girl. Once he married the shrew, he'd never be able to look at another woman again. If he did, he was sure the Frenchwoman wouldn't make life easy for him. "I am going to ride to the village and introduce myself to the serfs to let them know I'm their new lord. Do you want to accompany me?"

"Sure. Why not? I'm here to support you and help you in any way I can. Let's go."

~

"Stop here, Phineas," Rose told the man a little while after they'd entered the forest. "This looks like a good place to find the sticks we need for the wattle fences."

"Aye," said Phineas, slowing the wagon. His wife, Thomasina, sat between him and Rose on the front bench seat. Georgiana and the other gardeners were in the back with their tools. Traveling along with them on horses were Lady Lark and Lady Raven. The noblewomen said they wanted to come along and also gave their permission to enter the woods since Rook had already left for town and Rose couldn't ask him.

"What kind of wood do ye need to collect?" asked Lark from atop her horse.

Rose jumped down from the wagon and looked around the area. "It works best with branches that are pliable. Usually hazel or alder, or even maple, would suffice." She peered up into the trees. "There are a lot of oaks here." She groaned. "We can use some of these for now, but we'll have to keep searching."

"I'm sure you'll find what you need," said Raven from atop her steed. "However, I suggest you all stay together. The woods are not the safest place to be, so you are better protected in groups." Raven had her sword strapped to her side. She looked back and forth, inspecting the wooded area.

"Let's work quickly," said Rose, handing out rakes and shears and even axes.

They managed to find a good amount of branches that they loaded into the back of the wagon. Still, Rose wasn't happy.

She really wanted some hazel or alder branches because those made the best fences.

"I think it's time to go," called out Raven from her horse. She and Lark never dismounted, just watched the workers from atop their horses since they were nobles and didn't do manual labor.

"All right, load up the tools," Rose called out to her workers. "And head back to the wagon." Rose spotted some branches deeper in the woods that took her interest. They looked like hazel and were exactly what she'd been searching for.

"Cousin, are you coming?" asked Georgiana.

"In a minute," said Rose. "I want to collect a few more branches. I see some good ones just up ahead." Holding her shears, she started forward to get them.

"Rose, mayhap you should listen to Lady Raven and stay with the group. It's time to go," said her cousin.

"It's fine. I'll be fast. Go back to the wagon and help the others," said Rose, keeping her eye on the branches hanging down from a tree deeper in the forest. More pliable branches were even scattered on the ground. She hurried over and yanked on a branch and smiled. "Hazel. Yes. These are pliable, thin, and perfect." She was so busy snipping the branches and loading them into her arms that she didn't even realize there was someone else in the woods up ahead.

"Well, look at that. I found myself a nice piece of meat," came a man's gruff voice.

Her gaze shot over to the voice and that's when she realized she was in danger. Four scraggly men dressed in dirty and tattered clothes must have been poaching in the forest. They carried dead rabbits and squirrels with them hanging from rope. All of them had knives. One man even had a bow and arrows.

"She's mine," called out the one in the lead, moving closer. "I saw her first."

With her arms filled with branches, Rose took a few steps backwards. The men were moving in, and she figured she should turn and run. She spied her shears on the ground and dropped the sticks, lunging for the tool. She gripped her shears in her fist, holding them out to protect herself from the men who were now standing in front of her.

"Leave me alone," she warned them.

"What are you goin' to do?" laughed one of the filthy men.

"I warn you, I have others with me," said Rose, her gaze shifting quickly back to where she'd left the wagon, but she couldn't see anyone from her position. That made her realize she must have wandered deeper into the woods than she thought.

"Others? Really?" One of the men looked in the direction where Rose had just glanced. "Mayhap we'll all get lucky today after all."

"Go see if there are more wenches," one of the men told the others.

"Nay. I'm going to have this one," said a man with rotten teeth, while two of them headed toward the wagon at a run.

"You hold her for me and I'll hold her for you," said the fatter of the two who stayed behind. Rose felt ill and wanted to retch.

"Nay! Leave me alone," she cried, deciding her only chance would be to run. She turned and ran after all, hoping to make it back to her friends before she was accosted. She didn't get far before one of the men brought her to the ground. She fell atop her shears, unable to move under the man's weight. When she looked up, the feet of the second man were right in front of her face.

~

Rook and Robin rode back into the courtyard after having visited the serfs. Everyone seemed eager to have a new lord. He hadn't stayed long, but would return again to inspect his fields and crops at a later time.

Lark came barreling into the courtyard after them atop her horse.

"Rook! Robin!" she shouted. "Help them. They're bein' attacked." She seemed panicked and Rook had no idea what was happening here.

"Slow down," said Rook, still atop his horse. "Now, what's the matter?"

Lark stopped her horse. "Raven and the gardeners are in the forest," she screamed, pointing back at the woods nearby. "We were approached by ruffians, and Raven sent me back to get ye while she is fightin' them off."

"God's eyes, nay!" Rook turned his horse. "Stay here, Lark. Robin, come with me." Rook rode like the devil, able to hear the fighting as soon as he entered the woods. Up ahead, he saw Raven swinging her sword from atop her horse at men who were attacking them with long, sharp knives. Phineas swung a shovel at one of the men who was holding a bow and arrows. He hit the man in the head. Thomasina was like a madwoman with sharp shears in both hands, running after another of the attackers, snapping the tools like lobster claws. Georgiana and several other workers were hiding in the back of the wagon.

"Raven, take the others and get back to the manor," shouted Rook, ripping his sword from his scabbard to go after the attackers.

"Run!" yelled one of the attackers to the other as soon as they saw Rook and Robin approach. The two poachers dropped the animals they'd hunted and hightailed it through the forest.

"I'll get them," said Robin, but Rook stopped him.

"Nay. Leave them for now. It's more important we get everyone back to the manor safely. Is anyone hurt?" asked Rook.

"I don't think so," said Raven. "However, I wounded both of the attackers with my sword."

"Good job," said Rook, suddenly realizing he didn't see Rose with them. "Where is Rose?"

"She's out there. In the forest, all alone," cried Georgiana, pointing in the direction that her cousin went.

"Damnation, why didn't someone stay with her?"

"I told her not to go, but she was insistent upon it," said Georgiana. "Lord Rook, please. You've got to help her."

"Raven, Robin, guard the workers and get them and their things back to the manor at once. I'm going after Rose," said Rook, taking off at full speed deeper into the forest. He thought he heard voices and headed in that direction. When he made it through the clearing, he saw Rose on the ground on her stomach. One man sat on top of her, holding up her skirt, while the other had his trews pulled down and was getting into position.

"Nay!" shouted Rook, going mad with anger. He jumped off the horse, pulling the man with the lowered trews off of Rose, throwing him to the ground. Rook plunged his sword deep into the man's chest. "You filthy bastards!" he spat, retrieving his sword. He spun around to see the other man already up and running. Rook pulled his dagger from his waist belt, flinging it at the man. The blade went right into the attacker's head. The man gasped and fell dead to the ground.

"Lord Rook?" whimpered Rose from behind him.

"Rose!" Rook tossed aside his sword and ran to her, pulling her gown back down to save her modesty. She sat up, crying. She still had a pair of shears clutched in her hand, and there was blood on them. "God's eyes, Rose. Are you hurt?"

"Nay," she said, looking down at the shears. "I cut my arm on my shears when I fell, but I'm fine. I was going to use the shears as a weapon, but the man sat on me and then I couldn't move." She threw down the shears, wrapping her arms around him and cried.

"Shhhhh," said Rook, pulling Rose tighter into his embrace. He held her, rocking back and forth from a sitting position, tamping down her hair and kissing her atop the head. "Did they... did they... have you?" He hated to ask, but he needed to know.

"Nay," she answered, pulling back and sniffling. "They would have, if you hadn't saved me. Thank you," she said, throwing herself into his arms once again, holding him so tight that he thought she would never let him go.

Rook's heart went out to the girl, but all the while he kept his eyes open for more attackers. Rose had almost been raped today, and he felt as if he were responsible for the situation. Rook was lord of the manor and should have known Rose and the others were out here. He should at least have accompanied them on their quest for sticks. Rook had failed to watch over his people today, and this didn't sit well with him at all.

"You're safe now," he said, reaching down and wiping away a tear from her cheek. Rose looked up at him with her big brown eyes, and he saw fear mixed with gratitude within them. "I'm sorry I wasn't here to stop this from happening in the first place." He got to his feet, bringing her with him.

Rose looked over and saw the attackers dead on the ground, covered in blood. The one still had Rook's dagger sticking out of his head. She screamed and hid her face against his chest so she wouldn't have to see the gory sight.

"Get on the horse," he told her. "And try not to look at them." He helped her mount his horse. Then he picked up his sword and walked over and pulled his dagger out of the dead man's head, wiping the blood on the forest floor. He checked the other man to make sure he was dead as well. Satisfied that they'd cause no more trouble, Rook replaced his sword in the scabbard and collected Rose's shears from the ground.

"Rook, I heard a scream. Is everyone all right?" Robin came barreling through the woods atop his horse with his sword raised. "Oh, I guess I'm too late," he said, eyeing up the dead men.

"I told you to take everyone back to the manor," growled Rook. "Why are you still here?"

"Raven's got them. They're safe." Rook inspected the situation from atop his horse.

"Robin, can you help out and make sure these rotten slugs get buried?"

"I can do that," said Robin with a nod, replacing his sword. "When I get back to the manor, I'll have a few of the workers come back with shovels."

"Good, because I've got a very frightened girl that I need to guard. I won't let anything happen to her ever again."

Rook climbed up and seated himself in back of Rose, putting his arms around her and directing his horse to the manor. This was one hell of a day. Sadly, something told him that being lord of a manor was going to be a lot harder than he'd ever anticipated.

CHAPTER 6

By the time they rode back to Horrabridge Manor, Rose had finally calmed down and stopped shaking. With Rook's arms wrapped around her, she felt warm and well protected. She would be ever grateful to this man for saving her from being accosted by those swine in the forest. It was the most frightening thing she'd ever experienced in her life.

"Rook, you're back!" Raven had already returned with the workers. She rushed over with Lark at her side. Rook's mother saw him from across the courtyard and hurried over as well.

"What happened?" asked Devon.

"We were attacked by poachers in the forest, Mother," said Raven, in a calm and cool manner.

Rose admired Lady Raven. She was a noblewoman but also could protect others as well as herself. She also seemed to be able to keep her emotions at bay. Rose wished she could be more like Raven.

"Was anyone hurt?" asked Devon.

"I injured at least two of the attackers, but everyone here is fine, as far as I know," said Raven.

"What about ye, Rose? What happened to ye?" asked Lark.

Rook dismounted, holding out his arms and helping Rose to the ground.

"I was... I was..." she started, not even wanting to say aloud that those ruffians hurt her and almost had their way with her.

"Don't answer that," Rook told her softly. Then he looked out at the others. "Rose is fine. She is just shaken and needs to rest."

Robin rode in right after them. "I need a few men to help me bury some bodies," he announced.

"Bury bodies?" Devon's gaze swept over to Rook. "What exactly happened out there?"

"Never mind, Mother. I took care of it," said Rook. "Now, who will help Lord Robin?"

"I will," said Phineas.

"Me, too," added another of Rose's men.

"Good. Then grab some shovels and follow me," said Robin, leading the way.

"Phineas, bring back the sticks I dropped," Rose called out, not wanting to lose her good find.

"Sally, come here." Rook beckoned to the kitchen maid that had slept with him. Rose wondered why Rook was looking for her at a time like this.

"My lord?" The girl smiled and ran over to him. "What can I do for you?"

"You and the kitchen maids heat water and fill a bath in my solar anon."

"Aye, my lord," said the girl, still smiling. "I'd be more than happy to help you with your bath in any way possible." She curtseyed and ran off to do as told.

"Really, Rook? You're going to take a bath with your trollop? Now?" Raven shook her head in disgust.

"Nay, of course not," he growled. "The bath isn't for me. It's for Rose."

"It is?" That surprised Rose. She wasn't sure what to say or how to respond. Usually, she and her workers bathed out of a trough or in the lake when the weather allowed. Baths indoors were only for nobles.

"She's filthy from the woods," said Rook. "Plus, she's got blood on her gown."

"Blood?" asked Devon. "What happened? I thought you weren't hurt."

"It's just a scratch, and nothing to worry about," Rook explained.

"I fell on my shears," said Rose, wrapping her arms around her, not wanting to think of what almost happened to her.

"Raven, do you or Lark have something clean Rose can wear?" asked Rook.

"Oh, that's not necessary," said Rose. "I can wash out my gown and hang it by the fire to dry overnight."

"Do you have other clothes with you?" he asked her.

"Well, nay. Not with me," said Rose.

"Then mayhap my sister or cousin will lend you something until your gown can be cleaned."

"Of course they will," said Rook's mother, answering for the girls. "Rose, you'll come with me, and we'll fix you up, don't you worry."

"Thank you," said Rose, looking over at Rook. She still felt so shaken that she didn't want to leave his side.

"Go on," he told her, with a slight nod. "You'll be fine. My mother will take care of things. You're safe inside the manor walls."

"Thank you," said Rose, with a slight nod and a half-bow to Rook. "My lord," she added quickly, knowing that she needed to sound respectful since Lord Rook was a noble. She headed toward the manor with Rook's mother, feeling her legs shaking again.

"Rose?" Rook called out, causing her to stop and turn around.

"Yes, Lord Rook?"

"I want you to stay in my solar tonight, instead of sleeping in the great hall on the floor."

Rose wasn't sure what Rook meant by that, and didn't know how to answer. Was he saying he just wanted her to be comfortable after her harrowing experience in the woods? Or did he mean he wanted her to spend the night with him? Together? Her head spun, and she started to shake again. She felt so weak that she was afraid she'd fall.

"Aye, my lord," she answered in a mere whisper, closing her eyes.

"You can hold on to me if you'd like," offered Devon, putting her arm around Rose's waist. "You don't look so well. After your bath, I'll make sure some food and wine is sent up for you."

"Oh, please, no wine," said Rose, her head already dizzying. "Just a little spiced mead, if you have it, would be great."

"I'll be up to check on you later," Rook called out as they walked away.

Why did his words excite her and terrify her at the same time? And why couldn't she stop wondering if Rook meant to bathe with her, bed her, or just to make her comfortable? Also, why did she keep longing to be held in his arms once again?

~

"Robin," Rook called to his cousin later, seeing him emerging from the stable. "How did it go?"

"The bodies are buried," said Robin. "Everything is taken care of, and it's over."

"That was fast."

"Phineas is a madman with a shovel." Robin chuckled. "How is the girl?"

"I think she's all right. I'm going to go check on her now."

"What about the rest of the attackers? Shouldn't you hunt them down and punish them somehow? After all, they were poaching in your woods."

"I killed two of them today," said Rook, not feeling good about what he did since the men were no match for him with his sword. However, he went mad when he saw them pinning Rose to the ground and about to rape her. At first, he hadn't been sure they hadn't already done so. "I think that is enough to get the message across."

"Still, this kind of behavior shouldn't be tolerated," protested Robin. "You need to take action, Rook."

"I did," Rook said with a sigh. "The two who tried to accost Rose have paid their dues. As for the others... yes, they were poaching on my lands and if they return, they will pay as well. However, I can't be sure what kind of agreement Crazy Clive had with them."

"Who?" asked Robin, making a face.

"The last lord of the manor. He was eccentric. I'm going to need to speak with the villagers about it, and see what was allowed while the earl was alive. After all, he just died recently, and not everyone may know that they are under the rule of a new lord."

"I see your point," said Robin. "Still, you need to rule with an iron fist. Put fear into these commoners."

Commoners. The word sat sour in Rook's gut. Before Rose arrived at the manor, Rook's thinking would have been the same as his cousin's. But since meeting Rose, he started to realize that mayhap he'd been too harsh with commoners in the past. Rook did what he had to do today to protect Rose. But then again, killing never felt good, not even when it was a war.

"I saw commoners with fear in their eyes today, cousin, and it didn't feel good," said Rook. "If you could have seen how terrified Rose was, you would understand why I think I may have misjudged some... commoners. Or at least those who are not guilty."

"You make no sense, cousin. What are you saying?" asked Robin. "What kind of Lord of Horrabridge will you be?"

"I haven't decided yet. But one thing I know is that I want the commoners to respect me, not fear me. There is a difference, you realize."

"I guess so. I never really thought about it in that way."

"If you'll excuse me, I want to check on Rose." Rook left his cousin standing there and hurried into the keep. At the foot of the stairs, he met the promiscuous servant, Sally, with a tray of food in her hands.

"Lord Rook, how can I please you?" asked the girl, batting her eyes at him. Usually, that was her signal that she wanted to couple with him. He never turned her away. Until now.

Rook pretended not to notice the lust dripping from her pores, as well as her provocative stance. "Where are you going with that tray?" he asked.

"Lady Devon asked me to bring it to your solar. For the garden girl who you had me prepare the bath for."

"I'll take it to her," said Rook, collecting the tray from Sally.

"But, my lord. This is the job of a servant." It seemed to upset her that Rook wanted to do it himself. Somehow, he knew it wasn't because of respect, but rather because the girl was jealous of Rose.

"That'll be all. Now get back to the kitchen," he told her, watching as she pouted and stomped away.

Rook took the stairs slowly, balancing the tray that had a covered silver dish of food and a decanter of mead with a goblet. He chuckled to himself. No commoner ever ate off silver or drank from a goblet. The food on the dish was meant for nobles. His mother had a kind heart and often said she wished the commoners could be treated better. He was sure this would be the gossip of the kitchen wenches once Sally got back and started wagging her tongue.

He didn't care.

Carefully balancing the tray on one hand, he pushed open the door to his solar with the other. He stopped in his tracks. The room was dark since the shutter was closed. It was cold in here, and there was no fire on the hearth.

Rook placed the tray of food on a nearby table, finding a candle and lighting it.

"Rose?" he asked, thinking she was already sleeping. He looked over at the bed, but didn't see her there. However, there was one of his sister's gowns and a shift laid out on the bed for her. Next, he made his way over to the hearth and lit a fire that brightened the entire room. "Rose, are you in here?"

He turned around and froze. There, asleep in the wooden tub with her ears submerged under the water, was Rose. Firelight danced on her sun-kissed face, making the lines of her pale skinned form, normally hidden under her clothes, stand out noticeably.

Her long blonde hair floated atop the water like a mermaid's tresses, and her perky bare breasts poked up like two pale full moons. He should have looked away, but couldn't. Her taut nipples begged him to suckle them, and he felt his loins tighten at just the thought. Bid the devil, he wanted this girl.

She stirred and pushed up until her head was out of the water. Rook stood still, unable to move or to say a thing. Then her eyelids fluttered open. When she saw Rook standing there, she screamed and covered her breasts with her arms. "Nay, leave me alone. Don't hurt me!"

"Rose, it's me. Rook," he said, holding up his palms and backing away from the tub slowly. "I'm not going to hurt you, I promise."

"Lord R-Rook?" she asked, stopping her screaming. "What are you doing here?" Her thin brows dipped, and she sank back under the water to hide her exposed body from his sight.

"I'm sorry. I thought you'd be done bathing by now. I brought you food." He motioned to the food with his arm. "See? It's right here on the table by the door." He hurried over to get it.

"Leave," she demanded.

Rook picked up the tray, shaking his head as he let out a breath. She was only a commoner, and he was a noble, yet she was giving him commands. As much as he wanted to think differently about commoners, her words were something he couldn't ignore.

"This is my solar, Rose," he said, turning to face her. "You can't talk to a noble that way."

"My lord," she added quickly, as if that would make everything better, but it didn't.

"Get out of the tub and dry off," he commanded. Rook turned away from her to give her privacy, taking the tray over to a small table and two chairs. He spoke with his back to her as he took the food and drink off the tray. "It looks like my sister lent you a gown and shift. On the bed."

"I see it," he heard her say, hearing the water slosh as she removed herself from the tub. "Thank you."

Damn, this girl was confusing him. One minute she seemed angry he was there, and the next she was thanking him for something that he didn't even do. His thoughts went back to the way she looked, lying in the tub of water. It was tempting not to turn around and peek at her right now. He found himself wondering about the girl's every curve. He cleared his throat and tried to ignore the protruding bulge below his waist.

"Did you enjoy the bath?" he asked, trying to make pleasant conversation, although this wasn't one of his strong points at all. Especially not with women. Usually, when he was in his bedchamber with a beautiful woman, there wasn't much talking going on.

"Yes, thank you. It was relaxing." He heard the rustle of her clothing as she dressed. Once again, she thanked him, so he really couldn't be angry with her. He had probably just frightened her, being half-asleep, and that is why she spoke so brashly to him. She had been through a lot today, he realized.

"I'm sorry I scared you," he apologized, even though this wasn't one of his strong suits either.

"I—I fell asleep in the tub. I only screamed because I thought you were one of those men from the forest at first."

"Never," he said, hearing her bare feet padding across the room, so he turned to face her. "Oh, my," he said with a catch in his breath. Dressed in Raven's gown, she looked like a cross between a wet mermaid and an elegant noble.

"What's the matter?" she asked, looking down and tugging at the strings of the bodice. "Am I still exposed?"

"Nay," he said, with a shake of his head. "It's just that you look like a noble in that gown."

"That's because it is the gown of a noble," she stated the obvious. "Lord Rook, I shouldn't be wearing this. It's not right. I'll take it off." Her hands went to the bodice.

Rook quickly stepped forward, taking her hands in his to stop her. He felt her soft skin under his palms, still damp from the bathwater. "Nay. Leave it. Please," he said, barely able to get the words out since he wanted her so desperately. If she removed the gown, he wasn't going to be able to control himself any longer.

"What's that?" she asked, her gaze roaming with interest over to the table.

"My mother sent food for you." He released her hands and picked up the cover from the silver dish. The aroma of venison, root vegetables and a savory herbal sauce floated in the air.

"What is that?" asked Rose with wide eyes, leaning over the food and taking a deep breath. "Mmmm, it smells good."

"It looks like venison stew and white bread," he told her. "It's one of my favorite meals."

"Venison?" she asked. Then, so innocently, she batted her eyelids, reminding him of a doe.

"Deer meat," he told her, getting a scowl from Rose in return.

"I know what venison is. I've just never had it before."

"You haven't? Then sit down and try it." He pulled out a chair for her. She looked up in surprise. "Have a seat, my la— my little one," he said, almost getting lost in the moment and accidentally calling her 'my lady.' God's eyes, what was wrong with him? Mayhap she shouldn't be wearing that gown after all. It befuddled his mind.

"I'm not sure I should," she said, inspecting the dish, but doing nothing to taste it. "This isn't the food of commoners." She picked up the chunk of white bread and studied it, too. "This is the food of the nobles."

"You've never had white bread either?" he asked, pulling out a chair and sitting down at the table as well.

"Nay," she said. "I'm not sure this food is really for me."

"Of course it is."

"I'd better not." She put down the bread, brushing her fingers together. All the while, she stared at the meal, almost looking spellbound by it. Her eyes devoured it, but she did nothing to taste it.

"If it'll make you feel better, I'll eat some too," said Rook, to try to ease her discomfort. Rook picked up a spoon and dipped it into the bowl, his eyes focused on Rose as he opened his mouth and ate some of the stew. He moaned slightly. "It's so good with the rich ginger and herb sauce."

"Ginger?" That took her interest. "I've harvested ginger for many lords and ladies in their gardens."

"But you've never tasted it," he said, not bothering to ask since he already knew the answer.

She pressed her lips together and shook her head. All the while, her eyes stayed focused on his mouth. And when his tongue shot out to lick his lips, he swore he saw her squirm in her chair. He wasn't sure if the want he saw in her eyes was for the food or for him. Then again, did it really matter?

"Here. Try some." He scooped up a spoonful and held it up to her mouth. "Open," he said, watching her lips part. He put in the spoon and she closed her mouth, taking in the food.

"Mmmm," she said with her eyes half-closed. Her tongue shot out to lick her lips, the same way he had. Now it was his turn to squirm in his chair.

"You like it?"

"More than you know."

"Here. Have more." He handed her the spoon and quickly stood up. He noticed her eyes on the bulge in his trews and so he quickly sat back down again.

"I thought you just moved to the manor. Where did you get venison?" she asked curiously. "Did you go on a hunt?"

"Nay. We brought food with us, plus there was some left behind by the earl. His larder was nearly filled with salted meat. The man was rich. And very eccentric."

"I see." She spooned some more food into her mouth, not

able to eat it fast enough. "By eccentric, you mean because of the condition of the grounds?"

"That, and other things." He couldn't watch her eat anymore. One more lick of her lips and he'd be lunging over the table to taste her lips for himself. Unknowingly, the girl was arousing him.

"Did you want any more of the stew?" she asked, still chewing.

"Nay," he answered, walking over to stare into the fire. "You eat it."

"Well, then, at least have some bread." She hurried over to him with bread in her hands. She tore off a piece and held it up to his mouth. "Open up," she said with a giggle, saying back to him what he'd said to her.

Their gazes interlocked.

His mouth slowly opened.

Rook took the bite of bread and chewed, taking in her beauty in the light of the fire.

"Let me get some spiced mead for you. That's my favorite drink." She hurried back to the table, poured a goblet of mead, and walked carefully back to him, her eyes focused on the full cup so she wouldn't spill the contents.

"Here you go, my lord," she said, still staring at the goblet.

"You first."

Rose didn't object. She took a sip of mead. Rook watched her long, slim neck move as she swallowed. She then handed him the cup.

Rook's fingers closed over hers, and slowly her gaze lifted. He stared into the depths of strength and innocence intermingled with something he couldn't quite decipher. It was something he hadn't really seen before from any of his servants. Her big brown eyes drank him in. With their gazes interlocked, he couldn't look away.

"I feared for your life today," he told her, barely above a whisper.

"Thank you for saving me," she answered in a soft voice as well.

The firelight danced in her eyes, drawing him in deeper and deeper. Rose Ashdown was so unlike any of his servants. Although a commoner, she held skills as well as knowledge beyond her years. She looked alluring and strong. Then he remembered the fear he saw in her eyes in the forest, and it about broke his heart.

"I don't ever want you to have to experience such an awful situation again." His thumb brushed over the back of her hand. She jerked slightly in surprise, but he did nothing to release his hold on her.

"Neither do I," she told him.

He wanted, needed, to taste her lips. If he didn't do it soon, he was sure he would go mad. Rook dipped his head forward, pressing his mouth up against hers. The kiss was fast and simple. While she didn't push him away, neither did she return it. That confused him. He wasn't sure if she enjoyed it or disliked it now.

"Rose, you are beautiful," he said, unable to stop himself from stating his emotions aloud.

"My lord." Her eyes took on a tinge of fear again, and he didn't understand why. "Take your mead. Please."

"Aye. Of course." He took the cup from her and downed all the contents at one time. Her presence in his life was forced by the hand of his father; but his feelings for her seemed as if they were fate alone. Somehow, he felt as if their meeting was something more, but he couldn't explain it. By now, any commoner he desired would be naked and in his bed, willingly accepting him and all that went with it. Rook wanted Rose right now, more than any of his past follies.

But he wouldn't take her.

Nay, he couldn't.

Not after what she'd been through.

She deserved more than a lord ordering her to couple with him. Primrose Ashdown was a woman who deserved respect from everyone, no matter what their status.

"I am curious about your intent, my lord," she said, her arms going around her again in a form of self-protection. This disturbed him.

"My intent? What do you mean?"

"You told me you wanted me to sleep in your solar tonight." She looked at the floor instead of directly at him when she spoke. This told him that the thought bothered her.

"I was not insinuating I wanted to couple with you, if that is what you think."

"You weren't?" Her eyes flashed upward. Damn, he could no longer tell if she was pleased or upset by his admission. This woman confused him once again. He no longer knew how he was expected to act around her. She yawned, covering her mouth slightly. He could see her eyes already starting to drift shut, and it gave him the answer he needed.

"You use my bed tonight. I'll sleep in the great hall," said Rook, starting for the door.

"Wait," she called out, making him stop and turn around. "Don't leave me. Please."

"Nay?" Rook's eyes flashed to the door and then over to her again. The wench was still sending mixed signals. "What do you mean?"

"I don't want to be alone. I am still frightened by what happened to me in the woods today."

"I understand, but I told you that you are safe now."

"I know, but my body still shakes. Will you at least stay until I fall asleep?"

God's eyes. She didn't know what she was asking. Unknowingly, the little vixen was tempting him and testing his resolve. All he could think about was how she'd feel, naked and in his arms.

"All right," he agreed. "I'll stay. For now. Get in bed. I'll stroke the fire. Stoke," he quickly corrected himself, feeling embarrassed that his thoughts were leaking out into his conversation.

He stoked the fire, turning to see her getting under the covers dressed in only her shift.

"What are you doing?" he asked, surprised she was half-undressed. Rook felt as if he needed more mead or mayhap something stronger, like whisky.

"I didn't want to ruin your sister's nice gown. I put it on the chair. I'd better sleep in just the shift."

"Aye, of course." He dragged a hand through his hair in thought. This wench was either severely naïve or just playing the vixen. Either way, didn't she understand she couldn't undress in front of a man and expect him not to touch her?

"Sit down," she told him, patting the side of the bed.

Now, to make matters worse, she was inviting him to settle himself atop the bed, so close to her.

"All right," he agreed, sitting on the edge of the bed, trying to look at anything in the room except her.

"Tell me what you want to see in your pleasure garden."

"Nay," he groaned, not wanting to talk about pleasure or gardens right now. That only brought his mind back to things like making love. "Just go to sleep."

"I would, but I fear my body is still shaking, my lord. Will you ...will you ..."

"Will I what?" he asked, his heart racing. Did she want to be intimate with him after all? If so, should he agree to it or turn her away? God's eyes, this wasn't easy.

"I wondered if you'd hold me."

"Hold you," he said, swallowing forcefully. That is how intimacy usually began. Part of him told him to turn around and run out the door, but his heart told him he needed to stay. "All right," he said, although this sounded like she was offering what he was more than willing to take.

"Just hold me to comfort me. Nothing else," she said with a stern look in her eyes, setting things straight between them.

He exhaled. So that is what she meant. "Of course," he said, feeling slightly disappointed. He walked over to the other side of the bed, laying fully clothed atop the covers next to her. He rolled to his side and placed his arm over her.

She smiled and turned toward him, snuggling up to his chest.

"Is that good?" he asked, feeling his body coming to life being so close to her soft, warm self.

"Mmmm," she said with her eyes closed, pressed up to him. "I feel so safe...... in your......" She fell asleep before she could even finish her sentence. The poor girl was most likely exhausted, physically as well as emotionally, and it was taking a toll on her. It was probably for the best, he decided. Another minute of this, and he would have something straight between them as well.

Rook looked over at the sleeping beauty in his arms, gently smoothing back a lock of her long, wet hair. He brushed his lips against her forehead, kissing her, wanting to do so much more. But he wouldn't.

He waited until he was certain she was asleep. Then he slipped his arms from around her, standing up, feeling so hot and lusty that he thought he would burst. Spying the bath, he walked over and skimmed his fingers over the surface of the water.

Cold.

Just what he needed to quench the fires burning deep within him.

Quickly removing his clothing, Rook stepped over the edge of the tub.

Rose rolled to her side, her eyes opening slightly, thinking she was dreaming at first. She saw Rook's bare back end as he stepped naked into the tub of water. When he turned sideways before sitting, she almost gasped aloud at seeing his erection. The man was big and hard. He wanted her, and the evidence proved it. She wondered now how he had lain in bed holding her without even trying to couple with her. The man must have control made of steel.

Mayhap she should be afraid of him, but somehow she wasn't. She smiled and rolled back the other way, closing her eyes once again. Could it be that the pompous nobleman wasn't so heartless after all? When he'd kissed her, she felt warmth go through her. Then, when he saw that she was frightened by the thought of him possibly coupling with her, he didn't pursue it. That alone was a noble act that made him different from most lords. It earned respect in her eyes. Respect she freely gave him, without him demanding that she give it.

Yes, she decided. She was safe here with Lord Rook and it felt right after all. As she drifted off to sleep, she realized that there was nowhere else in the world at this moment that she would rather be.

CHAPTER 7

"Good morning, Rose," came a voice from the door of the solar the next morning. Rook's eyes popped open to find himself asleep in the bath that was frigidly cold. "I brought you your gown," said Raven, walking into the dark room, holding something. "It's clean and dry."

"It looks like it'll be a bonnie day," Rook heard next.

Oh, crap. Lark was with her.

Rook groaned inwardly. Since the room was dark, the women hadn't seen him and he hoped they'd leave before they did.

"Oh, good morning." Rose stretched and sat up in bed.

"Open the shutter, Lark," said Raven. "We can't see a thing in this darkened room."

"Damn," Rook whispered, realizing this couldn't end well. He quietly stepped out of the tub, grabbing a towel and holding it in front of his groin. He thought he heard a gasp from the corridor, but when he looked up, all he saw was a shadow, as if someone had walked by.

"My, it's a bonnie bright day," said Lark, opening the shutter. Streams of sunshine filled the room. Lark turned around and saw Rook. She screamed and covered her eyes.

"What's the matter, Lark?" Raven spun around to see Rook standing there.

"Good morning," said Rook, doing a sidestep, bending down to pick up his braies from the floor.

"Rook! You're naked again?" spat Raven.

"You two need to stop entering my room without knocking." Rook turned away from them and quickly dressed.

"Rook?" Rose sat up, pulling the sheet to her chest.

The door opened wider and Robin entered. "Have either of you seen Rook?"

"More of him than we want to see," complained Raven, motioning with her head toward her brother.

"Oh!" said Robin when he saw Rook.

Raven turned back to Rose. "Here, put these on. Your workers are ready to start on the pleasure garden and are looking for you for their instructions."

"Pleasure garden?" asked Robin with a chuckle. "I'd say my cousin has had enough pleasure for a while."

"It's not what you think," said Rook, his voice muffled as he pulled his tunic on over his head. Then he picked up his weapon belt and donned it.

"Of course not," said Robin, chuckling again, and turning for the door.

Rook put on his boots and ran out into the corridor after Robin. "Wait," he called out.

Robin stopped and turned back to him. "Yes?"

"I didn't sleep with the girl," said Rook, wanting to clear the air.

"Of course you didn't," said Robin with a grin. "I'm sure no sleeping happened at all. How was she?"

"Nay, really. I'm telling you the truth."

"I know you too well, cousin. So, when I find you with a pretty wench in your bed, half undressed, and you standing there stark naked, I'm not going to believe anything other than you coupled with her." He turned and started walking.

"All right, don't believe me. I don't care," said Rook, although it bothered him immensely. "Just refrain from mentioning anything to anyone about what you think might have happened, even though it didn't."

"What?"

"Keep your mouth shut about this."

"Why?" asked Robin. "It's not like anyone will bat an eye over it. Not with your lusty reputation."

"I don't care what they think about me. I am just trying to keep Rose's reputation untarnished."

"Whatever for?" Robin looked sideways at Rook and squinted. "Since when do you care about any commoner or servant's reputation at all?"

"Rose is different."

"She's a commoner, isn't she?"

"Well, yes."

"Then, there is no difference from any of the other wenches you've taken to your bed." He continued to walk.

"I didn't couple with her, and it's because she is not like the rest of them, I tell you."

Robin stopped. "You're serious, aren't you? You really didn't bed her?"

"Nay," said Rook, shaking his head. "I mean, aye, I'm serious and nay, I didn't bed her, I swear. I only gave her one kiss and held her until she fell asleep."

"What is happening to you, Rook? This isn't like you at all."

"I know," said Rook, not able to understand it himself. "But when I'm with Rose, it's almost like...... like I...... respect her."

"Respect? You make no sense."

"I can't explain it, but I like her and want to get to know her better before anything happens between us.

"Know her?"

"Aye. Not just in a sexual way, either."

"This is odd coming from the man who is about to be married to a noblewoman. Shouldn't you be thinking of your betrothed instead?"

"Don't remind me of that," said Rook, releasing a deep breath. The last thing he wanted to think of was that he was about to marry a woman he didn't know, and one he surely did not want.

"Phineas, you did a great job on digging the post holes and making the posts sturdy. Keep it up," said Rose, inspecting the stakes sticking out of the ground that would be used to make the wattle-woven fences to go around the raised beds in the garden. They'd already started weaving branches through them. "Thomasina, be sure to prune off all the sharp edges of any branches that stick out. I don't want anyone to hurt themselves." Rose bent over, using her shears to prune off a sharp edge that was sticking out from the knee-high fence.

"Aye, Rose," said Thomasina.

"Thank you, Rose," called out Phineas, continuing to use his hammer to drive more posts deep into the earth. Areas were sectioned off to make raised beds for planting. Some were for vegetables, and others for herbs. These were the closest to the kitchen, to make it easy for the cooks to gather food. Rose was happy to discover that even after all these years, the perennial plants were still growing on their own.

Her cousin, Georgiana, walked up with her arms loaded down with branches. "Rose," she whispered, and leaned in closer. "There is talk amongst the kitchen maids that you spent the night with Rook."

"What? Nay," said Rose. Then she thought about it and decided that wasn't exactly the truth. "Well, aye, sort of," she said softly and shrugged.

"What?" Her cousin almost dropped the branches. "What happened? Tell me all about it."

"Nothing happened. Not really." Rose looked one way and then the other before leaning closer and telling her cousin more.

"Rook kissed me." Rose smiled, thinking of what a wonderful kiss it was. She had enjoyed it immensely.

"He did?" Georgiana's eyes opened wide. "What else happened?"

"It's true I spent the night in his bed, and he was there all night too, but we didn't...... do it."

"Are you sure?" asked Georgiana, giving Rose a look that said she didn't believe her. "The kitchen maid named Sally said Lord Rook was naked this morning, and that you were half-undressed under the covers when the ladies Raven and Lark came to your room."

"Who told her that?"

"She walked past and saw it," said Georgiana.

"Oh, no," said Rose rather loud. She noticed Thomasina looking over and lowered her voice. "I mean, yes, that's what happened, but it's not what everyone thinks. He held me to calm me down, but I swear nothing happened between us."

"For truth?" Georgiana looked at Rose from the sides of her eyes.

"So I said." Rose held up a pinky finger and interlocked it with her cousin's in a quick shake, even though Georgiana was still holding a bundle of branches. It was what they used to do as children, to let each other know they weren't lying.

"All right. I believe you," said Georgiana, breaking the link between them. "But if something does happen, you know I'll expect to be the first one to know the details. I have to put these branches down now. They're getting heavy." Georgiana walked over to Thomasina to help with weaving a garden fence.

"What's all this?" came a deep voice from behind her, causing her to jump and hold her hand over her heart. Startled, Rose whirled around so fast that she nearly lost her balance. "Careful, sweetheart," said Rook, reaching out and grabbing her arm, helping her to gain her footing.

"Rook," she said, shyly smiling at him. She hoped he hadn't overheard her talking with Georgiana.

"I hope I didn't frighten you. Next time, I'll be sure to blow a horn to make my presence known long before I enter the garden."

"Nay, I'm glad you're here," she told him.

"You are?" He still held on to her arm and her workers were starting to stare.

"I wanted to show you the progress we've made in the garden and to ask you a few questions." She quickly stepped away from him, breaking the connection between them.

"First, let me ask you something, Rose." His eyes scanned the grounds. "What are all these posts for?"

"Oh, those are for the wattle-woven fences."

"The wattle-what?" he asked, making her giggle.

"You really don't know much about gardening, do you?"

"I can't say I ever go in a garden, to be honest with you. My days are usually spent on a practice field or inside the keep. Mayhap you can teach me about it?"

"Really?" she asked, surprised to hear him say this. "You are interested and want to learn about gardening?"

"I'm more interested than you think." Since his eyes were

on her and not on the fencing, Rose realized this could be a play on words. Still, she rather liked it. Rose decided to teach him since he asked.

"All right," she said. "First of all, we need fences to hold the plants off the paths and to section off different herbs and vegetables."

"Is that what I see growing there?" He pointed at the herb garden.

"Yes. The sage and thyme have come back each year. So has the mint. And in the vegetable beds, there is already a good patch of garlic and wild onions growing. Not to mention wild strawberries on the hilly area in the sun over there." She pointed and he looked.

"Interesting," he said. "So, you're building high fences?"

"Nay. Just short fences, like this one," she said, leading the way over to where Thomasina and her cousin were down on their knees weaving branches in and out around the posts. "The pliable branches are woven in between the posts to make a wall."

"Is that hard to do?" asked Rook, sounding genuinely interested.

"Nay, not really. I can teach you, if you'd like to try it."

Thomasina and Georgiana looked up, watching. Rose didn't think Rook would accept if anyone was staring at him, so she told them to go. "I'll take over this section if you two would like to go help rake the paths."

"Come on, Thomasina," said Georgiana, standing up and helping the oversized woman to her feet. "They want to be alone."

"Really? What for?" Thomasina looked over her shoulder as Georgiana pulled her to another section of the garden.

"What did she mean by that?" asked Rook, seeming suddenly uncomfortable.

"Oh, that's just my cousin being silly. She didn't mean anything by it. Here, watch me. First, I take one of the long, thin branches, and I weave it in front and then behind the posts, almost in the same manner as weaving a basket."

"Weaving a basket," he mumbled.

"Don't tell me you've never done that either?" she asked, amused at how little about the common things a nobleman really knew.

He made a face and shook his head. "Nay. I can't say that I have any interest in basket weaving."

"Well, it's simple and very similar to the weaving of a fence. Here, you try this." She handed him a long, flexible branch. "Move it in and out, opposite of the one I just placed."

"In and out," he said. "I can do that." He stared at her with sultry, hooded eyes, and she knew he was talking about something besides fences.

"Over here," she said, pointing down to the fence.

"Right." He let out a deep breath, trying to place the branch. "Like this?" he asked, attempting to weave it, but he was too forceful and the branch snapped. "Damn! Was that supposed to happen?"

"Don't worry, it happens," she assured him with a giggle. "Try another one." She handed him another long stick. "This time, work the branch and try to bend it. If you are too forceful and the branch is brittle, it will snap. If you are gentle, it will do exactly what you want."

"Exactly what I want," he mumbled, his eyes raking down her before going back for a second attempt with the fencing. It seemed as if he were really struggling. Rose could tell the branch was about to snap again.

"Wait," she said, taking his hands in her. "Bend it by stroking and caressing it, a little at a time. Gently. It will make the stick pliable, and then it will conform to your will. See?"

Rose used her hands over his, guiding his big fingers to caress the wood, wiggling and moving it back and forth until they were able to weave it through the posts without it breaking at all. "Understand?" she asked. Still bent over, she looked at him. Their faces were so close that they could kiss easily right now and no one would even know it.

"Aye, I think so," he said, looking directly at her mouth. "Be gentle. A little at a time to get exactly what I want. Kind of like foreplay."

"I don't know about that," she answered in a breathy voice. Rose was staring at his mouth, thinking about his kiss yesterday and how she'd been surprised. She wondered if he'd try it again. Part of her hoped so. Heat spiraled up inside her. The scent of wood smoke and leather coming from his clothes made her feel heady. Thoughts of doing more than just kissing flitted through her head next. Then she remembered the rumors surfacing about her and Rook in bed.

Rose quickly released his hands and stood up straight. He stood up as well. She took a deep breath, trying to calm herself. This time, it wasn't from fear, but rather from desire. She needed to focus, so she continued talking.

"To move the branches of the fencing closer and tighter together, you need to do this." She picked up her skirt, almost laughing aloud when his mouth fell open. Rose used her foot to tamp down the work, causing the branches of the woven fencing to move closer together.

"Tighter," he muttered the word, seemingly lost to say anything else as he stared at her legs that were exposed by her action.

"When the fences are about knee-high, we'll fill in the enclosures with a raised bed of worked dirt to plant the rest of your herbs and vegetables. Then, daub, or mud or manure, or whatever we have, will be packed in around the spacing of the branches to make solid fencing."

"Remarkable," he said, looking at her instead of the fencing. Rose had a feeling this lesson had come to an abrupt end.

"Did you want to take a walk with me?" she asked Rook. "I'll show you the labyrinth of bushes that was hidden under all the overgrowth. We've almost got it cleaned up. My father put it in for the earl about ten years ago. The bushes were small at the time."

"Yes, I'd like to see that," he told her.

"This way." She walked side by side with him, making sure she didn't get too close or more rumors about them would surface. "Years ago, this was one of my father's first jobs. He drew up an elaborate design, and the earl hired him to fix up the grounds. It took months to finish. I remember, because I was only ten at the time, but I helped him do it. The labyrinth of bushes was fun to construct. Now they are huge and overgrown and need trimming. I'll have my workers trim them down to form square shapes."

Rook nodded a greeting to the gardeners working like busy bees as he strolled through the gardens with Rose at his side. The tangled mess he'd seen when he first arrived was starting to disappear. In its place were what looked like planned paths and geometrical patterns of spaces that contained flowers. Tall, purple wild flowers swayed back and forth in the breeze. The scent of several species of perennials drifted on by, giving the air a sweet, magical quality.

"Good morning, Lord Rook," called out one of the workers.

"Hello, my lord," another greeted him with a nod and a bow.

The workers acknowledged him one by one, standing up quickly to show respect with a curtsy or a bow as he passed by.

Rook's thoughts went back to Rose. When she'd touched his hands and talked about gently working the branches, he couldn't help but thinking about stroking her in the same way. It had been torture staying in the same room with her all night and then nothing really happening between them. Then again, he reminded himself that Rose wasn't his usual light skirt. She was a smart, talented, skilled woman, and he respected that about her. Even if she was only a commoner. She came into his life like a breath of fresh air.

"Let's see that maze," he told her, trying to think about gardening instead of kissing her.

She stopped in her tracks and shook her head. "It's not a maze. It's a labyrinth."

"Same thing. Nay?" he asked, getting the feeling he was showing his ignorance about gardening once again.

"Nay, not the same thing at all. A maze of bushes is like what my father and I put in the king's garden. There are many paths, and many places to enter and exit. Some of the paths lead nowhere and you have to turn around."

"It sounds easy to get lost."

"In a way, yes. But not with a labyrinth." She held out her arm to show him the bushes. "There is only one way in, and one way out. In the center is the pleasure garden."

"I see. So this here is the entrance to the center of the late earl's pleasure garden?"

"Exactly." Rose led him through the labyrinth of very tall bushes. The two of them were hidden from sight of anyone else. "When we worked on the king's garden, we were there for nearly six months putting in his maze of bushes."

"Are labyrinths easier and faster to construct?" he asked her.

"Yes, the labyrinth is easier since it is a continuous path that leads to the center. There is less planning involved than with a maze, and also less chance for error."

"So, it's like a puzzle in a way," he said.

"Yes, I suppose so." She took his arm, holding on to him as she led the way. "When we get to the center, you'll see the pleasure garden. Or what's left of it, I should say. It hasn't been maintained so it won't be very impressive."

"I can't believe Crazy Clive had a pleasure garden since in his later years he never went outside," said Rook. "Or so I hear. I didn't know the man personally, although my grandfather and the earl at one time were friends."

"I remember the earl as being a kind man," Rose said, recalling the past. "I assure you, at one time, this was a very beautiful garden." She stopped in the garden and Rook saw an old bench with peeling paint and a pavilion built over it. It was weathered from the elements and an eyesore. A small pond, void of water, was in the center. Tangles of rose vines climbed up trellises, and tall, weedy-looking flowers grew wild, some already in bloom, though it was still early in the year. A few tall stone statues that looked to be Greek gods and goddesses peeked out from between the overgrown bushes, and some of them were toppled and half-covered by dirt.

"I'm sure it was beautiful at one time, but it has much to be desired now," he told her. "Especially that bench that is a true eyesore."

"I remember this bench fondly." A smile lit up Rose's face as she walked over to touch it. "I was just a child when my father built it. I helped him paint it. I even carved my name on the back, but never told him about it."

"You did?" he asked. "You knew how to write?"

"Yes, and read, too," she told him. "My father gave shelter to a traveling friar once who had taken ill on the road. In gratitude, the friar taught me to read and write while he was healing."

"Well, you were a sly child, putting your mark on that bench."

"I prefer to think of it as being creative and trying to express it."

"Creative, that's a good way to put it," he answered with a chuckle.

"Let me see if my name is still here." She hunkered down behind the bench, using her hand to feel around for the carved letters. When she started giggling, he bent down next to her.

"What's so funny?" he asked. "Did you find it?"

"Yes. It's still here," she answered excitedly. "As well as the picture of a rose I carved right next to it. Look."

"I don't see it."

"You need to look lower. Remember, I was a child at the time, not to mention I was trying to hide it from my father."

"I still don't see it," he said, stretching his neck, but only seeing an old, worn wooden bench.

"Here. Give me your hand." She took it without him offering. "Run your fingertips over the wood. Gently, so you don't get slivers."

"Gently," he replied, hearing that word again.

"The wood is weathered, but you can feel the letters, R–O–S–E, right here." She held on to his hand and used his finger to trace her name and then the picture of the rose.

Rook no longer cared about the letters or the flower. All he cared about was the feel of her hand on his. The scent of sunshine and nature wafted from her body, making him want to kiss her again and taste her sweet lips that to him were like honeyed mead.

"Feel it?" she asked, turning and looking at him with those earthy eyes that made him think of her as a magical being, mayhap an elemental of nature or a fae. "Do you feel it, Lord Rook?"

"I will tell you what I'm feeling, Rose, but it has nothing to do with carved letters on a bench."

"I don't understand." She frowned, still holding his hand. "What do you mean?"

"I'm feeling an attraction to you that I've never felt with anyone before."

"Oh!" She abruptly released his hand and sprang to her feet as if his words startled her. He followed. "Do you think these bushes should be trimmed down to waist level, or do you like them higher?" she asked, ignoring what he'd just told her altogether. "I like them a little higher, I think. After all, since it's a labyrinth, it should be mysterious. Don't you agree?"

"I like them high as well."

"You do?"

"Aye. It gives me the privacy I want when I'm with you." He reached out and cupped her cheek, watching her eyes close partially as she leaned in, resting her face in his hand. "Rose, I want to kiss you," he said in a deep whisper.

"I'd like that," she answered in a breathy voice, more than welcoming the suggestion.

He gently pulled her into his arms, pressing his lips against hers in a slow, lingering kiss. To his surprise, her arms encircled his waist, and she pressed her chest up to his, standing on her tiptoes. Her face turned up toward the sun like a bud waiting to bloom.

Rook only meant to kiss her once, but when he started to pull away, she held him tighter, this time pressing her mouth against his for another kiss.

God's eyes, he was in heaven. This woman kissed like no other. Such passion, such life. It wasn't just an action done in lust, the way it always felt with light skirts or whores. With

Rose, he felt her heart in the kiss. It was as if she put all her energy into every little thing she did, this kiss included.

His heart raced and his hands slowly trailed down her shoulders as they continued to kiss and his body grew hotter. His fingertips lightly caressed the sides of the swells of her breasts before his arms circled around her small waist.

"I like that," she whispered, doing nothing to pull away, but rather giving him permission to continue to explore. Rook's hands trailed down to her ass next. This time he felt so excited by her that he let his tongue enter her mouth. And when he heard her slight moan of pleasure at the back of her throat, he cupped her buttocks and pulled her up against his hardened form. His hips started to rock back and forth on their own, mimicking the dance of making love, even though they were fully clothed and he wasn't entering her at all. Still, his mind went crazy with want for this sensuous, passionate woman. And when he reached down to pull up the hem of her skirt, she pushed away and slapped him hard across his cheek, ending everything so fast that it made his head spin.

"What the hell was that for?" he groaned, rubbing his cheek.

"You went too far too fast," she snapped, sounding really upset by his actions.

He decided to make a jest to lighten the mood. "Well, it's a pleasure garden, isn't it?" He smiled at her, but she was not smiling back.

"That's not the type of pleasure one is supposed to feel in the garden," she retorted. "Lord Rook, I know I am naught but a commoner and also your hired help, but I must say I am highly offended by your actions. I told you before, I am not one of your strumpets!"

"Strumpets," he mumbled, running a hand through his long hair, wondering how things turned sour so quickly. Rose was confusing him again. One minute she seemed to want him, giving him signals to continue. Then, the next, she was pushing him away and slapping him, saying she was offended. The girl didn't make any sense at all.

"Rose, I didn't mean to offend you, but you told me you liked it," he said in his defense.

"I meant the kiss. Not being groped in the garden." Her eyes looked like narrowed slits now. Her mouth was pursed, and she crossed her arms over her chest. Damn, she seemed threatening. He didn't expect that from such a gentle creature. Rose had another side to her that he had yet to see.

"I didn't mean to do that." He stepped back, wanting to keep his distance from her. "I think it would be best if I left now, and you got back to work." He turned to go, but her words made him stop in his tracks.

"I did like it," she said softly, admitting what he knew to be true.

"What?" He turned around and stared at her, waiting for more of an explanation.

"I liked all of it, actually."

"You did?" he asked in astonishment. "Then why the hell did you push me away and slap me?"

"Because." Her arms slowly fell to her sides, and her gaze went from him to her feet when she spoke. "I cannot allow myself to fall for a man who will only use me for his own needs and push me aside when he finds his next folly. I'm sorry, but I am not that kind of girl. My lord," she added.

"I don't understand," he said, not sure where this was coming from. He'd told her he had feelings for her, but she didn't seem to believe him. "Rose, you will never be just a night of pleasure to me, I assure you. I admit you excite me and I have trouble containing it, but I see you as so much more than a strumpet or light skirt like Sally."

By the look on her face, he realized he never should have mentioned Sally. It wasn't winning him any points where attraction was concerned.

"Excuse me, my lord, but I have work to do now. I promise I will not be so easily distracted again." She rushed past him, but he reached out and grabbed her arm, swinging her around to face him.

"I haven't dismissed you yet, and you will not speak to me in that tone of voice."

Her eyes went to his hand on her arm and then to his face. Hurt showed in her gaze, making him regret his words already.

"Why not?" she asked. "Because I am just a commoner and that is all I will ever be?"

"I didn't say that."

"You don't need to, my lord. We both know it is true. No matter what we feel for one another, it doesn't matter in the end. You are a noble and I am a commoner. Besides, all I can ever be to you is nothing more than a mistress since you are about to marry a noble. I assure you, when I give myself to a man, it won't be to a lord who wants me only as his plaything. Neither will I ever be with a man who is married. Now, if you'll release my arm, I will gladly get back to work. My lord."

His hand slipped off of her arm, and his heart felt as if someone had just stabbed a knife through it.

"You're dismissed," he said, watching her go, doing nothing more to try to stop her.

Rose was right.

He was a betrothed man, soon to be married. She was naught but a commoner, a woman from below the salt. If he wanted her, there was no other choice other than she be his mistress or just a quick release like the rest of the light skirts. Rook had lived his life flitting from one wench to the next like a bee going from flower to flower. But now that the queen bee was about to arrive, he felt like shackles were being placed around him. He didn't want Lady Adelaide or Adeline, or whatever her fool name was, and he didn't care about the French wench at all. What he wanted was a woman he could lose himself in, and one with whom he could awake each day looking forward to spending it with her in his arms.

Rook had never known love in his life, but he was getting older now and things were changing. What didn't seem important before suddenly seemed like the only thing that mattered now. He honestly didn't want to marry a stranger for nothing more than an alliance the way nobles were expected to do. None of the women he'd met from above the salt ever interested him the way Rose did.

Something inside him had changed. Mayhap part of this had to do with the fact he saw how happy his twin sister was with the commoner she married. They'd found love, and in a way that made him feel jealous. Rook wanted to be in love with a woman. It shouldn't matter to a nobleman, but somehow it did. Now, that is all he could think about, and it was driving him mad. Time was ticking down to his wedding date. If he didn't do something about this soon, it would be too late. Then, he would be stuck and most likely miserable for the rest of his life.

Damn, he didn't know what he could possibly do concerning Rose. The only thing that was clear to him was that when he was with Rose, he felt things he had never felt with any other woman.

Aye, he couldn't deny it. He wanted Primrose Ashdown, a commoner, who had been hired to plant his garden. He wanted her for more than just a night or two. He wanted her forever. This was not good, he realized. Rook desired a woman from below the salt and one he could never have.

"Damn it," he spat, knowing if he gave into his feelings, he would let down his father, which is something he never wanted to do.

Rook was a noble with a manor now. He was expected to marry someone of his status. He was the one who had to keep up respect for the Blake family name.

Or was he?

He felt more than determined to win Rose's heart now. Why was her rejection of him making him feel so devastated? Why did it really matter? God's eyes. This only made him want her even more. Perhaps now that he was Lord of Horrabridge, in the end, he was going to go crazy just like Earl Clive.

Then again, mayhap he was only finally being true to himself for the first time in his life.

Something happened in this moment. It was something that Rook knew would change his life forever. He wasn't sure, but somehow he felt like mayhap he was actually falling in love. It was either that or he was truly going mad, because he decided the only place he wanted to plant his seed was in Rose's garden.

CHAPTER 8

A week later, Rook paced the grounds out back of his manor, watching Rose work in the garden, feeling as if she were avoiding him. He'd tried to talk to her more than once about the kisses they'd shared and his feelings for her. She wouldn't listen. Each time, she just changed the subject, bringing the focus back to the project at hand.

"My lord?" came a voice from behind him. He turned to see Godwin, the man he'd hired as steward for his manor. Godwin wasn't a peasant, he was from a wealthy family. He had worked for the earl as his steward. Rook was able to find him by talking with the peasants in the village.

"What is it, Godwin?" he asked, his mind still on Rose. Her work in his garden was exquisite, and she paid such attention to the smallest of details. He had watched her from a distance, pruning the wildflowers, being careful not to crush any blooms already there. It was as if she cared for all wildlife. Even when a rabbit hopped through the garden, she was kind and talked to it in the most sensitive way.

Aye, she must be a fae of the earth because she seemed so connected with it.

The garden was really starting to shape up, pleasing him immensely. He now had raised beds with wattle fencing that would be used for vegetables and herbs. The plants that came up by themselves were getting woody and too bushy. So, Rose trimmed back the thyme and sage and even the mint, giving it to the cooks to use in the meals.

Today, Rose had her workers on ladders, trimming the labyrinth of very tall bushes that led into what she'd told him was once the earl's pleasure garden.

"I have prepared the ledgers, recording everything the earl left behind, as well as what you have brought from Blake Castle," Godwin told him.

"Good. Good," said Rook, hearing a dog barking. He turned back to see Rose down on her knees in the garden, laughing and petting a mangy-looking mutt. "Where the hell did that thing come from?" he mumbled.

"That looks like Earl Clive's hound," said Godwin, stretching his neck to see the dog. "The mutt's name is Bandit. He's very old."

"Well, I don't want it here," Rook told him. "Get rid of it."

"I'm afraid that won't be easy, my lord. The dog has lived here, but outdoors, since he was a puppy," Godwin continued. "He got his name by stealing things from the earl, hence the reason he was banned to the outdoors. I haven't seen the hound since right before the earl passed away. I thought he ran away or died. I guess he decided to return."

"Mmmph," groaned Rook, not wanting any dog but his own at the manor. Of course, since he didn't have any dogs of his own yet, and his kennels were empty, he decided to let the matter go for now. After all, Rose did seem happy with the dog there. "How did the earl die?" asked Rook, not knowing the full story and curious as to the last owner of the manor.

"He died in his sleep, my lord."

"Was he ill?" Rook looked back at Godwin.

"I couldn't say. He mainly kept to himself, and for the last five years, or mayhap more, he never stepped foot outside the keep."

"He didn't? Why not?" asked Rook.

"He seemed to develop a fear of being anywhere but indoors," stated Godwin. "That is partially why the gossipers called him eccentric. The last months of his life, he didn't even come out of his room at all. I brought food to his door and emptied his chamber pot, but he wanted to be left alone. He said he no longer liked people."

"Really. That is strange. Was he always so odd?"

"He was eccentric, my lord," said Godwin, not wanting to speak ill of his previous lord. Godwin was old enough to be Rook's father. Stout and balding, Godwin still dressed accordingly and paid respect in all the proper ways.

"How so?" asked Rook. "Tell me more."

"Sometimes the earl even gave money and jewels to people he barely knew, just because he felt like it," explained Godwin.

"That is odd," said Rook. "He did that from inside his room?"

"Oh, nay. That happened long before he became a recluse."

"Didn't he have any family? Children, or a wife?" asked Rook. "An heir?"

"Nay. Not to my knowledge. As I told you, he said he didn't like people."

"Were you always his steward, Godwin?"

"Aye. Ever since the earl moved into Horrabridge Manor."

"Then you remember when the master gardener first designed the grounds?"

"Oh, yes. I remember it well. Bandit was a puppy and kept digging up everything the gardener planted. It made Oliver Ashdown angry. Oliver always wanted everything to be perfect."

"Do you remember Oliver's daughter? Rose? She's out there right now tending to the garden." Rook looked back at Rose when he said her name. Rose threw a stick for Bandit. Since the dog was old, he couldn't run fast anymore, but he limped after the stick to fetch it and brought it back to her, wagging his tail. Rose laughed and talked to the dog like she was speaking to a child, petting him and kissing him on the head.

"Yes, Rose was only ten at the time, I believe. However, she was mature for her age and also a fast learner. Her father taught her everything he knew about gardening. I remember, she could even read and write."

"I see," said Rook, impressed by the girl's skills.

"I must say, Rose turned out to be quite a beauty," continued Godwin. "Too pretty to be just a hired hand digging in the dirt, if you ask me."

"Yes. I agree," said Rook, not able to stop thinking about how Rose had looked so much like a lady when she'd been wearing Raven's gown.

"My lord?" Harold, Rook's squire, walked into the garden holding a missive in his hand. Harold was eighteen and hoped to someday be a knight. His blond hair looked even brighter with the sun shining down upon it. There wasn't a cloud in the sky today. It was a perfect spring day.

"What is it, Harold?" asked Rook.

"I was tending to your horse when a messenger arrived at the gate with a missive." He handed it to Rook. "It's from Lord Morcant in Somerset."

"Lord Morcant?" asked Rook, taking and inspecting the missive with the stamped wax seal.

"Isn't he who the gardeners were working for before coming here?" asked Harold. "I thought I heard Rose mention it."

"Yes. I believe that's right," Rook answered. "I wonder what he wants?" Rook opened the message and scanned it quickly. "Oh, no," he said when he read the news.

"Is something wrong, my lord?" asked Godwin.

"What is it?" asked Harold curiously.

"I'm afraid it's bad news for Rose. Excuse me, I must tell her at once." Rook headed out to the garden where Rose was still laughing and playing with the dog. She was down on her knees, not afraid of getting dirty, or of the mangy mutt licking her face. She seemed to enjoy it. Rook liked the sound of her giggling. It struck a chord in his heart.

"Rose," Rook called to her. "Rose, come here, please."

"Of course," she said, looking down at the hound. "Bandit, go play with Georgiana. Go on." She swished the dog away with her hands, flicking at air.

The dog barked a few times and then ran over to Georgiana, who was loading cuttings from the bushes into a push cart. The dog barked, stealing the girl's gloves and running away with them in his mouth.

"Get back here with those," yelled Georgiana, chasing the dog through the labyrinth of bushes.

"Bandit is such a cute dog, but troublesome," said Rose, wiping the dust from her clothes. "He always was. Can you believe Bandit remembered me from when I worked in the earl's garden with my father? That was ten years ago. Isn't that amazing?" She put on her work gloves as she chattered away nonstop.

"Rose, listen to me. I received a missive from Lord Morcant."

"You did?" She looked up in surprise. "Oh, is my father

105

asking about the gardening? He was very insistent that we do a good job for you." She was still smiling.

"It's not from your father, but it is about him," Rook told her, knowing she wasn't going to react favorably to the news.

"Is something the matter?" Rose's smile slowly faded. "Is my father all right?"

"I'm afraid he's taken a turn for the worse."

"What?" she asked with a gasp.

"It seems his leg became infected and the healers are no longer able to help him. Lord Morcant suggests you come quickly to say your final goodbye."

"Nay!" she cried, shaking her head. "You must have read it wrong. This is not true. My father is going to be healed."

"I'm sorry, Rose."

"Let me see it." She ripped the missive from his hand to see the message for herself. Rook, by rights, should have reprimanded her for that action, but he said nothing. He felt sorry for Rose and didn't want to upset her even more right now.

"It's an unfortunate circumstance," said Rook.

"Well, I don't believe it. This can't be true." Rose read the missive, her bottom lip quivering. Tears streaked down her cheeks. Finally, she accepted the truth. "I must go to him immediately."

"I agree," he said, even though Rose hadn't even asked for his permission to leave the manor.

"Lord Rook, I can't lose my father," she said, handing the missive back to him. Her eyes were filled with tears. "He is all I have."

Such desperation Rook had never seen in his life.

He felt choked up just by the thought of how close Rose must be with her father. He also didn't like to see any woman cry. He had no words for Rose and wasn't sure how to comfort her at a time like this.

"I understand," was all he managed to say.

"I must hurry." She looked back at her other workers. "Can I at least take Phineas with me for protection? I will leave the rest of the workers here, since I know you need the job completed quickly."

"Nay," he said, shaking his head. Rose looked more than surprised, and also a little angry.

"Then I'll go by myself. I don't care. I just need to get there. I want to be at his side should he pass away. He needs me." She started to sidestep Rook, but he grabbed her arm to stop her.

"I'll be the one to go with you to protect you," he told her.

"You?" Her eyes flashed up to his. "I don't understand. You are lord of the manor. You have important things to do. Why would you even consider such a thing?"

"I want to travel with you, Rose, because I see how important this is to you. Besides, I feel responsible for your safety. After what happened in the woods, I will make sure that no one ever tries to harm you again."

"All right," she said, with a sniffle. "Still, this changes nothing between us. My lord," she quickly added.

"I know," Rook answered, wishing Rose would understand that he truly cared for her. That was the reason he wanted to guard her and be with her. Not just to bed her. "Rose, I want you to realize that I wouldn't do this for any of my other servants, workers, or villagers."

"You wouldn't?" she asked, still staring into his eyes. "Then why do you bend the rules for me, my lord?" Her innocence mixed with determination made Rook want to hug her, or perhaps kiss her again. But he wouldn't. This was about so much more than physical pleasure. He saw the girl hurting and wanted to be there to help her heal her heart, and mayhap even her soul.

"You are special to me, Rose. That's why," he told her,

knowing she wouldn't understand, but not sure how to explain it.

"Special? I am no different from any of the other commoners, my lord."

"Nay, that's not true. You are different, and that is what I like about you."

"How?" she asked in defiant challenge. "How am I different from anyone else, my lord? I don't understand and need to know."

Rook took a deep breath and then released it. He wasn't one for baring his feelings, his heart or his soul, but at a time like this he figured it was important he try to do so.

"You are a light in a darkened night," he told her, taking her hand in his. "A breath of fresh air on a gloomy day. There is strength and an elegance deep inside you that most commoners will never possess. You, my dear, are like a blooming flower in a garden filled with weeds."

"I am?" She looked up into his eyes and blinked twice in succession.

"Aye," he said, gently running his thumb over the back of her smooth hand. "You may not know it, but you are a diamond in the rough, Rose. Yes, you are truly a rose among thorns."

Less than a half hour later, Rook, Rose, and Rook's squire, Harold were packed with a few items and ready to go see Rose's father. Rook stood in the courtyard, fixing the straps of his travel bag, noticing Georgiana running over to Rose, who was mounted on her horse, ready to leave.

"Oh, Rose, I wish I could go to say goodbye to Uncle Oliver too," cried Georgiana, reaching up and holding Rose's hand.

Rook almost felt bad for the girl, but he couldn't allow her to leave as well. If he started bending the rules for everyone, there would soon be no one left to see to his estate. They were workers and needed to stay and finish the job they started.

"I'm sorry, but I need you to stay here and help the others," Rose told her. "We are behind schedule with the gardening project. I'll have to work twice as fast when I return."

Robin emerged from the great hall and ran over to talk to them. "Rook, why are you going with her instead of sending a guard on the journey?"

"I feel I'm responsible for her safety." Rook continued to close up the bag.

"You are smitten with the wench. Just admit it," said Robin under his breath.

"This has nothing to do with that." Rook turned to face him.

"Nothing to do with what?" asked Raven, approaching with Lark and Rook's mother, to see them off.

"Nothing, sister. Don't worry about it," snapped Rook, not wanting everyone to know he had feelings for Rose. God's eyes, the tongues were already wagging.

Actually, Rose was all he could think about lately, and that concerned him even more. After all, he was about to become a husband to a noblewoman. That was something else he didn't want to consider at all.

"Rook, give our regards to the master gardener," said his mother. "Your father will be upset to hear about this when he returns."

"There will be a lot of sad nobles, including the king, when they hear Oliver died," said Raven.

"Aye," agreed Lark. "It's so sad. Rose doesna even have a mother or siblings."

"Stop it. All of you," Rook ground out, pulling himself up

109

into the saddle. "The man isn't dead yet. Hearing talk like this isn't going to help matters any. Rose is already very upset."

"Rook is right," said his mother. "We dare not distress the girl. Mayhap things will take a turn for the better where Rose's father is concerned. I will go wish Rose a safe journey."

"Us too," said Lark. She and Raven followed Rook's mother over to Rose.

Rook liked the fact that his family seemed to like and accept Rose. Then again, it was only going to make it harder when he had to let her go. Rook's father would most likely die if another of his children married a commoner. Nay, Rook couldn't keep letting his feelings for Rose get in the way of his duty as a noble. He was the eldest son and had a responsibility to do what needed to be done. Rook needed to make decisions with his head, not his heart.

"Don't do anything you'll regret," said Robin jesting, looking up at Rook with a smile.

"Too late for that," mumbled Rook, turning his horse to go. He might not have bedded the girl, but he had kissed Rose and that was something he could never forget. He was sure those kisses were going to cause problems, because Rose seemed to like them just as much as he did.

Rose rode in silence most of the trip, not able to focus on anything other than the fact that her father was dying. It frightened her more than even the thugs who tried to accost her in the forest. How would she be able to go on living without him if he died? She wouldn't be able to survive alone. She just couldn't.

"Would you like to share your thoughts?" Rook rode up next to her. Harold was leading the way.

"Not really." She continued to ride, keeping her gaze forward. Looking at him would only make her feel worse, since she had feelings for Rook even if they would never amount to anything. He was about to be married, and she would most likely end up alone forever.

"I know this is hard for you, but I want you to know I am here for you, Rose."

"Thank you." She still didn't look directly at him.

They rode in silence for a few more minutes before Rook spoke once again.

"So, Lark said you don't have any siblings?"

"Nay," she answered.

"And your mother is gone too?"

"Aye," she told him, not saying more.

"Can you tell me about it? I'd really like to know about you and your family."

Finally, Rose looked over at Rook. She didn't really want to talk about any of this right now, but couldn't ignore the fact that Rook genuinely seemed interested in her and her life. She supposed talking with him would make the trip go faster.

"My mother died when I was only a few years old. I don't really remember her."

"I'm sorry," he said. "I know that can't have been easy."

"It wasn't. However, I became very close to my father. He started bringing me along on his jobs, and that is how I learned all about gardening."

"I see. And where is your home?"

"My father, Georgiana, and I live in a village in Somerset, on Lord Morcant's lands. Our home is a small cottage made of wattle and daub. Phineas and Thomasina live with us, since they never had any children of their own. It is a one room house, but since we travel most of the time, it doesn't really matter."

ELIZABETH ROSE

"One room?" Rook sounded shocked. "I don't understand. Your father gets paid well for the jobs he does, and he even once worked for the king, no?"

"Yes, that's right," she answered.

"Then why didn't he ever buy or build a bigger house for you to live in?"

"My father thinks of everyone, but never himself," said Rose.

"Please, explain." Rook shook his head in confusion.

"Any money he has goes to not only our family but every family in our village. He helps others, sacrificing things he needs or wants, because he believes every commoner deserves a good meal and a place to lay their head."

"I see. That is very thoughtful of him."

"My father even helps plant the fields for Lord Morcant and also a garden for everyone back home. He does so, even though we are free tenants and don't work for Lord Morcant. My father wants all the serfs to be able to grow their own food as well as their lords. So, he helps them make small gardens next to their house that are for their personal use."

"Your father is very resourceful."

"He is also all I have. I don't know how I'll go on without him." Rose felt despair growing inside her.

"Of course you'll go on," said Rook, probably trying to cheer her up, but it wasn't working. "You can carry on your father's gardening, just like he's taught you."

"Nay, I can't," she told him.

"Why not?"

"Because the only reason we have the jobs in the first place is because my father is a master gardener. Besides, no one would hire a woman to do any work on her own or to be in charge of a job, and you know it."

"That's not true."

112

"Really?" She raised a brow. "You didn't want me to work in your garden when I first arrived. You didn't think a woman could head the workers and get things done. Or perhaps you didn't think women deserved to be paid for the same job men do. Am I right?"

"Well, I...... I mean."

"My life will be over without my father."

"Don't say that," said Rook. "You'll be married someday and raise a family."

"And do what?" she asked. "All I know is gardening."

"Your husband will have a job, I'm sure. He will take care of you and your children."

"Is that really what you think? Or just what you think I want to hear right now? Because no man in my village has much, and neither will he ever have since he is naught but a serf. If it weren't for my father, many of the villagers would have starved to death or died by now."

"Surely, you are exaggerating."

"Am I? You have never lived in a village sleeping on the floor with the animals and eating thin pottage and brown bread, only on the good days. So how would you know?"

"Well, I... nay, I haven't," he softly admitted. "I'm sorry life has been so hard for you, Rose."

"I don't wish to talk anymore. We should be at Somerset Castle within the hour."

"It looks like a storm is approaching," said Harold from in front of them.

"Then, we'd better speed up." Rose dug her heels into the sides of her horse and sped down the road, anxious to once again be at her father's side.

CHAPTER 9

B y the time they arrived at Somerset Castle, they were drenched from the rain. It was only midday, but so dark that it seemed as if the sun had already set. Rose had wished for better conditions, but it didn't really matter. All that concerned her was her father and his health and that she was here now to be with him.

"We've arrived, my lord," called out Harold from in front of them. They rode over the drawbridge, being stopped by the guards atop the guard tower.

"Who goes there?" shouted one of the men.

"It is Lord Rook from Horrabridge Manor," Rook called out, and then mumbled, "God's eyes, I need to change that name soon."

"Did you say Lord Rook?" asked one of the guards, obviously never having heard of him.

"Yes. Rook Blake. My father is Lord Corbett Blake of Devonshire."

"Oh, I know who you are," said one of the guards, leaning

over the battlements to see him better. "Your sister is that noblewoman who just married that blacksmith."

"Yes," said the other guard. "She's the one who married a commoner."

"Her husband is not a blacksmith, he is a master armorer, and has received the title of lord," Rook corrected them through gritted teeth. "Besides, this has nothing to do with them. Now open the gate before I have your heads. We're soaked to the skin."

"Is Lord Morcant expecting you?" asked the first guard, still doing nothing to let them in out of the rain.

"Please," Rose called out. "Lord Morcant sent a missive saying my father, Oliver Ashdown is dying. Please, let us in. I need to be with my father."

"Rose?" asked one of the guards. "Is that you?"

"Yes," she called back.

"Well, why didn't you say so," said the other guard. "Open the gate," he called out. "Rose needs to see her father."

Rook watched in awe as the gate rose up to let them enter. His name, and being a noble, seemed to do little to get the guards to obey. However, once they heard Rose was there, they lifted the gate with no qualms at all.

God's eyes, what was happening here? Rook wondered. Since when did commoners get better treatment than those with noble blood?

"I'm sure they didn't mean any disrespect, my lord," Rose said, almost as if she could read his thoughts. "Please, don't be angry with them." The rain dripped off the ends of her long hair and he noticed her shivering.

"They knew you, Rose," said Rook.

"Of course they did." Rose followed Harold into the courtyard. Rook rode alongside her. "My father and I live in the village. Plus, we just did extensive work in Lord Morcant's garden."

"I see," said Rook. "Those guards really seem to like you."

"My father and I always try to be friendly to everyone we meet. Actually, those guards, Hector and Peter, played dice with my father occasionally, when everyone else was in bed."

"They did?" asked Rook in surprise.

"Aye. Just don't mention it to Lord Morcant, because although he is a benevolent lord, he might not be happy to hear it."

"I suppose not."

"You see, the guards were on the night shift and my father brought them ale and fruit he'd harvested from the garden. A little kindness goes a long way. No matter if it comes from a noble or a simple commoner."

"I guess you're right," said Rook, impressed and also surprised. He didn't know anyone as selfless as Rose or her father.

The stable boy ran out to tend to their horses, while the steward met them at the stable and led them into the keep.

"Hello, Rose," said Lord Morcant, coming from the great hall to greet them. "Oh, Lord Rook. I didn't know you were accompanying her here. That wasn't necessary." Lord Morcant reached out and shook Rook's hand. "Why would you come instead of sending one of your guards?"

"I felt it was the right thing to do," said Rook, looking over at Rose. "After all, a little kindness goes a long way."

Rose scowled at him and approached Lord Morcant. "Please, may I see my father now, my lord?" she asked.

"You are soaked from the rain," said Morcant. "Your father is sleeping, so why don't you all have a cup of ale and something to eat while you dry off by the fire. The main meal is over, but I'll have my servants bring food and drink."

"No, thank you," said Rose. "All I want is to see my father."

"Of course," said Morcant. "My steward will show you the way."

"I'll take an ale by the fire while I dry off," said Harold. "I mean, if you don't mind, my lord."

"This is my squire, Harold," Rook introduced the boy.

"Of course. Lord Rook, why don't you join us?" asked Morcant.

"I thought I'd go with Rose to visit her father." Rook didn't want to leave her when she was so upset.

"Have it your way. We'll be here when you get back," said Morcant.

Rook and Rose followed the steward to a bedchamber. The steward opened the door and Rook saw a man lying on a bed in a nearly darkened room with only one candle burning.

"The healers say there is no more they can do for him," said the steward in a low voice. "They've just left his bedchamber. The priest was here to see him earlier and give him his final blessing. Rose, I'm sorry, but your father will most likely be gone by morning."

"Nay!" cried Rose, rushing into the darkened room, making her way over to the bed. "Father. Father, it's me, Rose. I'm here now."

"Thank you," said Rook with a nod, dismissing the steward. Rook entered the room, lighting several more candles, and closing the door behind him.

"Rose... you... came," said the man on the bed, his voice so feeble Rook could barely hear him.

"I'm here now, Father. I'll heal you. You'll be back to normal in no time. You'll see." Rose seemed to be in denial of her father's serious condition.

"I believe it's... too late for me... Rose. I am dying."

"Nay, you're not," she screamed, tears running down her cheeks.

"Now that I've seen you, I can... die in peace."

"Father, stop it." Rose continued to cry, reaching down and hugging her father.

Rook walked up and put his hand on Rose's shoulder.

"He needs to rest," said Rook.

"Who are... you?" Oliver squinted, trying to get a good look at Rook.

"I am Lord Rook from Horrabridge Manor," Rook told him. "I accompanied your daughter here to see to her safety."

"Thank you. For taking care... of my... Rose." The man's eyes started to close.

"Of course," said Rook. "I promise I will watch after her."

"Rose," said her father, his breathing labored. "Rose, I want to... talk to you... alone."

"Yes, Father." She turned around and looked at Rook. "I'd like to say my goodbyes in private, please," she told him.

"Of course. I'll wait for you in the corridor." Rook nodded goodbye to Oliver and turned and left the room.

"Father," said Rose, climbing right up in bed with the man, throwing her arms around him and hugging and kissing him.

"Rose, listen... to me. I... don't have long... to live."

"Of course you do. You're going to be healed now that I'm here. I'll even take you back to Horrabridge Manor with us so you can see the progress of the garden."

"Oh, I wish I could... see it... once more. I wish that more... than anything."

"You can and you will," said Rose, refusing to believe the

man was dying. "We are working hard, and it is starting to look so much better than when we arrived there."

"When I'm gone... it won't be easy... for you."

"You're not going anywhere," she told her father, holding both of his cold hands in hers.

"I once had a way that you... that you'd be provided for. Once I died."

"Stop this talk at once."

"Nay, listen. Earl Clive... he gave me a... purple pouch of money... and jewels."

"What are you saying?" asked Rose, wondering if her father was going mad. "He never gave you anything like that. I would know about it."

"He did, Rose. It was to... provide for you... once I died."

"Now, that is nonsense. Why would an earl care about my life at all?"

"He was crazy, I admit. But I... took it... for you."

"What are you saying?" asked Rose, not sure what to think.

"I had it... in my hands. I felt like a king. But then... it was stolen."

"Stolen? By who?"

"I don't... know. I looked and looked... but it was gone. I... was ashamed. So I... never mentioned it to you... or even the earl."

"Father, none of that matters anymore. We'll make a lot of money on future jobs once your leg heals." Rose pulled back the blanket and gasped. Her father's leg was wrapped with boards to hold it straight. However, she could see that the skin peeking out from under the wrappings was green. Red lines traveled up his body, and now she noticed that even his arms were a shade of blue. "Father. Is this the infection spreading?"

"Aye," he said, seeming as if he could barely speak or even

breathe. "I am sorry... I lost the money... that would secure... your future."

"I don't care about money. All I care about is you." She touched his forehead to discover he was burning up, but yet his body shivered. "Why isn't a healer here? You are burning up with fever. Healer! Someone get me a healer," she shouted at the door.

"Nay, Rose. Let... me go," said her father. "My life is... over."

"Father, I will be right back. I need to find someone to help you." She looked into his eyes, seeing the life draining from him fast.

"Lord... Rook," whispered her father.

"Yes, he is in the corridor," Rose answered. "I'll get him."

"He can... protect you. Take... care of you."

"Nay, Father, he can't." Tears dripped down her cheeks as she shook her head, knowing this would never be her future.

"Marry him... Rose."

"Father, what are you saying? You have truly lost your mind."

"Is he... married?" asked Oliver.

"Nay, but Lord Rook is marrying another woman in a few weeks' time," she explained. "Besides, he is a noble, and I am only a commoner. It can never happen."

"I knew his... grandfather. And his... father," said Oliver, struggling hard to breathe. "They are... good people." His eyes drifted close. "I'm sorry... daughter. I love you... Rose."

"I love you, too, Father," said Rose, crying and kissing him on the forehead.

"Goodbye, my... dear." His eyes closed, and he didn't move.

"Father? Father, speak to me," said Rose, crying harder now. "Wake up! Talk to me." She shook his shoulders, and that is when she realized he was no longer breathing. She lowered her head to his chest but didn't hear a heartbeat either. Slowly, she released him. "Nay. Don't go. Please. You can't do this to me. Don't leave me. Father. Father!" She threw her body at him, hugging him tightly.

"Rose?" she heard from behind her, but she was crying too hard to look up or to release her father. "Rose, are you all right?"

She felt the warmth of Rook's hand on her shoulder, turning to look up into his bright blue eyes. "H-he's gone," she told him. "My father is—he is," She burst out crying, diving into Rook's strong arms.

Rook sat on the edge of the bed holding her tightly, kissing her atop the head and rocking her gently. "Shhhh," he said. "I'm here now, Rose. Everything is going to be all right."

As much as Rose wanted to believe that, she knew it wasn't true. Her father was dead, and she was all alone now. There was nothing anyone could do to stop the pain twisting in her heart.

CHAPTER 10

"Oliver will be buried in the morning," Morcant told Rook a little while later. They stood in the great hall having an ale in front of the fire. The rain had stopped outside, and through the windows they could see the sun getting low on the horizon.

"Is Rose still in there with him?" asked Rook, not having wanted to leave her, but she had told him she needed time alone with her father.

"Aye, she is, but the undertaker has just arrived," Lord Morcant told him. "I asked the steward to bring her here while they box up her father's body."

"Rose is having a hard time with this," said Rook, bringing the tankard to his mouth for another swig of ale. He didn't like to see the girl in so much turmoil.

His squire talked with the occupants of the castle, flirting with a few of the serving wenches over by the fire.

"Oliver was a good man," said Morcant. "I'm sad to see him go."

"You say that like he was a friend." Rook had a hard time

understanding the relationship Morcant had with simple commoners. "Rose told me she lives in your village. Was she once one of your serfs?"

"Nay," said Morcant, sitting on the edge of a trestle table. "However, her late mother was my serf."

"Really. Tell me about it," said Rook, wanting to know more about Rose.

"Iris was her name," said Morcant, taking a swig of ale. "Oliver lived in a nearby town and met her years ago when he first came here to do work in my garden."

"Interesting," said Rook, sitting on the table as well. "Tell me more."

"Well, they were married. Oliver wanted to move Iris to town, but since she was my serf, he had to buy her freedom from me in order to do that."

"Did he? Buy her freedom, I mean?"

"He did, in time. However, Rose was born right afterwards, a free tenant like her parents, of course."

"Why didn't they leave here? I hardly think someone would stay living in a village if they didn't have to."

Morcant flagged down a serving girl and took two more tankards of ale from her, handing one to Rook. "I asked myself the same thing. However, Iris' brother and his family still lived in the village, and they were not free. She didn't want to leave them."

"I see."

"Oliver was a selfless man. He never thought about himself. He thought of others first."

"Rose is the same way," said Rook, thinking of all the things she did to help her workers before herself.

"Well, over time, Oliver kept buying the freedom of more and more of my serfs."

"He did?" This interested Rook.

"He was damn good at his craft. Oliver cared about the fine details and only wanted to give his best."

"I heard he even worked for the king at one time."

"Yes. He did. And he was paid well. With that pay, he came back and bought the freedom of all of Iris' family, swearing he would do the same for the rest of the villagers in time."

"Did he?"

"Nay. He bought the freedom of Phineas and Thomasina and a couple of others who helped him to garden. Still, he stayed living here in the village like a pauper, when he could have had a nice shop in town. He and Iris helped the others in the village, doing work that they didn't have to do."

"My, that really is selfless."

"Yes. Then, the sweating sickness hit one winter. That is what took Iris' life, as well as the life of her brother and his wife. It left Oliver to raise a ten-year-old daughter and a niece by himself."

"Georgiana," said Rook, realizing he meant Rose's cousin.

"Yes, Georgiana. That's right. Thomasina and Phineas moved in with him to help out with the girls."

"I didn't know that," said Rook, starting to understand more about Rose's family now.

"I lost a lot of serfs that winter," said Morcant. "That is when Oliver took the girls, as well as Thomasina and Phineas, and a few others and started gardening for other lords."

"They were free tenants, so they could come and go as they pleased," said Rook.

"That's right," said Morcant. "They were free, but paid rent to live in one of my cottages and on my land."

"What about the other villagers?" asked Rook. "Did Oliver continue to buy freedom for more of the serfs?"

"Nay. He seemed to lose that ambition once his wife passed. His focus was then on his daughter and her future."

"My lord, we are ready to move the body now, but the girl won't leave the dead man's side," said one of Morcant's guards.

"I'll get her," said Rook, standing. "I think a funeral at first light would be best. I am preparing for my wedding and need to return to Horrabridge tomorrow."

"Of course," said Morcant. "You are welcome to stay here at the castle for the night."

"With Rose?" he asked.

"I don't usually allow peasants in the bedchambers, but if you'll be with her, I will allow it this once."

"Thank you," said Rook, going to find Rose and wondering how he was going to comfort her in her time of tremendous despair. He also wondered how he was going to convince her to stay the night with him once again.

"Nay, I won't leave him. Go away," shouted Rose, clinging to the lifeless body of her father. She didn't want the undertaker or anyone to take him away from her.

"Rose," said Rook, walking into the room. "You need to let your father go now."

"Never," she said, still clinging to the corpse.

"She's been like this since I got here," said the undertaker with a shrug. "I'm not sure what to do."

"Is there any way the funeral can happen tonight?" asked Rook in a low voice. "I think in this case, the sooner the better."

"Nay." The undertaker shook his head. "The church will only do funerals during the daytime."

"I see."

"Plus, the gravediggers have to be notified, and it looks like it's about to rain again," said the undertaker. "That will complicate the process and slow things down."

"Then morning is fine." Rook reached out and gently pulled Rose away from Oliver, holding her tightly to his body. "Come, Rose. It's time for us to leave your father now."

Rook escorted her out the door, meeting the steward in the corridor.

"Lord Rook, Lord Morcant asked me to show you to your chamber. Your squire can sleep in the great hall. I've had the servants drop off food and wine for you in the chamber. Plus, they started the fire on the hearth."

"Thank you," said Rook, leading Rose away with him. She was still crying softly. "Give Lord Morcant my regards and tell him I will see him in the morning."

It wasn't until Rook entered the bedchamber and closed the door that Rose stopped crying. She looked up and wiped her tears with the back of her hand.

"What's this?" she asked, looking at the ornate room. There was a large raised bed with red velvet curtains surrounding it, taking up most of the floor. Two windows were shuttered, and there was a small table with two chairs in front of the fire. On the table was a covered platter, a flagon of wine, and two goblets.

"Rose, we have to stay the night. Lord Morcant has given us this room to use. In the morning, at first light, will be your father's funeral."

"I see," she said, looking around and then shaking her head. "Nay. I will go back to my home in the village and spend the night there. I don't belong here."

"I think it would be wise to take Lord Morcant up on his offer. He thought highly of your father and is fond of you as well."

"He said he wanted me to spend the night here?" she asked, sounding suspicious.

"Yes. As long as I was with you."

"Oh." She sniffled and her body shivered since she still wore her wet clothes.

"It seems we find ourselves in a similar situation once again," said Rook. "We'll need to dry our clothes by the fire."

"I'm fine. I'll just stand by the fire until they're dry." She walked over to the hearth and held out her hands. The fire popped and crackled as water dripped from her clothes to the floor.

"I'm sorry about your father, Rose." Rook poured two goblets of wine and handed one to her. "Here, drink this. It will help to ease your pain."

Rose turned to see Rook holding out a goblet to her once again. She wanted to object to it, but she felt so drained from crying and her body was shivering, so she took it from him.

"I don't know how I will go on without him. He was all I had." Rose took a sip of the wine, feeling it warming her insides on the way down.

"You are strong, Rose. You'll find a way."

"This wasn't supposed to happen. He wasn't supposed to die." She took another sip of wine.

"We are all going to die someday. It's a part of life, and we can't escape it," Rook told her in a low, calming voice. "What we do after we lose a loved one, and how we keep their memory alive, is what really matters."

She turned to face him. His words of wisdom were just what she needed at a time like this.

"You're right," she said. "My father wouldn't want me to cry and fall apart right now. He would want me to be strong, raise my chin high, and carry on. When my mother died, he told me that her spirit is what kept him living here in the village. He said that he wanted to be around the people who knew and loved her. That is what I want now, too."

"Oliver was a good man. Lord Morcant told me how your father bought your mother's freedom, as well as the freedom of many others."

"Yes. That is all that mattered to him." Rose smiled slightly. "I swear, if he thought he could buy the freedom of every serf in England, he would have done it. Actually, I'm not sure he wasn't trying to do just that."

"Rose, you're shivering. You need to get out of those wet clothes. I will ask Lord Morcant if he has something you can wear."

"Nay. I won't wear the gown of a noble again. It's not right, and we both know it."

"Then at least use this blanket to cover yourself. Put your wet clothes by the fire to dry." He handed her a blanket from atop a trunk.

Rose thought about it for a minute. She was alone with Rook once again. Knowing his reputation with women, she wasn't sure she should stay, so she hesitated.

"I promise I won't touch you. Now, I'll turn around while you undress. Then we'll have something to eat."

"I suppose that would be all right." She felt hungry. Just the aroma of whatever was under the covered platter made her stomach gurgle. "Turn around, and don't look," she commanded.

"Don't worry, I won't."

"It was nice of you to accompany me here," said Rose as she undressed and laid her wet clothes on a bench near the hearth, close to the flames. "After all, you have a wedding to prepare for, and don't have time for things like this."

"I would have it no other way."

She finished, wrapping the blanket around her and holding

it tightly. When she turned around, she gasped. Rook stood there bare-chested, with his wet clothes in his hands. His legs and feet were also bare, and he only had a small towel drawn around his waist.

"What are you doing?" she asked him.

"My clothes are wet, too. I couldn't find another blanket besides the one on the bed, but I didn't want to get that one wet. This towel will work fine."

Rose's legs almost gave out from under her when she watched Rook hunker down at the hearth, spreading his clothes out to dry as well. His legs went out to the sides, and the towel rose higher. If she'd been in front of him, she was sure she would see what lay underneath.

"I need to sit down," she said, settling herself atop a chair at the table. The sight of the muscles in his arms and the smattering of dark hair covering his wide chest made her feel warmth rising up from her belly.

"Are you warm enough, or shall I stoke the fire?" He stood and picked up the poker. The firelight danced on his skin, making him look so handsome.

"Nay, I'm fine. No need for that." She figured he would have to bend over to do it, and that would only make her view of him even more seductive. "Please, come and join me. This food smells delicious."

"All right." He put down the poker and sat across from her at the table. Reaching for the lid, he stopped and pulled his hand back. "Rose, I want you to know that I didn't plan this."

"Of course, not. Who plans someone's death?" she answered.

"Nay, not that. I'm talking about us. Spending the night together again. Alone. Undressed."

He didn't even look at her, and she could see how hard this was for him. He was a handsome lord, used to having any girl warm his bed that he desired. For him to promise not to touch her meant a lot to her. Especially because of his status and who she was.

"I know you didn't," she said. "I also know you'll keep your word and will not touch me at all during the night."

"Aye," he said, seeming to bite the inside of his cheek. "Have some more wine." He poured her more wine and then refilled his goblet as well.

"Oh, no. My head is already spinning. This wine is stronger than I am used to."

"Then you'd better eat." He pulled the lid off the platter, revealing a delicious looking array of meats, fish, cheese and fruit. There was white bread formed into the shapes of seashells and sprinkled with what looked like saffron and garlic.

"Oh, that is beautiful," she said, picking up a piece of bread to examine it.

"It looks like cold pork and chicken, with pickled herrings and salted cod. I'm sure Lord Morcant is sending us cold food since their main meal ended a while ago."

"I don't mind. This all looks delicious." Her eyes drank in the food meant for the nobles, and this seemed like a dream. "Mmmmm, it's good," she said, taking a bite of the bread and then a herring. Rook ate as well. There was another dish on the table still covered.

"Are you feeling better?" Rook asked, pouring her more wine when they were almost finished eating.

"Much better. Thank you for being here with me."

"You already thanked me and don't need to keep doing it," he told her.

"Oh, I'm sorry."

"You don't need to apologize either."

"What is under that lid?" she asked, her gaze roaming across the table.

"One way to find out." He lifted the lid and made a face. "What the hell?"

"Ooooh, violets," she said, seeing the small seed cake with candied violets gracing the top of it.

"I think someone is playing a trick on us, putting flowers on the food."

"No, they're not. You can eat them. Watch." She picked up a violet and popped it into her mouth. Flavor exploded on her tongue. "Try one. They are delicious."

"Nay, I don't think so." He looked horrified at the thought of eating flowers and that was so funny that it made her giggle.

"Are you laughing at me?

"Just at the way you are looking at the flowers," she told him.

"Well, I'm not a goat," he commented. "I won't eat flowers."

"This is different. Many flowers are edible and very good."

"Many?"

"Yes. For instance, did you know that you can eat primroses? I bet if you tried eating one you'd like it."

When she looked back up at Rook, his eyes were hooded, and he seemed dangerous and sexy. "Yes, I'm sure I would. As a matter of fact, I'd like to taste primroses more than you know." His eyes settled on her lips and she realized her mistake. He wanted primrose, but not the flower. The thought of him tasting her made her feel even warmer.

"Here, taste a violet," she said, plucking one off the cake and holding it up to him. When he opened his mouth to protest, she popped the flower between his lips.

His mouth closed and trapped her fingers between his lips as well. It felt hot and wet and it made her stir. Then he wrapped his long fingers around her wrist, slowly pulling her hand from his mouth, letting his tongue flick out to lick the tip of each of her fingers.

"Oh!" She felt a tingle between her thighs. His action had excited her and awoken something within her.

"Did you like that?" he asked in a deep, low voice.

She didn't answer. He was a mysterious man at times, and she wasn't exactly sure what he wanted her to say. The firelight flickered, and shadows danced across his face. Her head spun from drinking so much wine.

Then her gaze dropped, settling on his chest. She couldn't help but wonder how it would feel if she reached out and touched it. Rose lifted her hand to do so, but stopped and dropped it back down to the table.

"I am tired and think I'd like to sleep now," she told him.

"There's the bed," he said, holding out his arm.

"Where will you sleep?" she asked.

"It's big enough for two."

"Yes. It is." She got up to walk over to the bed, but became dizzy. She reached out for the chair, but knocked it over. She wobbled.

"Rose." Rook sprang out of his chair, reaching out for her right as her legs gave way. He scooped her up in his arms, and she held on around his neck.

"You continue to save me," she said, thanks resounding in her voice and words.

"That's what I'm here for." His mouth came closer to hers, but then he stopped, obviously remembering his promise.

She, in turn, reached up and kissed him, needing to feel the comfort of his lips upon hers right now. It was a sensuous kiss that heated her down to her very core. Pressed up against his bare skin felt amazing. Rose wanted Rook more and more.

Their lips parted, and he carried her to the bed, placing her between the soft sheets. When he released her, she noticed his towel sticking straight out from his erection beneath it. It lifted the towel so high that she was able to see part of what dangled between his legs.

"I'm sorry. I shouldn't have kissed you," she said. "It only makes it hard for you not to touch me now and keep your promise."

"Harder than you'll ever know." His eyes flashed down to his groin and then back up to her. "You initiated that, Rose. I had every intention of keeping my promise. I still will, if you want me to, although it won't be easy."

Now Rose felt horrible for leading him on. She knew with just a word from her, they would be making love in each other's arms. Part of her wanted to do just that. Actually, she could think of nothing more right now. Then, thoughts of her father's lifeless body lying before her filled her mind, quashing any feelings of wanting to be intimate with Rook.

"I—I can't Rook. All I can think of is my father dying in my arms." She rolled over and hugged the soft pillow, feeling like crying again, but honestly being too tired to do so.

"It wouldn't be right," he agreed. "You just lost your father. I don't know what I was thinking." He walked over to the other side of the bed, running a weary hand through his long hair. "I will lay next to you, Rose, but I won't take you unless you want me to."

"I—I don't know," she said. "It feels... wrong right now."

"Then I will hold you as you sleep if you need to cry. I will comfort you and be here to help you ease your pain. But you'll need to give me a little time to calm myself first." He lay next to her, but turned in the opposite direction. She could hear him taking deep breaths and releasing them, trying to wipe away the thought of making love from his mind and to bring his body back to normal.

"I'm all right," she told him, not wanting to tempt him further.

"Then mayhap it would be better for me to sleep in the great hall tonight." He got out of the bed.

"Nay. Your clothes are still wet. Besides, how would it look if you, a noble, slept in the great hall while I, a commoner, occupied the bed? I'm not sure Lord Morcant would like that."

"Nay, you're right. Then I'll just sleep here in the chair tonight." He sat down on the chair, facing the fire, stretching out his long legs, not looking at her at all.

"My father was right," she said softly.

"Hmmm?" he asked, turning his head slightly.

"He said the Blakes were a good family. He told me you were a good man."

"Thank you for your confidence, but I'm not sure everyone would agree with that. Just ask Raven."

"You are a good man, Rook," she said, drifting off to sleep, no longer able to keep her eyes open.

Rook awoke during the night sleeping with his head down on the table. The room was cold and totally dark. The fire had gone out. He got up and stoked the embers, bringing the flames back to life, throwing more wood on the fire. Noticing his clothes were dry, he hurriedly dressed.

Thinking Rose might be cold, he turned back to the bed to find it empty.

"Rose?" he said aloud, looking around the room, but she wasn't there. His eyes shot back to the hearth. Her clothes were gone too. It seemed that sometime during the night she must have dressed and left the room.

He didn't think she'd gone to the garderobe since there was

a chamber pot in the room. That meant she was walking around the castle, or possibly even outside, unprotected.

"I have to find her." He took his things, donning his weapon belt, and left the room. Lone torches flickered in the corridor. Making his way down to the great hall, he saw Harold sleeping atop a bench by the fire. Servants lay on the floor around him.

He was about to wake his squire to ask him to help him hunt for Rose when a thought made him turn around. If she was missing her father, where would she go? He headed out of the great hall and into the courtyard. The full moon shone down on the cobbled stones, lighting the area around them. The gate to the castle was closed. Still, he had a feeling she wasn't within the castle walls.

Taking the stairs two at a time, he bolted up to the wall walk and over to the guardhouse.

"My lord." Two guards were sitting on chairs half asleep, but jumped up when they saw him. "Can we help you?"

"You're Hector and Peter," he said, remembering Rose telling him the names of the guards when they'd entered earlier that day.

"Aye, my lord," said Peter.

"Did either of you see Rose tonight?"

They looked at each other but didn't answer.

"I have a feeling she is out there alone and unprotected. Tell me, did she leave the castle?"

"She asked us not to tell you, my lord, but yes, she left here hours ago," Hector informed him.

"Where did she go?"

"She went home," said Peter. "She said she missed her father and that she wanted to go home where she belonged."

"She lives in the village, doesn't she?"

"Aye," said Hector. "I suppose she's safe there."

"You never should have let her go by herself and at night. Now, open the gate. I'm heading to the stable to get my horse and I'm going after her."

"Aye, my lord, right away," said Peter, jumping up and cranking the winch to raise the gate.

"God's eyes, I hope she's safe," mumbled Rook, going after Rose and hoping he wasn't too late.

He rode to the village, slowing his horse as he entered, not knowing where to look for her. He jumped off his horse and walked it, surveying one small cottage made of wattle and daub after another. In the moonlight, he could see that each of the small homes had thatched roofs made of straw. He had no idea which house was hers.

He neared an enclosure of chickens that started squawking when he walked by.

"Shhh," he said, not wanting to rouse any of the villagers, but the damned birds were spooked by his horse and wouldn't stop squawking.

The door to a cottage burst open, and a man with an axe ran out, hopping on one leg, trying to pull up his trews. "Those damned wolves must be back," shouted the man, stopping in his tracks when he saw Rook.

"I didn't mean to alarm you," said Rook, holding up his hands. "I promise I am not here to steal the chickens."

"Who are you?" asked the man, trying to see him in the moonlight. A woman came to the door, and she rushed outside with a blanket wrapped around her.

"My lord," she said with wide eyes, bowing down before him. "Osbert, put down that axe and bow to him. He's nobility," scolded the woman, grabbing the axe from the man's hand.

"Well, I don't see so well at night, dear. You know that," complained the man. "Please forgive us, my lord."

"I am Lord Rook Blake from Horrabridge Manor. I came here with Rose because of the death of her father."

"I am Ida and this is my husband, Osbert," said the woman.

"Aye, we heard Oliver died. He'll be missed," said the man.

"Have either of you seen Rose tonight?"

"Nay," said the man with a shrug.

"Where is her home?" asked Rook.

"It's that one, right there," said the woman, pointing. "The last house on the end. But she and the others haven't been back since they left for Horrabridge."

"Rose and I were at the castle earlier, but I've been told she missed her father and returned here," said Rook.

"She might have," said the man with a shrug. "Did you want me to go and check her home?"

"Nay. I'll do it myself," said Rook. "Can I pay you to watch my horse until I return for him?"

"Of course," said the man. "We have a barn I can use."

"We'd be happy to do it for free, my lord," said the woman.

"Ida," the man growled at her. "We need the money."

"I'll pay you half now and half when I return." Rook handed the man the reins and the woman the coin. "I'll be at Rose's home if anyone asks for me. I'm sure that is where she is."

"Thank you, my lord," said the woman, holding the coin up in the moonlight. When the man went to grab for it, she shoved it into the cleavage of her ample bosom.

"Don't think I won't go after it," the man warned his wife.

"That's what I'm hopin' for," answered the woman as the two of them headed to the barn with Rook's horse.

Rook walked up to Rose's hovel, slowly pushing the door open and looking into the one-room house. "Rose?" he said softly.

There was a tallow candle burning on the table, filling the

room with the stench of animal fat. He entered and closed the door behind him. That's when she saw Rose lying on a straw-filled pallet that lay directly on the floor. She had a blanket pulled up to her chin. He quietly walked toward her.

In the firelight, he could see tears staining her cheeks. He also saw her hugging a man's tunic that he decided must be her father's. She was sleeping soundly, and he didn't want to wake her.

"You poor thing," he whispered, unclasping his weapon belt and laying it on the table. He removed his boots and then blew out the candle before lying next to her on the pallet, carefully getting under the blanket and putting his arm around her. She moaned in her sleep and rolled toward him, snuggling her nose up against his chest.

"Rook," she mumbled, still half-asleep.

"Shhh," he told her, kissing her atop her head, holding her tightly.

He was a noble, lying on a lumpy straw pallet on a cold floor, with no fire on the hearth to warm the room. Rook should have been disgusted, horrified, and outraged. For some reason, he wasn't.

With Rose in his arms, it seemed to him like nothing else mattered.

Aye, he decided. This was exactly where he wanted to be.

CHAPTER 11

The rooster crowed in the village, stirring Rose from a sound sleep. She'd been dreaming first of her father, and then of Rook all night long. Feeling comfortable, warm and cozy, the thoughts of losing her father seemed easier to accept today.

Her eyelids flickered open, and for a moment she thought she was still dreaming. Instead of hugging her father's old tunic, the way she'd been doing when she fell asleep, now she was hugging... Rook.

"Rook?" she asked, still not sure this was real. Her eyes flashed around the room. The sun was starting to rise. Through the cracks in the shutters, light filtered into the small cottage, enabling her to see that she was home. "Rook, are you really here?" she asked in a half-whisper.

This couldn't be real, she told herself. No noble would ever be lying on a straw-stuffed pallet directly on the floor of a wattle and daub cottage.

"Rose," came Rook's deep voice, making her heart sing. His

eyes opened slowly and his mouth turned up into a smile. "Feel better this morning?"

"I do now," she said, feeling a blush rise on her cheeks. "How did you know I was here?"

"I woke up to find you missing. Your friends, Hector and Peter, told me you went home. I had a suspicion since you mentioned going home to me yesterday."

"So, you came after me?" she asked, not sure why he would do such a thing.

"Of course, my little blossom. I didn't want you to have to endure the grief of losing your father all alone. I am here to comfort you."

"I wondered why I was so warm and cozy, and now I know," she told him, feeling honored that he would not only come after her, but stay the night with her as well. "Rook, you are a noble. You shouldn't be here sleeping on a prickly pallet on the cold floor of a simple wattle and daub cottage."

"And you shouldn't be telling me what to do," he answered.

"I'm sorry, my lord. I didn't mean to speak out of line."

"Nay, Rose, you didn't. That is not what I meant." He gave her a small kiss on her head. "I meant, I wanted to be here to comfort you in your time of great pain."

"Thank you, my lord."

"Please, Rose. Call me Rook when we're alone."

"Really? I don't know if I can."

"Using my title only reminds me of my status, and that is something I don't want to think about when I am with you."

"This means a lot to me, that you chose to be here with me, my lord."

He looked at her and raised a brow.

"I mean... Rook." There, she said it, but it still felt awkward to her. Mayhap he didn't want to think about his status when he was with her, but she couldn't push the thought from her mind. "Does anyone in the village know you're here?"

"Just Osbert and Ida. I paid them to keep an eye on my horse for me."

She giggled.

"What's so funny?" he asked, brushing back a lock of her hair behind her ear.

"In the village, what one person knows, everyone knows," she told him. "I'm certain that in the next hour, all the villagers will be standing outside my door, waiting for you to exit."

"Then we'd better make the best of the time we have together." He reached over and kissed her on the tip of her nose.

"Mmmmm," she moaned. "This feels so good that I never want it to end. I want to be happy again, the way I was when my father was still alive."

"I agree, I want that for you too," he said, then let out a deep breath. "Rose, I want to stay here with you in my arms, but unfortunately if I do, I'm afraid I won't be able to keep my promise of not coupling with you."

Rose didn't want him to leave. When he started to sit up, she blurted out her true feelings. "I don't want you to go."

"I know, sweetheart. However, I am not a saint." He smiled at her and reached out to softly stroke her cheek. "I made you a promise, and I intend to keep it."

"But, I don't want you to keep it."

"What?" Sitting up, he looked down at her. "What are you saying?"

"What if I told you I wanted to couple with you?"

"I'd say it's your grief talking. You'd only regret it later." Once again, he started to get up, but she reached out and grabbed his arm. He stilled, his eyes traveling from his arm up to her face. "What are you doing, Rose?"

"I won't regret it. Ever," she told him.

"You know, nothing can ever come of this. I don't want to lead you on. You deserve better than that."

"You won't be leading me on. Rook, I have feelings for you that I can't explain. I was being cautious because I didn't want to get my heart broken. However, the death of my father already did that. I want to make love with you. I don't want to go through life wondering how it would have been."

"You don't know what you're saying."

"I know exactly what I'm saying."

"Nay," he said, shaking his head. "I don't want to make you feel like another one of my strumpets, as you so bluntly put it."

"I did say that, didn't I? I'm sorry." Now, she wished she had never said such a thing to him at all.

"I suppose I deserved it. I haven't exactly been any woman's answer to her dreams."

"Then be mine. Now, in this place, in this moment. Please."

"Sweetheart," he said, reaching over and stroking her cheek. "As much as I am tempted by your words, I know it is only your grief talking. You want to feel happy again, and this is not the way to do that. It will take time for you to get over the loss of your father, but I am no savior, and neither do I intend to be."

"You're right," she said, feeling embarrassed by her words. "I suppose I am only trying to mask the sadness I feel in my heart at the loss of my father."

"There is a time for everything, Rose. This, unfortunately, is not the right time."

He reached over and kissed her deeply, causing her eyes to close and her heart to swell. Just being with Rook already made her feel better. It helped to fill that void of being so alone. Sounds came from outside the cottage, alerting her that someone was there.

"Rook, the villagers are stirring. We'd better get up now."

"Aye," he agreed. "Your father's funeral will be starting soon."

Rook looked around the cottage as he strapped on his weapon belt. "I know you said the cottage where you lived was small, but I had no idea it was so tiny."

"That's right. The villagers have small homes. We live simply and don't have a lot of money or possessions. Most of the villagers are still serfs and have to work for Lord Morcant just to have a roof over their heads. The rest of us pay him rent to live here."

"Yes, I suppose that is the way it has to be."

"See the other pallets rolled up in the corner? Those are for the others who live here."

"So, there is no privacy? How awful."

"We don't have a choice. It is the way we live."

"Why don't you and your father at least have your own home? He is a master gardener and I'm sure is paid well for his work by the nobles."

"Was," she corrected him, feelings of sadness filling her again just from looking at her father's pallet.

"Yes. Was. That's what I meant."

"I'm a commoner," she reminded him. "Our lives are nothing like the lives of a noble."

"I must say I am surprised at the conditions." Rook looked around the small surroundings once again. "I've never spent the night in one of these homes made of wattle and daub. It is less than desirable."

"Most of the time, the animals sleep in the house with us," she explained. "The only reason there aren't any in here now is because we were away."

"The animals stay here too?"

"Yes. It keeps us as well as them warm in the winter and protects them from predators."

There came a knock at the door. "Lord Rook, are you in there?" a man called out.

Rook walked over and pulled open the door to find Harold standing there with the reins of his horse in his hand. "What is it, Harold?" he growled.

"Ah, you really are here. Some of the villagers told me so, but I honestly didn't believe it. Then again, when I couldn't find you or Rose at the castle and discovered your horse was missing, I wasn't sure what to think."

"Well, now you know," said Rook.

"Did you really sleep here all night?" asked Harold, sounding as if he thought it was a horrible idea.

Rook looked up to see all the villagers standing in a crowd watching him.

"Does it even matter?"

"My lord," said Harold, his eyes glancing around before he leaned in closer and whispered. "The villagers are saying that you and Rose coupled."

"Bid the devil, don't listen to gossip," complained Rook.

"Then it's not true?"

"It's none of anyone's business, that's what it is."

"Rook? Is it time for my father's funeral?" Rose came to the door to join him. "Oh, good morning, Harold."

"Hello, Rose."

"Ida. Osric," she called out, waving to them. "Good morning, everyone. I hope you'll join us for my father's funeral."

"We're going to miss having Oliver around," said Ida, wiping a tear from her eye. Many of the other villagers joined in about how much Oliver had meant to them.

"I have the lord's horse," said Osric, bringing it over to Rook.

"I am most obliged," said Rook, pulling out a coin from his pouch to pay the man.

"Rook, I wish my cousin and the other gardeners could be here for the funeral," said Rose.

"*Lord* Rook," he gently reminded her to use his title, clearing his throat when he said it. "We have no time to wait for them to arrive. I need to get back to the manor."

"Aye, to prepare for the wedding. Of course," said Rose, sounding disappointed in Rook. It shouldn't have bothered him, but it did. After spending the night with Rose in his arms, talking about marrying another woman felt wrong somehow. Even if he and Rose had not been intimate, he still felt guilty.

"Here comes Lord Morcant now," said Harold. "As well as the undertaker with Oliver's body."

The undertaker drove a wagon with the casket in the back. Several grave diggers with shovels walked behind.

"Father," said Rose with a whimper when she saw the casket. She held her hand to her mouth, trying to hold back her tears.

"Shall I go back to the castle for Rose's horse?" asked Harold.

"Nay, not now," said Rook, reaching out and putting his arm around Rose's shoulders. "Rose will ride with me to the funeral. Let's go."

"Wait," said Rose, running back into the cottage and emerging with an old tunic clutched in her grasp. "This was my father's favorite tunic," she said, holding it up to her face and kissing it.

Rook realized that the girl was looking for comfort in whatever way she could find it, and he couldn't blame her. After denying her wish to couple he didn't have the heart to tell her to leave the old tunic behind.

The funeral was solemn, and many of the villagers shed tears for the man they once knew. Then, one by one, they dropped flowers atop Oliver's casket after it had been lowered into the ground. Rose clung to her father's old tunic like a lifeline, not wanting to let it go. She dropped primroses atop the casket, kneeling next to the hole, staring down into it with tears in her eyes.

"She's really upset," Harold whispered to Rook.

"Of course she is. He was her father. What did you expect?" Rook also felt shaken by the death of the man, although he'd never even known him.

The priest said a prayer over the gravesite and then it was all over. The villagers left, one by one, stopping briefly to talk with Rose and give her their condolences.

"Go quickly to the castle and get Rose's horse," Rook told his squire. "We need to get back on the road immediately."

"Is she going to be all right?" asked Harold, looking over at Rose.

"She's strong. She'll be fine," said Rook, wishing he could really believe it. Honestly, he was worried about her. The poor girl had been through so much. She lost most of her family, except for Georgiana, was almost raped in the woods, and now she was basically alone.

Harold left for her horse and Rook waited, giving Rose the time she needed to visit with the rest of the villagers.

"Thank you," Rose told the last of the villagers, an old woman, giving her a hug.

"Will you be back soon?" the woman asked her.

Rose's eyes flashed over to Rook before she answered. He felt very uncomfortable about this, and looked the other way.

"Yes, I'll be home soon. Right after I finish the gardening job for Lord Rook."

Rook walked over to join her as soon as the woman left. "Rose, we need to go," he said in a low voice. "Please, say your final goodbye to your father and let the gravediggers finish their job."

"Just give me a minute," said Rose, kneeling down again and staring into the hole that contained the casket.

Rook walked away to talk to Lord Morcant, who was still there, sitting atop his horse.

"Blake, I feel bad about the situation," said Morcant. "I lost my wife a few years ago, so I know how hard this must be for her."

"Yes, death is never easy."

"I feel partially responsible for the death of Oliver," said Morcant, surprising Rook to hear him say this.

"How so?" he asked.

"My hounds knocked him off the ladder when they were chasing a squirrel."

"It was an accident and no one's fault," Rook assured him.

"Still, I'd like to help the girl out with some money. Unless you've already paid her, that is."

"Paid her? I'm sure I don't know what you mean," said Rook.

"For last night," said Morcant. "I hear you took her in the hovel. I am guessing you wouldn't purposely take advantage of the girl at a time like this, so I figured she was trying to make money to live on now that her father was gone. After all, she'll lose the business, since no one will ever hire a woman."

Anger rose in Rook, and he had a hard time keeping it down.

"Insinuate something like that again, and I swear I'll cut out your tongue," spat Rook. "Rose is not a whore."

"Blake, I think it's time for you to leave now." Anger flashed in Morcant's eyes. "If I hadn't just attended a funeral for a good man, I would challenge you to a duel for speaking to me in such a manner. I want you off my lands immediately. Do you hear me?"

"I can't wait to go. Keep your damned money. Rose doesn't want it or need it from a man who thinks of her as naught but a whore," said Rook through gritted teeth.

Morcant turned and rode away just as Harold returned with Rose's horse.

"Lord Morcant seemed angry," said Harold. "I heard you arguing. Is anything wrong?"

"It's time to go," Rook told his squire. "Rose, we're leaving," he called out. "If you need to get anything from the house, do so quickly."

"Nay. I have everything I need," said Rose, still clutching her father's old tunic. She wiped away a tear with the cloth and started for the horse. The grave diggers shoveled dirt into the hole.

"Are you all right?" asked Rook, genuinely caring for Rose. He walked over and reached out to touch her on the shoulder.

"Yes, I think so," she said with a sniffle. "I will try not to cry anymore. It is what my father would have wanted."

"I'm sorry for all this, Rose. You know I will do anything to help you."

"You already have." She smiled at Rook. "Just staying with me last night makes me feel calmer and stronger. Thank you for your kindness."

"Of course," he said, shifting from foot to foot, not able to stop thinking of what Morcant said. Was that truly the way all nobles thought of commoners? Did Rook speak and act this way as well and not even realize it? It didn't feel good at all.

As much as he despised what Morcant said, Rook knew he

was correct in assuming that no one would hire Rose for a job as the leader of gardeners now. Not without her father and his reputation of being a master gardener behind it. She was a girl, and a commoner as well. Rose had everything working against her. The best she could hope for was to return here and take up work at the castle for Lord Morcant. That made Rook even more furious. If the man was truly such a benevolent lord, why would he ever think Rose would sell her body for money? "Let's go, Rose."

"Wait," she said, holding up a hand. She went back to the gravesite. Giving her father's old tunic one more hug and then a kiss, she slowly dropped it into the ground with the casket. Then she returned and mounted her horse. "I'm ready. I think I'll be all right, even without my father now."

"I'm happy for you, Rose," said Rook. "Tell me, what brought you to that decision?"

"You did," she told him with a wide smile. "Your kindness to me, and the way you seem to care about me, touched my heart. Just having spent the night in your arms made everything better and different. You are a noble, but treated me so much better than a mere commoner. That alone gives me the strength to go on."

As she rode away, Rook let out a deep breath. Yes, everything was different now, but the last thing he saw himself as was any kind of mentor or savior. Neither did he want to be. Nay, before this was all over, he was sure Rose would see him differently and it would probably be as naught but the devil.

CHAPTER 12

Rose rode through the gates of Horrabridge Manor later that day, feeling full of life after spending time with Rook. He may have turned her away when she wanted to make love, but he was right in saying it wasn't the right time. She wanted more than anything to be happy again, and oddly enough, Rook's surprising behavior of not wanting to sleep with her made her feel happy and much stronger. By doing that, it was like an act of respect. Rook was changing. From the stories she'd heard about him with women, he never would have turned down the offer unless he truly cared about her.

Rose's heart still felt empty without her father, but something changed within her because of Rook. She now held a confidence that she didn't hold before. This garden project was important to her father, and she was determined to do all she could to make it perfect—the way her father would have wanted it to be. She decided she would make her father proud in heaven.

Rose always took pride in her work, since that is the way her father raised her. But now—now she would go above and beyond to make certain the details were focused on, the way her father would want it. It would be her way of praising his memory.

"Rose, you're back!" Georgiana came running. Thomasina and Phineas were right behind her. They still wore their gardening gloves, and Thomasina held her shears in her hand. "How is Uncle Oliver?"

"Oh, Georgiana," said Rose, dismounting. "Father is dead."

"Nay!" cried Georgiana. "Rose, I am so sorry." She encased Rose in a big hug.

"Oliver was a good man," said Phineas.

"We will all miss him," agreed Thomasina, wiping her eye.

"I am sorry you couldn't all be there for the funeral, but Lord Rook said we didn't have the time to wait for you to arrive," Rose explained. She looked over at Rook next to her, dismounting his steed. He told his squire to tend to their horses.

"I am sorry about that," said Rook, joining them, having overheard their conversation. "However, we are short on time and have to move forward." He nodded at them and went to greet his mother, sister, and Lark.

"My, he is cold-hearted," said Georgiana, glaring at him. "How can you even stand to be around him?"

"Nay, he's right," said Rose. "We have a job to finish. Rook is a kind-hearted man, whether you think so or not. Now, how is the garden coming?"

"It's going fine," said Phineas. "Thomasina and I were just cleaning up for the night."

"Thank you," said Rose.

Once they left, Rose took Georgiana's hand. "Come with me. I have something to tell you."

"What is it?" asked her cousin.

Rose needed to confide in someone, and Georgiana was the

only person with whom she felt she could do that. She led her cousin through the labyrinth and into the pleasure garden. Bandit barked and followed on their heels.

"Hush, Bandit," said Rose. "You are making too much noise."

"Where are you taking me?" asked her cousin.

"I have something to tell you, and I don't want anyone else to hear."

When they got to the old bench, they both sat down while Bandit sniffed around and dug in the dirt.

"What is it?" asked Georgiana.

"Cousin, it was amazing." A smile spread across her face.

"What was?"

"I wanted to make love with Rook, but he turned me down."

Rose watched as Georgiana's mouth dropped open.

"You did what? And he did what?" she asked, seeming as if she thought she'd misheard Rose.

"It isn't like you think. I mean, he wanted me as much as I did him."

"Rose, the man is a philanderer and everyone knows it. This makes no sense at all."

"He wanted to couple with me, but pointed out that it wasn't the right time."

"Is there a right time?" asked Georgiana with a shrug.

"Yes, I suppose there is. However, Rook knew I was hurting and didn't want me to do it just trying to mask my grief."

"I see. I think. And you are happy or sad about this?" Georgiana seemed so confused.

"Both, actually. However, it showed me that he thought of me as so much more than just another of his strumpets. Georgiana, I think he respected me in a way, and that means the world to me."

"I suppose it should."

"I feel more alive now than I ever have before. I still miss my father, don't get me wrong, but now, I feel as if I can do anything. Even if I'm a girl and a commoner. I mean, does it really matter?" Rose looked up at the darkening sky, taking a deep breath of fresh air.

"Oh, Rose, you are sound addled now. Yes, of course, it matters."

"I disagree."

"Well, I think you're in love with Lord Rook and that is why you are acting this way," said Georgiana, looking at her from the corners of her eyes.

"Is that what it is?" asked Rose, never having really come to that conclusion.

"It must be. Why else would you be sounding so odd and acting so silly?"

"Well, mayhap I am falling in love with him," she said with a sigh. "Funny, but I never thought I would."

"Why are you smiling about it? This can bring you nothing but grief and you know it. Nothing can ever come of it. He is a noble and you are not."

"Cousin, I know my relationship with Rook can never go anywhere, but please, allow me a moment to feel happy. It so seldom happens in my life and I want to savor it."

"You call him Rook, but I don't believe you should. You need to use his title. He's a noble!" Georgiana looked terrified and shook her head violently. "Oh, this is not good at all. What has happened to you? What will happen now that you are in this addled state of mind?" Georgiana got up and started pacing the garden.

"Relax, Georgiana. He asked me to call him Rook. Only when we're alone, of course," Rose explained. "I didn't feel comfortable doing it at first, but now I think I like it."

"And how often do you figure that will be? When you are alone and can address him without his title? You do remember that the man is about to be married, don't you?"

"I know," said Rose, her smile slowly fading. "Georgiana, I must admit that part of me wishes that I was the one marrying him instead."

There was a rustling in the bushes, and then a servant boy ran out and away from the labyrinth. To Rose's surprise, Sally walked out next, tying the bodice of her gown.

"Sally?" Rose sprang to her feet. "How long were you in the bushes?"

"Long enough to hear that you wanted to couple with Rook and he turned you down. And now you think that he respects you and you're in love."

"You were spying on me!" Rose's hands went to her hips. "How could you?"

"You really think that's what I was doing out here? Spying on you?" The girl laughed and took a hold of her breasts, hoisting them up so they almost spilled out of her bodice. "If you believe that, then I guess you are really naïve enough to think Rook loves you."

"I never said that! I spoke of respect only."

"But it is what you are hoping, isn't it? If you think a man like Rook can respect or love any woman than you are even stupider than I thought."

"Stop calling my cousin names," shouted Georgiana. "She just lost her father."

"She also just got played by a man who only knows how to use women for his own pleasure," said Sally.

"Nay, it wasn't like that," protested Rose. "And we didn't do anything, so I didn't get played at all."

"That's what he wants you to think. Don't worry, he'll come sniffing around you again, and you'll want him even more because you believe he is the type of man that he is not. I assure you, I know better. Rook is a good time in bed, but he is incapable of ever really caring about anyone but himself."

"Stop talking that way about Rook—Lord Rook. He is a good man," said Rose, about ready to pull the girl's hair out. "You don't know him at all."

"Neither do you, although you think you have him figured out," said Sally. "Don't worry, you'll have more time to discover more about him, I'm sure. Even though he's getting married, he'll still have both of us on the side when he has an itch to scratch."

"Nay, he won't. Not when he is a married man," protested Rose.

"It won't matter to him if he's married or not. Actually, that will make it even more exciting for him to have a few mistresses."

"I'm going to kill her," Rose told her cousin, clenching her jaw so hard that it hurt. She lunged for Sally, but Georgiana held Rose back.

"Go on, get out of here, before we tell Lord Rook what you said about him," spat Georgiana.

"You wouldn't do that, because then I'd tell him what you said as well," Sally challenged them.

"Well, we might at least tell him you were lifting your skirts again," shouted Georgiana.

Sally chuckled. "As if he doesn't already know it. Besides, what does it matter? Isn't that what a pleasure garden is for?"

"Nay, it's certainly not," hissed Rose.

"I'm sure Lord Rook and I will find immense pleasure out here in the garden, sooner or later," Sally continued. "I'm going to ask him if I can stay here instead of returning to my duties at Blake Castle. Then he can make my gown green whenever he wants." She smiled proudly, turning and brushing grass and hedge clippings from the backside of her gown.

"Go!" shouted Georgiana, still holding Rose back.

Once the girl was gone, Rose pulled out of her cousin's hold and plopped down on the garden bench.

"Do you think Sally is right about Rook?" asked Rose softly.

"Nay. Not at all," said Georgiana. "Don't listen to that hussy."

"But you were just telling me the same thing, more or less."

"That is not what I meant, Rose. I was only pointing out that he is a noble and you are a commoner. I don't want to see you get your heart broken."

"Hmmm," said Rose, staring at the ground. "Mayhap I am being a fool."

"Don't think that, by going on the word of that whore. Look into your heart for the answer instead," said Georgiana. "Or at least wait until you have actual proof that he's a cur before you decide he really is one."

"You're right," said Rose, determined not to let anyone bring her down. It was hard enough dealing with the death of her father. She didn't need someone filling her head with lies about the man she was falling in love with, too. "Rook is a good man, and he really cares about me. I know he does. If not, he would have taken me in the hovel without a second thought."

"I'm sure that's true."

They started to walk out of the pleasure garden, with Bandit leading the way.

"Rose?"

"Yes?"

"Did you tell him you loved him?"

"Nay. I don't think so."

"Did he say it to you?"

"Nay. Of course not."

All of a sudden Rose started to feel insecure. That spike of confidence that had made her feel so alive was fading quickly.

"Do you think I should have told him?" asked Rose. "Would that have made a difference? Mayhap, since I didn't, he thinks I'm no better than Sally, since I wanted to make love with him."

"Nay, you did the right thing," Georgiana assured her. "I mean, it's good you didn't say you loved him. Not yet, anyway. It's much too soon."

"You're right. I'll wait until we actually make love, and then I'll tell him. That will be the right time, I'm sure."

Georgiana stopped her in tracks and her mouth hung open again. "You're still planning on coupling with him? Are you sure about this, Rose?"

"I can't say for sure what will happen. However, if the opportunity to make love with Rook arises, I have to be honest and tell you that I'm not going to be in a hurry to turn him away again."

Rook sat at the dais with Robin later that night, having a tankard of ale as the servants started to settle down on the floor in front of the fire to sleep. Rose was with them. It pained him to watch her sleeping on the floor like a dog. He didn't like it in the least. Now that he'd experienced the way she lived, he felt as if she should be treated so much better than the rest of the villagers. Rose was a beautiful woman, and her heart was filled with love. The girl was talented and had a deep strength within her, even though at times she seemed frail or even naïve. He liked that about her. She wasn't crude like that light skirt, Sally.

"What's got you so upset?" asked Robin.

"What do you mean?" Rook took a drink of ale.

"Ever since you returned from Somerset, it seems as if you're lost in your thoughts or something."

"Or something," said Rook, looking down into his tankard. When he looked back up, he saw Rose staring at him from the other side of the great hall. He flashed her a smile and she returned it.

"Did something happen between you and the gardener girl?" asked Robin suspiciously.

"I don't know what you're talking about." Rook held out his tankard as Sally came up and refilled his drink.

"My lord, would you like me to see to anything for you? Anything at all?" She leaned over, giving him a good view down her bodice. Her breasts pushed out, straining against the fabric. Seeing this usually enticed him, but tonight it did not.

"Nay, that'll be all, Susan, he said with little thought." His eyes went back to Rose.

"*Sally*," snarled the girl, storming away in a huff.

"God's teeth, I know what it is," said Robin with a chuckle. "You bedded the gardener girl, didn't you?"

"Her name is Rose, so use it. And although it's none of your business what I do, nay I did not bed her. Although, I was more than tempted when she wanted to do so."

"I don't understand," said Robin. "You turned down an offer to bed a beautiful woman, although I swear you seem smitten with the wench? Who are you, and what did you do with my cousin?"

"Don't call her a wench. That bothers me," said Rook. "She is a woman, and a beautiful one at that. And before you start sounding like that crude fool, Lord Morcant, the girl is not a whore."

Robin was drinking and almost choked on his ale when he heard that. "You just defended Rose, who you did not bed, yet you pushed away that sultry light skirt that is your favorite? I've never seen you turn down an offer of a whore, yet alone a willing wench. What is going on?"

"I don't know," Rook said with a scowl, burying his nose in his tankard. "Mayhap you are imagining things, and it doesn't mean anything at all."

"Nay, it does, although I'm not exactly sure what. After all, you're getting married soon, and it's to a noblewoman. You should be eager to bed all the women you can before that happens."

"Don't remind me about having to marry Lady Adelaide."

"I thought her name was Adeline."

"Mayhap it is." He looked back up at Rose, not able to take his eyes off her.

"Bid the devil, cousin. You're not going to end up with a commoner like Raven did, are you?"

"Nay. Of course not," said Rook, staring down into his tankard again. "I'm a noble and I would never marry someone from below the salt. It wouldn't be right."

When he looked back at Rose once more, his heart about broke. He saw her lying on the floor atop a thin blanket with that mangy mutt curled up next to her. He kept thinking about her home and how she had no privacy and had to share it with so many others. Then he thought about animals sleeping alongside her, and he felt a knot in his stomach. It was bad enough she had her arm over that dirty dog. He couldn't even picture her sleeping next to a pig or a goat. She deserved so much better than that.

Rook wanted nothing more than to bring her to his soft bed and to spend the night holding her protectively in his arms.

"Well, I'm glad to hear that, because I would hate to think you'd do something so stupid as to marry a commoner," Robin continued. "That will not only make Uncle Corbett furious, but it'll bring dishonor to the Blake name."

"Don't remind me. Now, if there is nothing you have to say that I don't already know, please stop talking." Rook pushed up from the chair and made his way out of the great hall, not able to look at Rose on the floor as he walked past her.

Something was happening to him and he couldn't explain it. All he knew was that he wanted to defend Rose to everyone. He also wanted to protect her and keep her safe in his arms.

"Oh, hell," he said, running a hand through his hair as he headed for his solar. Robin was right. He was highly attracted to a commoner, and he couldn't stop it from happening. He was making the same mistake as his sister, although it was what he swore he would never do.

Bid the devil, if he didn't know better, he would say he was falling in love with Rose Ashdown.

CHAPTER 13

"Bandit, stop digging holes!" Rose scolded the dog. Every time she planted something, Bandit seemed to come along and dig it up again. This was slowing her down immensely. It had been a week since they returned from her father's funeral. They should be close to finishing the job by now, but they still had so much to do. It was only because she wanted everything to be perfect. Just like the job her father would do. That is all that mattered to her now.

The garden was coming along nicely, but with only a handful of workers, it was a slow process. Rook's betrothed would be arriving in a little over a week. Rose had to make sure everything was perfect for Rook's wedding.

"What do you want us to do next?" asked Georgiana, brushing her hands together. "Prune the climbing roses?"

"Nay," said Rose, looking up at the vines that trailed over the stone walls of the manor and led right to Rook's solar window. "I'll do that. Mayhap you can help with pulling the vines off of the outbuildings. Lord Rook wants to be able to see just what he has. I sent Thomasina and Phineas to the orchard to check on the trees as well."

"All right," said Georgiana, turning to go.

"Can you take Bandit with you?" asked Rose, pulling the dog out of the herb garden. "If he digs up one more thing, I swear I am going to scream."

"Sure. Come on, Bandit. Let's go find a rabbit for you to chase." The dog heard the word rabbit and took off toward the bailey at a run.

"I'll just trim these roses and vines, and make everything look beautiful again," Rose said to herself, hauling a wooden ladder over to the side of the manor and leaning it against the wall. The roses were a tangled mess, with climbing jasmine interwoven between them. The little white flowers of the jasmine buds were already blooming and smelled sweet. The roses were in bud but being choked out by the jasmine. They were finding it hard to bloom. All Rose had to do was to separate the two, and she'd find order amongst the chaos.

She looked around for her gardening gloves, but they were nowhere to be found. "Bandit," she said, knowing the culprit who most likely took them. Not wanting to waste time looking for more, she decided to work without gloves, just being extra careful.

With her shears in hand, she climbed the ladder, snipping away the troublesome vines. When she got to the top of the ladder, she could see that the climbing vines were starting to go right up into Rook's window. She didn't think he'd like that, so she decided to trim them back.

Standing on the very top of the ladder, she could almost reach the vines, but not quite. So she went up on her tiptoes, stretching as far as she could.

. . .

Rook opened the shutters over the window to his solar, leaning against the wall and breathing in the fresh air. Something smelled sweet on the breeze. It reminded him of Rose and how she always smelled like fresh air, sunshine, and flowers. He heard a snipping nose below him and looked down to see Rose atop a ladder, trimming the vines right under his window.

"Hello," he said, putting his elbows on the window sill, leaning out to talk to her.

"Oh!" Startled, Rose looked up so fast that she lost her balance. Her shears fell to the ground as the ladder wobbled and she grabbed for the vines to right herself. Rook's eyes opened wide as he saw the ladder starting to topple with Rose on it.

"Nay!" he cried, reaching out the window as the ladder fell to the ground. His hands closed around Rose's arms at the same time, keeping her from falling.

"Rook! Help me," cried Rose, looking down at the ground. Her legs waved wildly in the air.

"I've got you, Rose, don't worry," he shouted. "I'm going to pull you up now, so hold tightly to my hands."

He brought her up and over the sill, her feet finally landing inside his room. Then he held her tightly to his chest, not able to stop thinking about how Oliver fell from a ladder and now he was dead. That could have easily been Rose's fate as well.

"You need to be more careful," he scolded. "You could have fallen to your death."

"You frightened me and I lost my balance."

He realized mayhap it was his fault after all. She hadn't expected him to be there, talking to her out the window. He must have scared her, and he hadn't meant to do that. This, being his fault, made him angry with himself.

"I'm sorry, Rose. I didn't mean for that to happen. Are you hurt?" He let go of his tight embrace, putting his hands on her shoulders as he looked her up and down. Shocked, he noticed blood on the front of her gown. "God's eyes, Rose. You're bleeding."

"I'm fine. I just got scratched on the thorns," she told him, showing him her arms. "The scratches will heal just as they have before."

"Sit down," he said, leading her to the bed. "I will call for my mother to tend to your wounds since I don't have a healer here at the manor yet."

"Nay, Rook, there is no need to bother her," she told him in a steady voice. She held one hand over her bleeding arm. "Just find me a strip of cloth that I can use to bind it."

"Aye, cloth. Cloth," he said, rushing over to his trunk and pulling out one of his tunics. "This will do." He ripped a strip off the bottom of his tunic and hurried back over to her. "Give me your arm before you bleed to death."

"It's just a scratch, Rook. Calm down, I'm fine. I'm sure you've seen much worse on the battlefield."

"True, but not on a woman. Plus, this is my fault since I startled you."

"Nay, it was not your fault. I was careless and wasn't wearing my gloves. Of course, I couldn't find them and I have a suspicion Bandit stole them. He steals everything and constantly digs up whatever I plant."

"I'll have the dog removed at once."

"No, you won't," she told him. "Bandit is my friend."

"Come here. Hold your arm over this basin and I'll wash off the scratch with water so it doesn't get infected." Rook helped her to the other side of the room.

After washing her hand and arm, Rook dried it and then kissed it before wrapping the bandage around the worst of it.

"Thank you, that is so much better," she said. "It barely even hurts at all anymore."

"Those thorns can be nasty."

"Yes, they can."

"I still think I need to get rid of that mutt, Rose. He's only causing trouble."

"No. Please, don't do that, Rook. I like him. Bandit was here when I worked with my father when I was just a child. It sounds silly, but having him here is comforting in a way. It makes me feel as if my father is still here with me, too."

"All right," Rook answered, blowing a puff of air from his mouth. "The dog stays. But when you leave, please be sure to take the mutt with you."

"Oh. Of course," she said, sounding sad instead of happy like he thought she would be.

Rook realized he probably shouldn't have said anything about her leaving, because that was upsetting her. Actually, it upset him as well.

"Did you want some wine?" he asked, picking up his goblet and holding it out to her.

"Nay. I'm afraid if I drink that, it might make me do something I shouldn't be doing."

"Like what?" he asked, coming closer to her.

"Like... making love with you." Her big, round eyes flashed up to him, and he felt excited just hearing the words coming from her mouth.

God's teeth why did she have to say that? He'd been purposely staying around a lot of people when he was with her, just so he wouldn't be tempted to couple with her like he really wanted to do. Their time together would be coming to an end soon, and he couldn't see anything good coming from being intimate with her. Or could he?

"Rose, don't tempt me," he said, kissing her atop her head. "Mmmm, you smell sweet like a flower."

"You probably smell the jasmine. It's in bloom. Didn't you

see the little white flowers when you looked out the window? Or the roses that are in bud?"

"Nay, the only rose I saw was you."

"Come here," she said, taking his hand and leading him to the window. "It is amazing, and I want you to see it. The jasmine is the vine with the little white flowers on it. The roses are in bud, but not in bloom yet. Oh wait. I see one in bloom right there." She smiled and her eyes lit up with excitement. "I love finding the first rose of the year. It's always brought me good luck. Let me pick it for you." She leaned over the edge of the window.

"Nay, you don't," he said, holding her around her waist, not wanting her to fall. Damn, it felt good to have his arms around her once again.

"I've got it," she said, holding up a pinkish-red rose with pride. Entwined around it was part of a vine with dainty white flowers. "Smell it," she said, holding the rose up to her nose. "It is the scent of rose mixed with the jasmine and is very intoxicating." Her eyes closed, and a smile pursed her lips as she breathed in the scent. The girl looked like a goddess, reveling in the smallest things of the earth that brought her to life.

Her eyes popped open, and Rook lost himself in the depths of her orbs.

"Go on, give it a sniff." She held the flower up to his nose.

Rook leaned over to sniff the flower, but it wasn't the flower he was really interested in. Instead, he took the opportunity to kiss Rose on the lips, not able to stop himself from doing so.

Her hands slowly went around his neck as the kiss deepened. When their lips parted, he released the breath he didn't even know he was holding. "Yes. Intoxicating," he said in naught more than a hoarse whisper.

"I know that look, Rook," she said, smiling up at him in a

playful manner. "You want it just as much as I do, and I don't mean the flower." She giggled, tapping him on the head with the rose, then stepping away from him to put the flower in the pitcher of water on the bedside table.

It was more than he could handle. Like a man possessed by the song of a siren, Rook needed Rose like a fish needed water.

"Forget the flower," he said, taking her arm and turning her toward him. "The only rose I want to experience the scent of is you." He scooped her off her feet and carried her over to the bed.

Rose's heart drummed in her ears. Excitement coursed through her just being in Rook's arms. Her feelings were stronger than ever now, and she found herself starting to lose control.

Rook gently laid her on the bed, causing her to become frightened, anxious, and exhilarated all at the same time. And when he started to climb atop her, she knew this was finally the right time to make love with Rook.

He stared down at her, but did nothing to remove either of their clothing and that made her think that he was going to turn her away again. By the rood, she hoped not.

"Are you sure you want to do this, Rose?" he asked, his eyes drinking her in. Leaning over her in this manner, his long, black hair hung down, brushing against her cheek.

"I do," she answered, barely able to speak. She reached up and ran her fingers through his soft hair.

"Even if it's only a onetime thing?" he asked, making sure she didn't want to change her mind.

She didn't.

"I have never felt this way before about any man," she told him. "You have showed me kindness and have been there when I needed you. No one has ever done that for me before."

"So, I'm to be your savior then?"

"Nay, not my savior. You're to be my lover. That is, if you want to be."

"Damn it, Rose, you know I do." He rubbed the back of his neck in thought and seemed to be weighing out the consequences in his mind.

"This won't affect the job you've hired me to do. I promise," she told him. "I also won't cause you any trouble when your betrothed arrives, if that is what's worrying you."

"Oh, Rose, I want to make love to you more than anything in the world. I have never met a woman who I feel so strongly about until now. Are you sure this won't be too much for you to handle?"

"My, someone is awfully certain of their prowess," she teased him, smiling and tapping him on the nose.

"You know what I mean. Can you handle it in your heart?"

"I promise, I can," she said, holding out her arms. "Now stop all your worrying and let's get lost in the moment. Being here right now, together, is all that matters."

"You're right," he said with a crooked smile that made him look so handsome that she wanted to throw herself at him, pulling him down to the mattress right now.

"Can I... can I see your chest again?" she asked shyly. "I must admit that when I saw it in the firelight at Lord Morcant's castle, I wanted to run my hands over it."

"Really?" He stood up and removed his tunic, throwing it to the floor. "I don't mind, but of course you realize that I'm going to have to ask to see your chest in return."

She felt her breath hitch as she answered. "I think that's only fair."

"Actually, why don't you just take a good look at all of me at once?" He totally undressed, standing in front of her stark naked. The sunlight coming in the window illuminated his body from head to toe.

"I might need help. Undressing," she said in a breathy voice.

"I'd be happy to oblige."

Rook was experienced around women and it was evident by how quickly he'd managed to undress her. Now, she lay on his big, comfortable bed, naked, and feeling like a lusty lady rather than a common gardener. After all, the only raised bed she'd ever experienced was in the garden. Now, she was in a noble's bed atop a pedestal with curtains that wrapped around it. Just closing the curtains around them would be more privacy than she'd ever experienced in her entire life. The coverlet beneath her felt like it was made of soft cotton and satin. The large pillow under her head was like a cloud sent directly from heaven. Commoners oftentimes slept with their heads resting on logs, since pillows were a luxury that could not be afforded.

"God's eyes, you are beautiful," he whispered, moving slowly over to her and climbing up next to her on the bed. "Can I kiss you, Rose?" he asked her permission, which made her feel special and as if he truly did care about her after all, no matter what Sally said.

"I wish you would." She raised her mouth to his, the moment feeling romantic and like something that she would never forget her entire life.

His hot lips covered hers completely while he cupped her cheek with his large palm. They shared a kiss, slow, hot, lingering. Every fiber of her being came to life, and she felt a happiness growing inside her like she'd never felt before.

Then he used two hands to hold her face, kissing her even more, letting his tongue slip between her lips and enter her mouth.

"Mmmmm," she moaned, liking the feel of part of him inside her. Just thinking of another part of him entering her made her heart beat even faster.

"Just kissing you is making my loins stir," he whispered into her ear, nibbling on her lobe. Then his tongue entered her ear, almost making her jump up in excitement.

"Rook," she whispered with her eyes closed. Her breathing became labored.

"Here. Feel me," he said, taking her hands in his and placing them on his hot chest.

She opened her eyes, slowly running her fingers over his chest, feeling the crisp curls of hair that ran down to his taut stomach. Then she lifted her hands and felt his biceps, giving them a quick squeeze. They were rock hard. "This is even better than I expected."

"The best is yet to come." He winked and nodded to his nether region. When she looked down she gasped at the size of his full erection.

"Go ahead. Feel that too."

"R-really?" she asked, a little nervous to do so. She wasn't a virgin and knew about men. It was actually only once a few years ago and more because she had been curious than anything else. Her limited knowledge of lovemaking made her anxious. Rose was afraid that perhaps she wouldn't be able to please Rook. After all, she didn't know what he liked, or honestly, what she was really doing at all. "Nay, I couldn't."

"Then let me feel your chest, like you did to me." He slowly reached out, caressing her breasts, using the tips of his fingers to roll her nipples, causing them to go taut. Then he lowered his head and closed his mouth over one, using his tongue, flicking it over the hardened nub. It felt wonderful, and Rose couldn't help but moan aloud.

"Oh, Rook," she said. "I am feeling so very warm right now."

"I promise, before we're finished, you'll feel like you're on fire." He trailed kisses down her chest and all the way to her stomach. His tongue swirled around her navel, and her back arched up off the bed. Then, to her surprise, he lowered his mouth to her nether regions, kissing her there as well. "Spread your legs for me, Rose," he said, and she did as he instructed. First, he used his fingers, playing with her womanly folds and bringing her to life. It sent tingles up her body from her inner core in the most delicious manner. When he lowered his face to her and used his lips and tongue to awaken her, she closed her eyes and threw back her head, whimpering softly as her entire body vibrated from his foreplay.

"Ooooh," she moaned, never having felt anything like this before.

"Let yourself go, Rose. Don't hold back," he urged her on.

This time, when he pleasured her with his mouth, she couldn't stop from crying out. She felt herself climbing higher and higher. Her knees rose up around him and she clung to the top of his head. Before she knew it, she was lifting her hips off the bed for him, giving him total access. Rose had to hold her hand to her mouth to muffle her scream when she reached her climax.

"There you go," he said, positioning himself between her spread legs. His manly attributes made him well hung, and once again, she found herself becoming aroused. Rook took her hands in his, and to her surprise, he placed them on his hardened form. "Do what you want," he coaxed her.

Her fingers wrapped around him and slid down his long shaft and then back up again. Rose reveled in the feel of silk over steel. Rook inhaled deeply and his eyes became hooded.

"Did I hurt you?" she asked.

"Nay," he said with a chuckle. "But I'm not sure how much longer I can refrain from taking you in the way I really want to."

"Do it," she told him, letting go of him and giving her permission.

"What?" His bright blue eyes stared down at her in question. "Rose, I'm used to whores who like it rough."

"I want to make love to you the way you'd do with any lover."

"Nay. You are a frail flower and I—"

"I'm not a virgin."

"Y-you're not?"

"I am stronger than you think," she told him, not really sure that was true. However, she wished to make this a memorable experience for him and she wanted him to let go the way he'd told her to do. "Don't hold back. I want you to make love to me fully in every way."

"I am not one for ignoring a lady's wishes."

She almost corrected him, reminding him she wasn't a lady. Then, she thought nay, this wasn't the right time. Just once, she wanted everything stripped away between them, whether it be clothing, inhibitions, or even status.

"Neither do I want you to ignore my wish now," she mumbled, allowing him what he seemed to want or need.

He mounted her then, entering her slowly and gently at first. She felt him sliding into her until his form filled her completely.

"Like a glove," she heard him mumble, knowing that he felt the same comfortable tightness as she did. They fit together perfectly, and this was right. It was as if here was where they both belonged.

Then, he turned into a wild man, his hips moving faster than she thought possible as he thrust his full length into her and back out again, doing the dance of love. A look of raw passion covered his face. For a second, it startled her, but when she realized it did not hurt, it calmed her once again. Something was happening inside her that made her want to pull him in and keep him there forever. She lifted her legs around his back, holding on for the ride of her life. Rook grabbed her buttocks, lifting her even higher as he made love to her atop the bed but on his knees.

"Rook. Oh, Rook!" she all but screamed when she felt that tingling sensation again, but this time it was even stronger.

"Rose, Rose, Roooooose," he growled like an animal, making her even more excited.

She squealed, and he continued to growl. Then he found his release and when she swore she felt his life seed entering her, that only excited her once again.

Finally, the dance of love slowed and Rook broke the connection, lowering himself next to her, breathing hard. She found it hard to gain her breath as well. That was the most exhilarating thing she'd ever experienced in her life, and something she would never forget.

He pulled her into his arms, not letting her go.

"That was nice," she said, her cheek against his chest as she listened to the rapid drumming of his heart.

Rook slowly released her, peering at her with his beautiful clear eyes that drew her in and made her want to lose herself to him once again.

"Nice?" he asked, seeming almost disappointed.

"Wonderful," she corrected herself, not wanting him to think it was anything but satisfying, because that would be the furthest thing from the truth.

"Heaven on earth, my dear little flower." He was gentle again, letting his fingers trail down the side of her face. She turned her head and sucked his finger into her mouth.

"Mmmm," he moaned. "Next time, try doing that, but somewhere else."

She released his finger from her mouth, the action making a popping noise. She knew exactly where he meant. "I will," she gave him her sultry promise, wanting to make love with Rook over and over again. Once wasn't going to be enough with this man. Because, now that she'd felt such tantalizing pleasure with him, she didn't want it to ever end.

CHAPTER 14

"Thank you for all your help, and I will see you soon." Rook stood in the courtyard the next day, saying goodbye to his sister and mother. Raven missed her husband, Jonathon, and Rook felt as if it was mean to keep the newly-weds apart so long, so he suggested she go.

He'd also gotten word that his father had returned to Blake Castle. Rook's mother thought she should be there to greet him, so she was leaving for now as well.

"We'll all be back for the wedding," said Raven, mounting her horse. Rook had sent a missive to the castle yesterday, and several guards showed up to escort the women home safely. They also brought with them some news. A missive had arrived at Blake Castle from France. Rook held it at his side, having read it earlier.

"I'll miss ye," called out Lark, waving to Raven.

"Are you sure you don't want to go with them?" Rook asked his cousin.

"Nay, I'll stay and help at least until yer weddin'," said Lark. "Ye need the hand of a lady around here."

Robin stood next to Rook and snorted. "And which wedding would that be?" he asked snidely.

Rook shot him a daggered look, warning him to keep quiet. It was probably a mistake to have told Robin he'd bedded Rose, but hell, Rook needed someone to confide in. Too damned bad Robin wasn't a little more supportive of Rook's feelings for Rose.

"What does that mean?" asked Lark, as Raven and Devon headed out the gate.

"Nothing," said Rook with a shrug. "Robin is a fool and everyone knows it. He is constantly spouting nonsense. Just ignore him."

"Me, a fool? Hah!" spat Robin. "We'll see sooner than later which of us is spouting nonsense, won't we, Rook?"

Rook didn't answer. He knew his cousin was talking about Rose.

"Lord Rook," called out Rose, rushing over to them. "Hello, Lady Lark. Lord Robin," she said with the utmost respect, curtsying to each in turn.

"The garden is lookin' beautiful," said Lark. "Ye do fine work, Rose."

"Thank you," said Rose, sounding delighted to be acknowledged for her skills. "Since we found so many herbs and vegetables already growing, the cooks have been using them. Some of the villagers here at Horrabridge gave me basil plants and rosemary that are in the ground now, too."

"Great," said Lark.

"Yes, everything is wonderful," said Rook, thinking he didn't compliment Rose enough and wanted to make an extra effort to do so.

"Yes, I hear it was pretty wonderful, wasn't it, Rook?" asked Robin.

"Robin, don't you have somewhere to go or something to do?" asked Rook.

"Actually, no," Robin answered.

"Wonderful," grumbled Rook, meaning that in an entirely different way.

"Lord Rook, I wanted to tell you that I am certain we can finish the gardens in time for your wedding," said Rose. "I, and my workers, are going to put in extra hours to see it is completed before the big event."

"Oh," he said, almost forgetting about the missive in his hand. "Actually, you'll have more time than you think."

"I will?" asked Rose.

"Yes. I received a missive this morning from the father of my betrothed in France. It seems she had some things to take care of and won't be here for at least another few weeks."

"That's wonderful!" Rose's eyes lit up when she answered.

Rook knew it wasn't because it gave her more time to work on the garden. She wanted to spend more time with him, and he couldn't deny that he wanted the same.

"Wonderful. Again," said Robin, laughing softly.

"Would all of you like to see what's growing in the garden?" asked Rose.

"I have to decline," said Robin quickly. "I have to... do something. Excuse me." He left at a near run. Rook took note of it. Now he knew how to get rid of Robin when he was being obnoxious.

"I'd love to see the plants in the garden," said Lark.

"Me too," agreed Rook, although he honestly wanted to run the other way and join Robin. Rook wasn't interested in plants and gardening. What he was interested in was Rose, and spending as much time with her as he could before his betrothed arrived.

"This way first," said Rose excitedly, leading the way.

• • •

Rose felt proud of her work and knew that her father would have been happy with the progress as well. First, she showed the nobles the raised beds that were nearest the manor.

"Here is the herb garden, close enough to the kitchen so that the cooks can run out and get what they need," said Rose. "The herbs that will be available are sage, rosemary, parsley, mint, savory, lemon balm, purslane, fennel, marjoram, anise, and basil."

"That's quite a list, and very impressive," remarked Rook.

"The herbs can be used in cooking, and even in making remedies for healing."

"That is amazin'," said Lark, looking at all the herbs.

"Each raised bed is surrounded by a wattle-woven fence," Rose continued. "The area is just wide enough so it is easy for one to weed or pick herbs and vegetables without having to actually step on other growing plants."

"How smart," said Lark.

"I helped make those wattly fences," Rook told Lark.

"Wattle-woven," Rose corrected him with a giggle.

"They're harder to do than they look," Rook told his cousin.

"There is a vegetable garden and also a garden that holds edible flowers. That's more of a luxury, of course."

"I've tasted some of those flowers," said Rook.

"Really?" asked Lark. "Which ones can you eat?"

"I'm not sure about all of them, but you can eat those little violets, and also primrose," said Rook. "The roses are the best by far."

Rose's eyes met his, and she felt a heat rise to her cheeks. She had a feeling he meant her and not the petals of the flowers.

"How is it that there are so many herbs and plants already growin' and bloomin'?" asked Lark. "It is still early in the year."

"True," said Rose. "But you have to realize that most of the larger plants are perennials that come up by themselves every year. They were here all the time, just hidden under all the tangle of weeds."

"Yes, we don't want weeds," said Rook, probably trying to sound like he knew what he was talking about. "Rose, I see a lot of dandelions you forgot to pull."

"Actually, a lot of weeds are also edible," said Rose, bending down and picking a dandelion. "Like this dandelion. Every part of the plant can be consumed." She pulled off a green leaf and popped it into her mouth.

"Nay! Don't eat that," warned Rook, with a look of terror on his face.

"It's perfectly safe," said Rose. "You can even make dandelion wine with the yellow flowers. Did you want to taste it?"

"Nay, no' me," said Lark.

"Lord Rook?" Rose pulled off a leaf and challenged him to try it.

"Well, I... sure, why not?" He took it and inspected it, making a face. Then he popped it into his mouth and chewed. "Tastes kind of bitter."

"Well, it could be an older leaf. Or hopefully Bandit didn't see to watering it." Rose almost laughed aloud when Rook's eyes opened wide as he figured out exactly what she meant. He spit out the leaf and even brushed off his tongue.

"Now, Lord Rook, don't look so disgusted by it," said Rose.

"I'm not used to putting things in my mouth that aren't normal food," he complained.

"Really, now," she said, smiling at him shyly. "Did you want to put anything else in your mouth?" asked Rose, getting a sultry look from Rook but no answer.

The day was windy and Lark had her head covered with a thin veil. The wind took it and she screamed.

179

"Nay! My veil," cried Lark.

Bandit ran up and grabbed it, taking off at a run.

"Get back here you mangy mutt," shouted Rook, starting to go after him.

"Nay, Rook, I'll get it. I'm no' sure the dog likes ye." Lark went after the dog, and Georgiana saw her and helped her.

"The dog doesn't like me?" asked Rook, seeming so disappointed.

"Well, you are always saying you're going to get rid of Bandit, and calling the poor thing a mangy mutt," Rose reminded him. "I suppose dogs can pick up on those things."

"Oh. I didn't know."

"Did you want to see the progression of the pleasure garden next?"

"All right," he answered. "Rose, this place looks nothing like when we first arrived. You have done a wonderful job of cleaning it up and organizing things. It is a true work of art."

"Thank you, but it wasn't only me. My gardeners have been working hard on it as well."

"Yes, of course. You'll all be paid well, I promise."

They walked past the symmetrical short hedges that enclosed flowers of every kind. Rose showed Rook the peonies, lilies, tulips, coneflowers, and even hellebores and anemones in vibrant hues of purple, pink, white and blue.

"Don't they look and smell pretty?" she asked, leading him into the labyrinth and to the pleasure garden next.

"None of the flowers are as pretty as you," she heard from behind her, and turned around to face him. "Where are the primroses?" he asked.

"Right here," she said, making sure no one was watching before she quickly leaned over and kissed him on the mouth.

"Rose, you should save that for when we are in private," he scolded.

"We are in private. These hedges are so tall that no one can see us."

They walked to the center of the labyrinth, stopping at the old bench where she'd carved her name as a child.

"I suppose I should have Phineas build a new bench," said Rose. "It is an eyesore, being so old, like you said."

"Nay, I decided I like this one," Rook told her.

"You do?" she asked in surprise. "But it is falling apart. I don't think your new bride will agree to keep it."

"I like it because it has your name on it, Rose. I will keep that bench forever, no matter what my new bride says."

"Oh. As a remembrance of me once I'm gone?" she asked, suddenly becoming very sad.

"I'd rather not talk about that now. I'm going to the village to try to get to know the serfs better."

"Are any of them free tenants?" she asked.

"Nay. I don't believe so."

"I wish my father could have bought the freedom of all the serfs on Lord Morcant's estate."

"So do I, Rose, but you know that is not possible. Besides, the nobles need those serfs to farm their fields."

"Also to collect rent from as well," said Rose.

"True. It's how we survive. It is all part of a noble's income, just like when the crops are traded and sold."

"Isn't there another way for nobles to make income?" asked Rose.

"I suppose. However, selling the crops and eggs from the chickens brings in a good price."

"Why don't you sell some of the oak trees in your forest?" asked Rose. "I'm sure that would bring in good money. Strong wood like that is well needed in constructing new homes and castles for the nobles."

"Yes, that is a good idea. Mayhap in time, I will." Rook sat down on the bench and Rose sat next to him.

"I'll miss Horrabridge. I'll also miss you," she said softly.

He didn't answer at first, and she wasn't sure that he would. Then he finally spoke, but it wasn't what she wanted him to say.

"Rose, since you are a free tenant, mayhap you can live here in Horrabridge from now on and not go back to Somerset at all."

"Live here?" Rose's heart jumped into her throat. Did he mean he wanted her to stay with him? In the manor? And did that mean he wanted her for more than just a gardener?

"Yes. In the village, of course," he told her.

"Oh. I see." Her heart dropped. He was still thinking of her as naught but a commoner. Reality hit her hard. He was never going to see her as anything else, because that was who she was. She stood up abruptly. "Since your bride isn't arriving for a few weeks yet, I think I'll have Phineas make a wooden arch, which I'll cover with flowers, for your wedding."

"Rose, that's not necessary."

"I helped my father make many of them through the years. It's easy. There is still time to plant climbing vines and flowers around the arch. As for the bare spots, I'll hide pots of blooming flowers inside the trellis to fill it out. It's very beautiful once it's finished."

"Aye, I'm sure it is." He stood as well. "There is really no reason for it. Why would you want to do that?"

"I want to do it because it is what my father would do. Plus, it is what I would want at my wedding." She looked him in the eye, feeling like crying, but she wouldn't—not in front of him. "I will never have a wedding where I can have an archway of blooming flowers, so this is the closest to really having one that I will ever get. Excuse me, I have work to do and want to make sure Lady Lark retrieved her veil from Bandit."

She ran out of the labyrinth, not waiting to be dismissed. Mayhap she had feelings for Rook stronger than what he had for her. Or mayhap, it was just that he could never give her what her heart longed for... to be Rook's bride.

CHAPTER 15

Rook had spent over a week getting his manor in order. He had nearly a full staff now, including guards, a steward, and a stablemaster to watch over the horses. He had hired chambermaids from the village as well as a laundress. It was decided that his kitchen servants from Blake Castle would stay, as well as his squire.

Eventually, when he acquired hunting dogs of his own, he'd take care of having a kennel groom then. The same for birds and a falconer, but that wouldn't be until later. He was used to living in a castle, so having limited room meant limited inhabitants, income, and limited positions to fill as well.

His mind was preoccupied today. The days were passing by so quickly. When he climbed the stairs to the church to attend mass with Lark and Robin, Lark pointed out something that hadn't been there before.

"Rook, look at that," said Lark, pointing to a parchment attached to the door of the church.

"What is it?" Rook pushed past Robin and several others to see it.

"It is yer weddin' banns. They've been posted," said Lark.

Wedding banns were usually posted several weeks before a wedding and read aloud three times in succession in the church where the wedding would take place. This was required before a couple could actually be married.

"It looks like it's becoming real," said Robin with a low whistle.

"Aye," said Rook, glancing at the writing on the parchment that announced that Rook would soon be marrying Lady Adeline Croiset from Bordeaux, France.

"Let's go, the mass is about to begin," said Robin, taking Lark's arm to escort her inside. The church was crowded today. All the peasants from the village, as well as the inhabitants of Rook's manor, were there.

Rook looked down the stairs to see Rose approaching with her cousin, Georgiana.

"Rose," said Rook, frozen to the spot.

"What are you looking at?" asked Rose, smiling from ear to ear.

"Mayhap, that?" asked Georgiana, pointing to the wedding banns.

"What is it?" asked Rose, taking a closer look at the parchment.

Rook half-wished right now that Rose wasn't able to read, but he knew that she could.

"It's nothing. Let's go inside," said Rook, taking a hold of Rose's arm.

"Wait," she said, looking closer at the parchment. Her smile dissolved. "Oh, I see your wedding banns have been posted."

"Aye," said Rook. "Shall we go inside now?"

She slipped out of his hold and took Georgiana's hand and hurried into the church without him. Damn, why did seeing the banns posted upset Rook just as much as it seemed to upset Rose?

Rook never felt as uncomfortable as he did today when the priest read the banns out loud at the end of the mass. He noticed Rose and her cousin leaving the church before the priest even said the mass was over.

Walking out of the church, Rook glanced once more at the wedding banns, feeling so angry about this that he wanted to pull them down. He reached out to do so, just as the priest exited the church.

"Congratulations, Lord Rook," said Father Avery. "It's so nice to have a new lord at the manor, and soon a lady as well."

Rook slowly lowered his hand to his side.

"Thank you," he mumbled.

"I'll bet you can't wait for your betrothed to arrive."

"Now, Father, don't go making any bets. Remember, you're a holy man," said Rook, trying to jest and brush off the comment.

"When will she arrive?" asked the priest.

"Lady Adelaide?" asked Rook, receiving a scowl from the priest in return. The man's eyes flashed over to the door.

"The missive says her name is Lady Adeline. Did someone make a mistake?" asked Father Avery.

Aye, thought Rook. Someone indeed made a mistake, and it was him.

"Yes, her name is Adeline, but I often call her Adelaide," said Rook, realizing how addled that sounded as soon as it left his mouth. "I must go now. Good day, Father."

He left the priest standing there scratching his head in confusion.

Rook looked down the stairs to see Rose and Georgiana heading back to the manor on foot. It was close by and no horse was needed, but still, the nobles arrived on horseback.

"Here is your horse, my lord," said Harold, handing Rook the reins as soon as he descended the stairs.

Rook noticed Rose glance back over her shoulder at him. He smiled and lifted his hand to wave to her, but quickly pretended to be pushing back his hair when he saw Rose frowning and doing nothing to even acknowledge him.

"My lord?" asked Harold, still holding the reins out to him.

"Harold, have my steward tell the cook to pack up some food and wine for two into a basket."

"What for?" asked Harold.

"I'm going on an outing and will be gone most of the day."

"Oh, that will be fun. I love outings," said Harold. "I mean, since you said food for two, I am guessing I'll be accompanying you on your little trip?"

"Nay, you fool, not you. I'm going down to the river to–" He stopped short, not really wanting anyone to know he planned on spending private time with Rose.

"To what?" asked Harold.

"If you must know, I'm accompanying Rose to look for... wildflowers. To... bring back and plant in my pleasure garden."

"Really," said Harold with a grin. "Pleasure garden, you say? How pleasurable?"

"Go!" snapped Rook, mounting his horse. "Have the cook prepare it at once, and tell the stable boy to saddle Rose's horse for a trip."

"Aye, my lord," said Harold, taking off atop his horse at full speed.

"Rook, we're waitin' for ye," Lark called to him, sitting sidesaddle atop her horse, ready to go back to the manor.

Rook rode over to Lark and Robin. "Go on without me. I want to ride through the village before going back to the manor."

"Whatever for?" asked Lark.

"I want to take a better look at the old mill," said Rook, speaking of the abandoned mill in the village. It sat right on the river that wound its way over Rook's new demesne.

"I'll join you," said Robin.

"Well, I don't need to see it. I'm going back to the manor," said Lark, leaving in the opposite direction as Rook and Robin headed to the village.

"You seem upset about the wedding banns," said Robin.

"Mmmph," grunted Rook.

"Since you want to look at the mill, I am guessing you're worried about money, too."

"Crazy Clive, I've been told, shut the mill down years ago and had the serfs plant the fields with his favorite vegetables of cabbage and carrots only, instead of wheat and barley."

"Oh, that is unfortunate," said Robin.

"Godwin told me that the serfs have really suffered since they still had to pay the earl rent, plus gave him and the church most of what they grew."

"The earl was really an odd man."

"I am thinking of getting the mill going again, Robin. It's a great source of income and well needed."

They got to the mill and walked inside, to find that the large stone wheels to grind the grain into flour were all covered with dust. On the second floor with the hoppers, part of the roof had caved in, and there was a lot of water damage. The same went for the basement.

"This isn't looking good," said Robin as they made their way back up to the main floor. "It's going to take some real time and money to repair."

"I'm not even sure it can be done," said Rook, blowing air from his mouth in frustration.

"Well, at least you'll have your betrothed's dowry to live on until you can get it running."

"Right," said Rook, not wanting to have to depend on the Frenchwoman's money. "Well, we might as well leave. I guess fixing up this old mill and getting it running again was a bad idea."

"It can be done," came a voice from the shadows. A peasant man walked out into the sunlight filtering in through the open holes in the roof.

"Who are you?" asked Rook.

"I am Thomas, my lords," said the man with a bow. "I live here in the village and used to be the miller before the earl closed down the mill and put me out of work."

"Oh. I'm sorry," said Rook. "Do you think it's possible to get the mill up and running again?"

"It is. However, it will take some time and effort. Plus, we will need to plant wheat and barley in the fields again."

"Is that grain in those barrels?" Rook walked over, using his dagger to pop open the lid of a barrel. He dipped in his hand and pulled out moldy, ruined product. Several mice ran out from a hole in the bottom. "Ugh," he said throwing the grain back down. "Are the rest of these barrels the same?"

"Yes. They are all ruined," said Thomas. "The earl wouldn't allow us in here and that is why everything is in such disrepair."

"How did the earl survive?" asked Robin. "I mean, what did he use for his main income?"

"He was naturally wealthy," said Thomas. "He didn't feel he needed the mill for income. But through the years, he... he..." The man looked up at Rook, seeming as if he were reluctant to tell him.

"You can speak freely, Thomas. I need to know what happened," said Rook. "This is my manor now and I want to make things right."

"The earl went mad, my lords," said Thomas. "The wealth

he had, he eventually squandered away, giving it to whomever he wanted. Sadly, that wasn't the serfs of his village."

"Aye, we can tell he certainly didn't use it for upkeeping the grounds of the manor either," said Robin.

"Many of the serfs have died each winter because of the bad conditions in the village, my lords," said Thomas. "If we weren't bound to the earl and his manor, we would have left to find a better place to live."

"But you farm the land," said Rook.

"Aye. However, the fields have nearly all gone fallow since the earl didn't give us enough seeds and the supplies we needed to keep it going. Plus, we need to mix quicklime with the soil to prepare it, and we have none. We had to feed the livestock as well," Thomas continued. "Of course, most of that livestock has been killed and eaten in desperation. Please, don't punish us for just trying not to starve to death, my lords."

"Nay, of course not. I had no idea things were so bad here," said Rook, realizing that these serfs were even worse off than the ones in Somerset.

"My lord, I beg you to forgive me for something else as well," said Thomas.

"What is that?" asked Rook.

"When I saw the grain going bad, I admit I kept half a dozen barrels of each, but only so it wouldn't be ruined. I had hoped to plant it again someday, but had to use most of it to help feed the livestock we had left, over the winter months."

"Is there any left at all? Where is it?" asked Rook.

"I have about a barrel of each grain left in my cottage."

"Let's see it," said Robin.

When Rook ran his hand through this grain, it was dry and fresh and a smile crossed his face. "Is the earl's reeve living here in the village as well?" asked Rook.

"He is, my lord," said Thomas.

"Good. Send him to the manor house to see me, tomorrow. I want the fallow fields plowed in the meantime. I'll have quicklime brought in to mix with the soil. I want those fields prepared as quickly as possible for planting this grain." He dropped the grain back into the barrel and brushed off his hands.

"Thank you, my lords. Thank you," said Thomas, bowing and looking so happy that Rook thought the man might cry.

"I have to leave now, Thomas," said Rook. "Tell the villagers now that I am lord, things and conditions will improve. I promise to take care of every single one of you."

Thomas dropped to his knees, still thanking Rook. This made Rook's heart swell. It felt good to help the less fortunate, and he swore he would never again shun those of a lower status just because they were from below the salt.

CHAPTER 16

Rose stopped in the kitchen on her way out to the garden, with Bandit following her everywhere she went. She decided if mayhap she could feed Bandit before going to work in the garden, then hopefully he wouldn't keep digging up the ground. Her underlying plan was that the dog would become tired and take a nap.

Even though things were progressing nicely, she still had work to do before Rook's betrothed arrived for the wedding. The wooden archway Phineas had constructed was positioned just outside the entrance of the labyrinth of bushes. She would need to plant quick climbing flowers and vines around it, as well as to find flowers to cover the rest of the arch, closer to the actual wedding. Rose also wanted to fix up the pleasure garden with more flowers and mayhap a new fixture or two would make it more intriguing. She still needed to clean out the pond, and replace and fix the fallen statues as well. If she had thought Rook would keep Bandit there, she would have built the dog a small house out of wood and keep it in the pleasure garden too.

"What's that mangy thing doing in here?" sniffed Sally, plucking the feathers from a chicken, standing at a wooden table inside the kitchen.

"Bandit is hungry," said Rose. "I thought if he had something to eat, then mayhap he wouldn't be so troublesome in the garden."

"We don't have anything in here for bitches," said Sally with a grin.

"Bandit is a boy, not a girl," she corrected Sally.

"Who said I was talking about the hound?"

Rose didn't like that comment, and if it hadn't been for the cook interfering, she would probably have had a fight with the hussy.

"Here, the dog can have this bone from the soup pot," said the cook, a fat man who looked as if he tasted everything he made. He put the bone on the floor and Bandit picked it up and ran away with it.

"Thank you," said Rose, seeing Rook's squire enter the kitchen.

"The basket is ready," the cook told Harold. "It's on the table. Take it."

"All right," said Harold, picking up the basket and then spying Rose. "Hello, Rose."

She stopped and turned back to be polite and talk to Harold. "Hello. How are you?"

"Going somewhere today are you?" asked Harold with a smirk.

"Yes. I'm going to work in the garden."

"Why?"

"To finish the job and make money, of course." She thought the squire was asking odd questions. Shouldn't it be obvious what she was there for?

"You don't need money," said the squire.

"Of course, I do," answered Rose. "Why would you think otherwise?"

"Because, I overheard Lord Rook telling Lord Morcant at your father's funeral that you didn't need or want the money he was offering to give you."

"Lord Morcant didn't offer me money."

"Nay, not directly to you, but he was trying to give it to Lord Rook."

"He was?" This made her angry. "So, Lord Rook said I didn't need it?"

"Aye. He said that you didn't want it, either. That seemed to make Lord Morcant angry for some reason. I only caught bits and pieces of their conversation so I don't know any more."

"I can understand being angry," she told him, thinking how much that money would have helped her to survive, now that her father was gone. She needed funds to live on.

"Squire, what is taking so long?" Rook entered the kitchen.

Sally saw him, throwing down the chicken and running over to greet him, wiping her hands on her apron. "Lord Rook. What can I do for you?" asked Sally, standing very close to Rook.

"You can get back to work, is what you can do," said Rook, stepping around her, and making his way over to Rose and Harold. "Hello, Rose. You're just the person I was looking for."

"Really," she said, glaring at him.

Rook looked at her oddly from the corners of his eyes, and took the basket from his squire. "I'll take that, Harold," said Rook, slipping the handle of the basket over his arm. Rose couldn't see what was inside since a cloth covered the top. However, she did see the neck of a bottle poking out from underneath.

"Excuse me, Lord Rook, but I really need to get back to the

garden," said Rose.

"You won't be working in the garden today. Come with me," he said, walking away. She had no choice but to follow.

He didn't say another word to her until they got out to the courtyard.

"It's Sunday, and I want you to take the day off," he told her.

"Oh, but I can't, my lord."

"Of course, you can. I saw some wildflowers down by the river that I want to show you."

"What for?"

"What for?" His head jerked around and his eyes scanned the area. Then he spoke louder than normal, as if he wanted everyone to hear him. "I found flowers I want at my wedding. I've had my squire load a shovel in the cart and you're going to dig them up for me."

"I am?" she asked, thinking he was acting strange. Especially since he knew nothing at all about flowers, and she knew he really didn't care. She followed him over to the stable where the stable boy had a horse and cart waiting for them.

"Thank you," said Rook to the boy, putting the basket on the floor by the seat of the wagon. "Get in, Rose."

"I think Phineas is the one you want with you," she told him. "He's better with a shovel than I am. I will get him." She didn't go two steps before Rook's hand was on her arm, stopping her from leaving.

"Rose," he said in a low voice. "We're not really going to dig up flowers."

"We're not? Then why did you say that?"

"I've got food and wine. In the basket," he said with a jerk of his head toward the wagon. "I thought we could spend some time together down by the river today."

As much as she would normally like that, right now she

was furious with Rook for turning away money that Lord Morcant wanted to give her. Who did he think he was to be making decisions for her like that?

"I don't think so," she said, but Rook was not taking no for an answer.

"Get in the wagon," he told her. "You are making everyone stare."

"Oh, so you're saying that you are embarrassed to be spending time alone with me? My lord," she added, along with a curtsy.

"Stop it, Rose."

"You care too much what people might say if they find out."

"I'm soon to be a married man, and would just rather not announce my doings to everyone in the manor, thank you."

"I deserve respect, even if I'm a commoner."

"Well, how much respect do you think you'll get once I throw you over my shoulder and put you in the damned wagon myself?" he ground out.

By the look in his eyes, she didn't doubt that he'd do just that. Not wanting to start trouble, she stormed over to the wagon and climbed up to the bench seat.

"That's better," he said, settling himself next to her and taking the reins. He directed the horse through the gates and headed for the river.

"You're awfully quiet," he said after a while.

"I have nothing to say."

"If this is about the wedding banns being posted and announced at church, I didn't know they'd do that," said Rook.

"It's not that, and of course you knew. Unless you're a simpleton," she said under her breath, crossing her arms over her chest.

"All right, I am going to ignore that snide remark because I can tell something is really bothering you."

"Nay. I'm fine."

"I order you to tell me what it is."

"You order me?" That was the last straw. She was keeping quiet and trying not to be disrespectful to a noble, but she was so angry with Rook right now that she could stay silent no longer. "All right, I'll tell you exactly what has me so upset. It is the fact that I am a commoner, a simple girl, with no real way to make an income or survive after I finish this job for you."

"Oh, is that all?" he chuckled. "You'll be fine. Don't worry."

"Don't worry? Don't worry?" she repeated, about ready to explode. "You might be a noble and don't need every penny you can get just to be able to live to the next day, but I am a commoner in case you've forgotten, and I do. I struggle for everything while your pompous backside rests on a padded chair and backbreaking work from servants is what satisfies your every greedy need. Nothing comes easy to me, but everything comes easy for you."

"Rose, where is this coming from?" asked Rook, seeming shocked by her outburst.

"There was no need for you to tell Lord Morcant that I didn't need or want the money he offered to give me at my father's funeral, because I do want it and need it more than you will ever know."

"Oh, that's what this is all about," he said, swallowing forcefully. "How did you find out?"

"What difference does it make?" She didn't want to rat out Harold and get him in trouble. "The only thing that matters is that you care so little about me that even when someone wants to help me, you won't let them."

He actually stopped the wagon, looking over to her in a serious manner.

"That's not true, sweetheart," he told her.

"Don't call me, sweetheart. You're to be married any day and shouldn't be speaking to me in that manner."

"You are angry for the wrong reason. You should be thanking me instead," he told her, making no sense at all.

"Don't tell me how to feel," she spat. "Why in the world would I ever thank you for denying me money that should have been mine?"

"Because, Lord Morcant was offering it, thinking you were whoring yourself out for money to survive now that your father is dead. He thought we coupled and wanted to pay for it." With a shake of the reins he continued to travel down the road, looking straight ahead instead of at her.

"Oh," she said, feeling lost for words. "H-he thought I was a... a whore? Really?"

"Yes. He thought we'd made love and he wanted to make sure I paid you enough for your services. I became angry with him and told him you weren't a whore and that you didn't need or want his damned money."

"I—I see." She looked down and played with her fingers, feeling bad now for what she had said. "I didn't know that."

"Rose, I didn't want to take the money, because I could never live with myself if gossip started up, saying you are a strumpet. You don't deserve that. It would have ruined your reputation, and I couldn't have that."

"Thank you," she said softly, feeling like crying now. "No one has ever stood up for me in that manner."

"I will say that I think it caused trouble between me and Morcant, but honestly, I don't care. I did what needed to be done. Well, here we are." He directed the horse off the road and toward the river, finally stopping altogether. "That is, if you want to share a meal with me at the river. If not, I understand and will turn around right now and take you back to the manor."

"Nay, don't do that." Her hand shot out and she touched him on the arm. "I would like to share a meal with you and spend time alone with you as well, Rook. I would like that more than anything, and I am sorry for my outburst. I didn't mean all those nasty things I said about you. Please forgive me."

"There is nothing to forgive, because honestly, I know what you said is probably true." He jumped out of the wagon and grabbed the handle of the basket. Then he walked around and held out his arm to assist her. "I can't say I've been the ideal noble, but I am trying to change."

"Nay. You have been the ideal noble, because that is what is expected of your kind." She took his arm and got out of the wagon. "However, I can't really say that you've always been the ideal..." She stopped and didn't finish.

"Ideal man?"

She was going to say lover, or husband, but wasn't sure that was appropriate since they'd only made love once and he was about to become a husband to someone other than her. Plus, it wasn't accurate, since his love-making truly was idea after all.

"What's in the basket?" she asked.

"I'm not sure, but I think we're about to find out."

The barking of a dog caused them both to turn around. Bandit was in the back of the wagon, standing with his front paws on the edge, looking over at them.

"Bandit!" cried Rose. "I thought you were back at the castle with a bone."

Bandit barked again, jumping out of the wagon and running toward them.

"I'll tie him up," said Rook, putting the basket down on the ground, meaning to go back to the wagon to look for rope.

"Nay, leave him. He just wants to run and play," Rose told

him. "He won't cause any trouble."

"No?" asked Rook, nodding with his head to the ground.

Bandit had his nose under the towel covering the food in the basket. He pulled out a string of sausages and ran down to the river to eat them.

Rook and Rose both laughed.

"Well, I'm not sure how much food we'll have now, but at least the dog didn't take the wine." Rook reached down, picking up the bottle, pulling out the cork. He looked for goblets and shook his head. "The damned cook forgot to give us cups of any kind."

"It's all right. We can drink right out of the bottle." Rose took the bottle from him and downed a swig. Then she handed it back to him and he did the same.

"Come, let's sit with our feet in the water. It's a warm day," he told her. He took her hand in his. Rose scooped up the basket with her free hand as they made their way to a flat rock at the edge of the water.

"I'm surprised nobles want to dip their toes into a river," she told him, sitting down on the rock and removing her shoes.

"I used to always walk barefoot in the water as a child when I hunted for frogs." Rook removed his weapon belt and then his boots.

"You went frog hunting?" The idea of Rook going after frogs while being half-undressed made her giggle.

"Of course," he said, taking another swig of wine and handing back the bottle. "Don't you believe it?"

"Mayhap," she said, lifting the bottle to her mouth.

"I did it so I could put the frog in Raven's bed and scare her and make her scream."

"Oh, all right. I believe it now," she said, and they both burst out laughing.

"Are you afraid of frogs?" Rook asked her.

"No."

"Then, I'll show you how to hunt for them. Here, come with me. Walk in the water." He held out his hand.

Bandit lay on the shore chomping on the sausages, quiet and finally content.

"Nay, I'll get my hose wet."

"Then take off your hose."

"Take it off?" The idea of undressing made her aroused. She started thinking about the last time they made love.

"Actually, I don't want to get my clothes wet either," he told her. Then, in one motion, he removed his tunic and threw it to the shore. "It would be better not to get my trews wet, in case I fall in." He removed his trews and threw them to the shore too, standing there only in his braies.

"Rook," she gasped, looking over her shoulder. "What if someone sees you? What will they think?"

"No one will see us. We're off the beaten path, and it's Sunday so no one will be traveling on the road. Join me. Take off your gown, so it won't get wet."

"Well, all right," she said, knowing this might be her last time ever to be alone with Rook. She removed her gown and hose and tiptoed over to the water wearing just her shift. Her hair was in a long braid down her back, and she wound it atop her head, using one of her hair ribbons to hold it there. The sun was hot today and actually the air on her skin felt good. "Do you see any frogs?" she asked him.

He held out his hand and she took it. Together they walked knee-deep along the bank of the river.

"Nay, not yet," Rook answered. "It's usually the best to hunt for them at night when it's warm and the frogs come up to sit on the shore."

"So, this is going to be all for naught?"

"Nay, not really. Oh, I think I see one." He dove for it,

ending up face down in the water. He came up spitting water from his mouth.

Rose laughed hard because it was so funny.

"Stop laughing," he told her.

"Did you catch the frog?"

He opened his hands to reveal a piece of bark. "Ooops," he said. "It's a lot easier with a net."

"I'll bet it is." She kept on laughing. He got up and trudged through the water toward her.

"You think it's funny I slipped and fell into the water, don't you?" he asked.

His long, black hair was wet and scraggly, hanging down over his eyes.

"Yes, you look funny," she said, still laughing, until he reached out for her.

"Nay, don't dunk me. I don't want to fall in."

He pulled her to him, and she screamed playfully. And just when she was sure he would throw her into the water, he pulled her into his arms instead, kissing her deeply.

His lips on hers were like heaven and a heat rose up from her belly. Their lips parted and he looked into her eyes, brushing back a stray strand of her long, blonde hair from her eyes.

"I would never purposely throw you into the water, Rose. I was just teasing you."

"I know."

Just then, Bandit ran up to the shore, barking. The dog jumped into the water and swam to them, wanting to play as well.

"Nay, get away from us, you mangy mutt," said Rook, pushing the dog away.

Bandit somehow sprang right out of the water, and with more force than thought possible, knocked into them.

"Nay, Bandit," cried Rose, losing her balance. Before she knew it, she, Rook, and the dog were all in the water splashing around.

"I'm sorry, Rose. I didn't mean for that to happen," Rook called out, trying to be heard over Bandit's barking.

"I'm not angry. It's actually refreshing," she told him and smiled.

He came up next to her, pulling her to him. "Wrap your legs around me," he said, walking out to deeper water. Bandit went back to the shore and shook. Water sprayed everywhere.

"What are you doing, Rook?" asked Rose.

"Have you ever made love out in the open and in the water?"

"Nay. Have you?"

With his foot, he tossed his braies over to the shore.

"I guess that means, yes?" she asked. "I don't want to be naked out in the open," she told him.

"You don't have to be." He looked down at her chest, and moaned.

When she looked down, she saw her nipples right through her wet shift and they were poking out like little peaks.

With her legs around him, she felt him place her over his hardened form, sliding her slowly down his shaft. His mouth claimed hers and then they made love right there in the water. It was the most invigorating, exciting thing she had ever experienced in her life.

"Oh, Rook," she said, still holding on to him after they'd both reached their peaks and been sated. "I feel so alive. So at one with nature."

"That's what I like about you, Rose. You are not afraid to try new things." He carried her to the shore and gently put her down on the flat rock. "We'll have to let the sun dry us before we dress. Just let me put on my braies."

Rook looked around but couldn't find them. Then, hearing Bandit barking, they looked up to see the dog with Rook's braies on the ground, ready to pick them up and run.

They both burst out laughing.

"I guess I'll go without them," he said, putting on his trews instead. Still, he had a bare chest.

"I think I'd feel better if I were dressed too," she told him. Her hair had come down and she used her fingers to unbraid it so it would dry faster.

"At least take off that wet shift, or you'll be uncomfortable." Without asking, he removed it for her. Sitting naked atop the rock with her long hair the only thing covering her, Rose felt like a water nymph.

"God's eyes, you are beautiful, my little Primrose." Rook bent over and kissed her again. If she hadn't stopped him, he probably would have made love with her right there atop the rock at the bank of the river.

"I don't feel comfortable with this," she said, grabbing for her gown. "In the water while wearing my shift was enough adventure for the day."

"Then let's have something to eat." Rook sat down with the basket, pulling out bread and cheese and even some herring as Rose dressed.

Bandit walked up panting, brushing his nose up against Rook's arm.

"You bring back my braies first, before I give you anything," said Rook, rubbing his hand over the dog's head. "And don't forget, you already ate all the sausages. You need to leave something for us."

"You didn't call him a mangy mutt," said Rose in surprise.

"Nay, I think I'm done calling him that."

"It seems as if you and Bandit might just be able to get

along after all," said Rose, happy to see this new relationship evolve.

"Yes, mayhap I am getting used to Bandit after all," Rook answered.

They ate the meal and drank the wine, talking and laughing in the sun. Rose felt as if it was the perfect day. That is, until they heard horses and crashing wagon wheels on the road above them.

"That sounds like quite an entourage," said Rose, turning to look. "They seem to be headed toward your manor. Who could it be?"

"Oh, hell," said Rook, standing up to get a better view.

Rook's heart jumped when he perused the entourage of people. His father was leading the procession, as well as a man whose squire was carrying a flag with a crest that looked very foreign to him. Then, a woman sitting sidesaddle atop a horse rode by, and Rook knew exactly who she was.

"Shit," he said, hunkering down, quickly reaching for his tunic.

"Who is it, Rook?" When Rose started to stand, he yanked her back down.

"Keep your head down," he told her.

Bandit barked and started to run toward the road.

"Dammit, Bandit, get back here," said Rook, and the dog actually turned and came back to them. However, the dog's barking had alerted the woman to their presence. His eyes met hers for a brief second before he yanked his tunic over his head and she passed on by.

"Rook? Who was that?" asked Rose.

"My betrothed," he said in a low voice, feeling like his world just came crashing down around him.

CHAPTER 17

"Rose, I'm going to have to ask you to stay here and wait until everyone is inside before coming back into the courtyard with the wagon," said Rook as soon as they approached the manor.

"What? Why?" asked Rose. "Are you really that embarrassed to be seen with me?"

"It's not that, sweetheart, honest it isn't. It's just that I have never met my betrothed and now she's here with her family and entourage, as well as my father. I think we'd better take things slow."

"Take things slow?" asked Rose. "It's a little too late for that, Rook."

"Oh, and remember to call me Lord Rook around them. You have to use my title." He stopped the horse and got out of the wagon.

"You're doing it again, and I can't say I like it," said Rose, starting to get upset.

"Doing what?" Rook shook his head like a dog, then ran his

fingers through his hair, trying to dry it. Bandit, in the back of the wagon, shook to dry off as well.

Interesting, thought Rose, that all curs acted in the same manner.

"You honestly don't know?" she asked him.

"Rose, if you have something to say, hurry up and do it." His eyes nervously roamed toward the manor house. "I really need to get over there."

"All right, I will," she said, no longer afraid to speak her mind when it came to Rook. "You are once again acting like you don't want to be seen with me. Like I am only good enough to be with you if we're alone and no one is watching. But as soon as we're in front of wondering eyes, you want to push me away and act like there is nothing going on between us."

"There isn't," he said, almost too fast. Her heart jumped into her throat. This only made her angrier to hear him say this after everything they'd been through together. "You knew all along I was getting married, so I don't know why you're making such a fuss. Now remember, wait until we are all inside before you bring the wagon into the courtyard." He took off at a near run, not even waiting to hear her response.

"I can't live this way," said Rose, not wanting to do anything to jeopardize Rook where his future was concerned, but neither was she going to be just another of his play things, like she said when she'd first met him.

Rook tried his best to sneak in through the gates, and thankfully with all the commotion of the guests arriving, no one saw him. He slipped into the stable, trying to make himself look presentable, and wishing his hair wasn't still wet from the river.

"Ah, there you are, cousin," said Robin, coming into the stable. "Your betrothed has arrived and your father is looking for you."

"Damn it," Rook ground out. "What is she doing here already? I thought the missive said it would be a few more weeks yet before she got here."

"I guess Lady Adeline wanted to surprise you."

"She sure as hell did."

"Rook, why is your hair wet?" asked Robin, squinting his eyes to get a better look. "And your tunic looks like it's got mud on it."

"You're wearing a cloak," said Rook. "Give it to me."

"Why?"

"Just do it. Quickly." Rook held out his hands.

"Nay. Get your own cloak. Or don't you think your betrothed will approve of that outlandish red one you like to wear?"

Rook picked up the hem of Robin's cloak and used it like a towel to dry his hair, rubbing it over his head.

"Damn it, Rook. Take the damned thing now. I can't wear it after you wiped your stench all over it." Robin took it off and handed it to Rook.

"Thanks." Rook donned the cloak and pulled the hood up over his head.

"You smell fishy. Like the river." Robin wrinkled his nose and made a face. "That's where you were, isn't it?"

"Yes. I took Rose to the river and we made love in the water, but don't say a thing to anyone or I'll have your head."

"You fool, what are you thinking? I can't even imagine what would happen if your betrothed had seen that!"

"She did."

"God's eyes, nay."

"I mean, not the actual lovemaking part, but she looked directly at me."

"This isn't good," said Robin, shaking his head. "This is going to cause trouble."

"We were a little ways from the road, so I'm sure she won't know it was me," said Rook, hoping that were true.

"She'll recognize your clothes."

"Nay, she won't."

"Why not?"

"I wasn't wearing any."

"What? She saw you naked? Are you insane?" Robin flailed his arms in the air and started to pace the ground.

"Just my chest was naked. I had my trews on, but don't worry. She won't catch on."

"Where is Rose?" asked Robin, looking around. "Did you drown her in the river rather than to be caught with her?"

"Stop it. Of course not. I just told her to wait until we're all inside before she enters the courtyard with the wagon. I thought it would be better that way. So, help me get everyone into the great hall quickly."

Rook pushed past him, feeling ill. He was about to make his presence known to the woman who was going to be his wife, and he didn't want to. All he really wanted to do was to turn around and go back to the river with Rose.

"Son, there you are," bellowed Corbett. "Come meet your betrothed, and her parents, Lord and Lady Croiset."

"Pleased to meet you, Lady Adelaide," said Rook, trying to remember if it was that or Adeline. He got his first look at his betrothed. She seemed to be about his age, with dark hair tied up under a headpiece and wimple that hung over her neck and around her shoulders too. Of course, she was so covered up that he couldn't really tell if she was comely or ugly. She wore a long green gown and over that, a long tan cloak. She had gloves on her hands even though it was a warm day. He swore he never saw anyone so covered up and hidden away under their clothes, except mayhap a nun. Or mayhap it was because he had just seen Rose naked that this seemed so extreme.

"It's Lady Adeline, not Adelaide," the woman retorted, pushing her nose in the air, sounding like the shrew she was gossiped about to be. "You would think my betrothed would at least know my name."

Damn, she sounded stuffy. Rook could have kicked himself for using the wrong name, but honestly, he could never remember which of the two it was. Names weren't important to him. He remembered the personalities of people more.

"Forgive me, my betrothed. It won't happen again," said Rook, feeling so phony, but knowing he needed to apologize. He wanted the first meeting between them to go smoothly, and that didn't seem to be happening.

"Kiss my hand," she commanded, pulling off her glove and holding her hand out to him.

Rook kissed it, as was proper. Her skin looked so pale that he was sure she never saw the sun. When he kissed Rose's hand it was golden and rosy from the weather, and looked so much healthier than this.

He went on to greet the shrew's parents next.

"I am sorry I wasn't here immediately when you arrived, but the missive you sent said it would be a few more weeks yet, so I wasn't expecting you until then," Rook told them.

"Aye, yes," said the girl's father. "That was my daughter's idea. She wanted to surprise you."

"And that she did," said Rook, not liking the girl's calculated, addled games. It was more than likely she wanted to catch Rook off guard, doing something he shouldn't be doing.

Which she did.

"Well, shall we all go into the great hall for some

wine or ale?" asked Rook, looking up to see Robin standing there as well. Rook tried to signal him with his eyes.

"Yes. Inside," said Robin, clearing his throat, finally catching on. "That is where we... get... drinks. And things."

Rook shot his cousin a dirty look. He wasn't being of any true help at all.

"Oh, my glove. I dropped it," said Adeline. She looked at Rook and opened her fingers. The glove fell to the ground. "Be a dear and pick it up for me, Lord Rook."

She hadn't really dropped it. Or at least not until after she said so. She was playing games again, and Rook didn't like it at all.

"Isn't it a little warm to be wearing gloves?" asked Rook, bending down to get it, since he knew he had no choice but to do so.

"You're wearing a cloak and hood," she pointed out, shutting him up quickly.

Before he could even touch the glove, Bandit ran into the courtyard barking, picked it up, and ran off with it in his mouth.

"My glove!" shouted Adeline.

"Dammit, that mutt is trouble," growled Rook. "Don't worry, I'll get it for you, Adelaide. Adeline. I mean, Lady Adeline." He was glad for a reason to get out of here right now since he was only making matters worse.

"Don't you have servants for that?" asked Lord Croiset.

"Yes, Rook. Let the servants chase the dog," said Corbett. "You need to escort your betrothed inside."

Before Rook could even offer his arm to the wench, the sound of a wagon barreling in to the courtyard and stopping just behind them took his attention.

"Bloody hell," he said under his breath as he saw Rose

climbing out of the wagon with her hair loose and dripping wet.

"What's this?" asked Lady Croiset with a sniff.

"Yes, Rook, who is this bedraggled girl and why is she so close to us?" asked Adeline, sneering at Rose and taking a step backward to make distance between them.

"Hello," said Rose, walking up with the basket over her arm. "I'm Rose Ashdown."

The nobles looked horrified that she was even speaking to them at all.

"She's the gardener," Rook explained. "She was out picking flowers and is on her way back to work, aren't you?" he said through gritted teeth, looking directly at Rose.

"Are you Lady Adeline?" asked Rose, making Rook cringe that she was speaking to his betrothed. He knew this could only mean trouble.

"Why does it matter to you who I am? I don't know you, and neither do I want to," said his betrothed with a sharp tongue.

"Oh, I just wondered because I saw you ride by when I was down at the river bathing earlier."

"Bathing? In that dirty water? Oh, my." Once again, Lady Adeline's nose was in the air. "Where is your half-naked lover that I saw with you?"

Rook's head snapped around and his eyes met Rose's. He slowly shook his head, praying she wasn't so heartless that she'd tell his betrothed the truth. Please, he thought, begging her with his eyes but not saying a word. Please, Rose, stay silent.

"Oh, I see you know about that," said Rose with a sardonic smile. "Well, he didn't want to be caught, so he ran away like a coward."

Rook didn't like Rose calling him a coward, but couldn't

say anything or his betrothed would know it was him she saw with Rose.

Bandit zipped through the courtyard, dropping the glove and jumping up on to the back of the wagon. By now, several servants, including Sally, were chasing after the dog.

"Here is your glove," said Rook, picking it up and slapping it against his hand to remove the dirt. It was wet and slobbery from the hound's mouth. He handed it to Adeline, but she just wrinkled her nose.

"You don't really expect me to touch it now, do you?"

"It might have a little dog drool on it, but it's not as bad as touching a frog, my lady," said Rose.

"Rook, do something," warned Corbett under his breath.

"I'll have the glove washed. Or buy you a new pair," said Rook, shoving it through his belt. "Why don't we all go inside now, shall we?"

"You haven't even seen the dowry yet," said the girl's father. "We've brought silks and satins, and jewels, and of course a lot of money."

"Yes, fine. Thank you." Rook held out his arm to Adeline. "May I escort you inside, my lady?"

She hesitantly took his arm, but when Rose started shouting at Bandit, he stopped and turned around. To his horror, Bandit had Rook's braies in its mouth.

"Give those to me," said Rose, yanking them away from the dog.

All the servants ran up and stopped to watch.

"Are those undergarments?" asked Adeline, sounding like she was very disgusted and possibly about to swoon.

"Nay," said Rook at the same time Rose said, "Aye."

"They're my lover's," said Rose, holding them up for the others to see. "We made love in the river and the dog stole them."

"Oh, my!" gasped Adeline, holding her hand to her mouth.

"Blake, you need to discipline your gardener, and whip that servant who was coupling in the river with her," complained Lord Croiset. "You need to rule these commoners with an iron fist."

"Yes. You do," agreed the shrew.

"Well, I'm sure the man is long gone, and I don't even know who those braies belong to," said Rook, almost choking on his words.

"Oh, I do," said Sally, laughing, walking up and grabbing the braies from Rose. She held them high in the air. "These are the braies of my lover as well, and he is right here at the manor."

"I think it's time I get back to work now," said Rose, yanking the braies from Sally and shoving them into the basket. "I am so sorry to have disturbed you. We all are." She curtsied and grabbed Sally by the arm, dragging her away.

"All right, then. To the great hall," said Robin, finally swooping in for the rescue, even though Rook figured it was already too late. If Adeline hadn't figured out by now that he was the lover of both Rose and Sally, then one of the girls was most definitely going to end up telling her before the day was over. That's all he needed.

God's eyes, Rook wanted to die right now. Then, at least, all his problems would end.

~

Rose ran back to the garden, still holding on to Sally, wanting to get her away from the nobles before she came right out and told Lady Adeline that Rook had slept with both of them.

"Let go of me!" snapped Sally. "What are you doing?"

Rose finally released her. "What am I doing? What about

you?" asked Rose. "You were about to come right out and tell the French nobles that those were Rook's braies."

"Well, they are," she said with a shrug. "Besides, you were there bragging that you made love with him in the river."

"I never said it was Rook." Rose felt horrible now. She'd been so angry with Rook that at first she wanted to ruin things for him with his betrothed. But when Sally showed up, Rose realized what a horrible mistake she had made. If she could take it all back now and just stay outside the gate like Rook wanted her to, she would.

"Cousin, what is going on?" asked Georgiana, running over with Phineas and Thomasina. They were dirty from digging in the garden.

"Nothing. Get back to work," she told the others. "We will finish up the job tomorrow and then we'll leave."

"Leave Horrabridge? Already?" asked Georgiana.

Rose felt as if she were about to cry and didn't want to do it in front of the others. She took off at a run, into the labyrinth of bushes, with Bandit running right behind her. She didn't stop until she got to the center of the pleasure garden.

"What did I do?" she said aloud, throwing herself down on the ground in front of the wooden bench that she'd carved her name into when she was a child. Hiding her face in her hands, she cried her heart out.

It had been a wonderful day and she'd never felt closer to Rook than she had at the river. Then, everything changed with the arrival of Lady Adeline. In the blink of an eye, Rose went from being happy to mad to sad. This was getting to be too much, and she knew she couldn't stay here in Horrabridge any longer.

Rose couldn't watch Rook marry another woman. It would kill her to witness it. She also couldn't stay here with a man who wanted to hide her away when her presence in his life wasn't convenient for him.

"Rose?" came the soft voice of Georgiana as she followed Rose into the labyrinth to comfort her. "Are you all right?"

"Oh, Georgiana," said Rose, uncovering her eyes and shaking her head. "I'm in love with Rook, but I've just made a terrible mistake out in the courtyard."

"I heard. Sally told me."

"I was angry at him, and jealous I suppose, that he is marrying that Frenchwoman."

Georgiana hunkered down and put her arms around Rose. Bandit kept busy, digging a hole under the bench.

"You knew what you had with Rook wouldn't last, Rose. You can't expect a noble to throw away his whole life for a girl who is only a commoner."

"I just hoped it could be different, I suppose. After all, Rook's sister married a commoner," Rose reminded her cousin.

"True, but Rook is Lord Corbett's eldest son and heir. It is important that he marry someone of his status who can bring much to the alliance."

"Yes, I suppose so. It was just a dream that made me happy for a while, that's all."

"Are we really leaving tomorrow?" asked her cousin.

"Yes." Rose brushed away a tear. "We'll finish up the arch of flowers for the wedding and then we'll go. I think the sooner I leave here, the better for everyone."

"Shouldn't you at least talk to Lord Rook first?"

"Nay. He has enough problems. I only wish I knew how we were going to survive."

"Bandit, stop digging," scolded Georgiana, walking over and pulling the dog out from under the bench. Rose could see the dog had something dangling from its mouth.

"What do you have there, Bandit?" Rose got up and walked over to the dog, taking the item from his mouth.

"What is it?" asked Georgiana curiously, still holding the dog and looking over the top of the bench.

"It looks like a purple pouch," said Rose, brushing the dirt off of it. "And it's heavy. There is something in it." She dumped out the contents atop the ground and gasped. "Georgiana, there is a lot of money in this pouch and even jewels."

"What? Let me see." Her cousin released the dog and came around the bench. "Oh, my!" she gasped and held her hand to her mouth. "What are you going to do?"

"I don't know," she said, suddenly remembering the story her father told her on his deathbed. "Cousin, I think this is the pouch of money and jewels that the crazy earl gave my father."

"Really? The one you told me about that he lost?" asked Georgiana, knowing the story as well, since Rose told her about it after the funeral.

"Yes. It was meant for me. That is what Father said. It was to be for my future life after he passed away."

"Rose, the dog must have stolen it years ago and hidden it here under this bench," said Georgiana.

"Yes. Yes, I am sure that is what happened," said Rose, the answer being so clear now. "I used to play by this bench with Bandit when I was a child. It was like a secret place where we'd go together. He was only a puppy, but he must have remembered. He also must have stolen the pouch so many years ago and buried it here. Since no one tended to the garden all these years and the bench was over it, no one ever found it."

"What are you going to do with the money and jewels?" asked Georgiana. "Are you going to keep it?"

Bandit started barking at something, and Rose figured it was a squirrel.

"I don't know," Rose answered.

"You found the money and jewels in Lord Rook's garden, so I suppose it really belongs to him now. Rose, you're going to have to hand it over."

"Nay! I won't do that," said Rose, scooping the contents back into the pouch and pulling the ties closed. "Rook has everything he'll ever want in life. He doesn't need this. I have nothing. This amount of wealth can feed us for a long time, Georgiana. I want to take care of not only me, but also you, and Phineas and Thomasina with this money. It is what Father would have wanted me to do. Besides, Rook doesn't even know about it, so he'll never miss it."

Bandit kept barking, and Rose saw the dog chasing someone or something out of the labyrinth. She didn't pay much attention to it because right now, nothing else mattered except this pouch of money that could secure her future.

"I have the means to survive now, even without Rook," said Rose. It was a bittersweet moment, in a way. With all her heart, she still wanted Rook, but she knew she could never have him. This was the only thing that would help fill that awful void that the death of her father left in her life.

"Georgiana, with this money, now we won't have to live in the village and pay taxes to Lord Morcant anymore. We can move to a town and mayhap I'll even find a job that is acceptive of women."

"Is that what you want, Rose? Is it right to keep that money and never tell Lord Rook about it?" Georgiana seemed troubled by Rose's decision.

"We are commoners, Georgiana, and have to do whatever it takes to survive," said Rose, tying the pouch to her belt. "I can't say I like it or that it feels right, but at least it'll keep us alive until I can figure out a plan for the rest of our lives."

CHAPTER 18

Rook felt as if he were in a living hell. His betrothed arrived yesterday, and already he despised the woman. She was constantly telling him what to do, belittling the servants, and complaining about every little thing.

Not to mention, Rook was upset with Rose because of the little stunt she pulled. It almost exposed his private encounter with her at the river. Thank goodness, Rose at least stopped Sally from saying those were his braies.

What was happening here? This should be the best time of his life and instead he felt as if he were in some kind of nightmare.

"The wedding will be next week," announced Adeline's father as they sat at the dais for the meal.

Rook's head snapped upward. "So soon? But the wedding banns were just posted."

"It doesn't matter," said the haughty Adeline, taking a sip of wine. She was still covered up from head to toe and Rook couldn't even imagine what a wedding night with her would entail. "Father will tell the priest to make two more announcements about our wedding during the week. Then we will have fulfilled the obligation. Rook, be a dear and cut some meat for me, please."

Rook didn't want to wait on the woman hand and foot. But when he saw his father staring at him, he used his eating knife to cut the meat in bite-sized pieces for his bride-to-be.

"We'll do everything necessary to have the wedding when you want it," Corbett assured the bride's father. Adeline's mother sat silently and never seemed to say much at all. Corbett's mother and sister hadn't arrived yet, and he found himself wishing they would. Rook felt as if he needed support. He really didn't want to marry this woman, but couldn't talk about it with his father.

"So, you are Rook's cousin?" Adeline asked Lark, who sat next to her.

"Aye. I am from Scotland," she told her.

"So, I've heard. The servants tell me that you have a bastard child and will never marry now that you've ruined your reputation."

"What?" asked Lark, her eyes opening wide.

"It wasn't Lark's fault," said Rook, trying to come to Lark's aid.

"Rook, I don't want her sitting at the dais. She needs to go back to Scotland before the wedding," Adeline demanded. "It's going to cause a scandal having her here at all."

"She's my cousin. She stays," said Rook.

Lark was so upset that she jumped up and ran from the room.

"Why did you have to upset her?" Rook asked his betrothed. "There was no need for that."

"Why do you expect me to live in this manor house instead of a castle?" asked Adeline, holding out her cup. "I want more wine."

Rook nodded to Sally, who was refilling the goblets of the nobles. The girl came over to pour wine for Adeline.

"I'm sorry, but I don't have a castle to offer," said Rook. "I'd think you would appreciate what I do have instead of tearing me down." This woman was trying his patience.

"My daughter will not be spoken to in such a rude manner," bellowed Lord Croiset. "Adeline, just be patient," he told the woman. "As soon as Lord Corbett Blake dies, his castle and demesne will be yours. I mean, Rook's."

Rook looked over at his father. Corbett didn't seem happy either, but said nothing to the man.

"Why is this tart refilling my goblet?" complained Adeline. "Where is your cupbearer?"

"I am still in the process of getting my manor set up, and some of the positions still haven't been filled," Rook told her. "The servants help out wherever they are needed."

"Hrmph," snorted the woman, glaring at Sally. "Well, I don't like this one. Neither do I like that gardener girl. Get rid of them both. I won't have them living in my household."

"I'm one of Lord Corbett's favorite servants," said Sally, sounding spiteful. "Besides, I'm not the one he needs to get rid of. I don't steal from him the way Rose the gardener does."

"What are you saying?" asked Adeline.

"Yes, what are you saying, Susan?" asked Rook.

"It's Sally, my lord," said Sally, becoming very frustrated. "Rose found a pouch of money and jewels in the garden that was the crazy earl's. She plans on keeping it and not even telling you about it." Sally stormed off in a huff.

"Is this true, Rook?" asked Corbett.

"Nay, I'm sure it's not," said Rook, having no idea but not wanting to get Rose in trouble. "I'll look into it later." He picked up his tankard and took a swig of ale.

"I think we should look into it right now," said Adeline.

"I agree," said her father. "Where is the girl?"

"I don't know," said Rook. "She's probably hard at work in the garden."

"Well, find her," snapped Adeline. "This kind of behavior will not be tolerated."

Rook wanted to say that the woman's behavior shouldn't be tolerated either, but because he was her betrothed and they were about to be married, he didn't think it would be a proper thing to do. Not now, anyway.

"Excuse me. I'll be right back," said Rook, happy to leave the table. He headed out to the garden to look for Rose.

Rose's workers had finished the garden for the wedding just in time. She couldn't wait to get out of here. The steward had paid her for the work, but it was much less than what they normally made or had agreed upon. Most likely, it was because her father wasn't here and the man didn't want to give more money than necessary to a woman.

While Georgiana and the others loaded up the wagon in the courtyard, Rose decided she wanted to go back to the pleasure garden one last time, thinking about how much her father liked it. She also hadn't said goodbye to Rook, but wasn't going to get that opportunity now that Lady Adeline was here. Rose's heart hurt. She couldn't stay here and watch as Rook married the woman. She wanted to go home and never come back here again.

One last time, Rose went over to the bench where she'd carved her name so many years ago. She reached out and ran her hand lovingly over the back of the bench and sat down. At least that would still be here with Rook, even if she couldn't be.

Or at least until Lady Shrew decided it wasn't good enough and got rid of it, which she surely would.

Life without Rook would seem so empty. Rose had really enjoyed the time she spent with him and never wanted it to end. She closed her eyes and lifted her face to the sun. Breathing in the sweet scent of tulips and lilies, she tried hard to embed this on her mind so she would never forget it.

Rose heard soft crying coming from the other end of the pleasure garden and opened her eyes, searching for where the sound came. "Lady Lark?" she asked, seeing the woman with her back turned, facing the tall bushes of the labyrinth, half-hidden behind the stone goddess statue of Aphrodite. Lark dabbed at her eyes with a cloth. "Are you all right?" asked Rose. She got up and walked over to comfort her.

"Oh, Rose. I didn't think anyone would be out here right now," said Lark with a sniffle.

"You're crying. What's wrong?"

"Nothing," she said, trying to fake a smile.

"You can tell me." Rose put her hand on Lark's shoulder. "I am here for you."

"Thank ye, Rose," said Lark, wiping at her eyes. "I'm just upset because my cousin's betrothed said some nasty things about me and wants me gone."

"Well, don't listen to her. She is not a nice woman. I'm sure she wants me gone, too."

"Are ye leavin'?" asked Lark, looking at the travel bag over Rose's shoulder.

"Yes, I am. Please tell Rook I said goodbye."

"Ye should tell him yerself, Rose. After all, he seems to be very fond of ye."

"Not anymore, I'm sure. I caused him trouble yesterday in front of his betrothed, but I was so angry at him for wanting to hide me away that I just couldn't help it. I guess, in a way, I had hoped we'd end up together someday."

"I wish ye would too, Rose. I like ye a lot. I dinna like that stuffy, pompous woman that he is about to marry. She is an awful person and very cruel."

"Well, looky what we got here," came a deep voice from the entrance to the labyrinth. Rose looked up to see two dirty men in tattered clothing standing there. One had a scar across his cheek and the other had his hand wrapped.

"Who are you and what are you doing here?" Rose demanded to know.

"Rose," whispered Lark. "Those are the two attackers from the forest. I can see where Raven wounded them."

"Are you sure?" whispered Rose.

"Aye. Positive."

Fear coursed through Rose but she tried to stay brave. "You don't belong here and need to leave at once," Rose told the men.

"Not until we both have a little of each of you," said the second man, lust dripping from his words.

"How did you get in here?" Rose backed up closer to Lark.

"The question is, how are you getting out of here since we're blocking the only exit?" said the other one with a raucous chuckle.

"Lark, we need to get help," whispered Rose. "I'll distract them. You try to run back to the manor."

"Nay, I willna leave ye," said Lark.

"What are we waiting for?" The men moved toward them. One of the men reached out and grabbed Lark. She screamed and fought against him.

"Let go of her!" Rose threw down her travel bag and jumped on the man's back, hitting him with her fists, trying to protect Lark.

"I've got this one," said the second man, pulling Rose off of his friend.

"Lark, run," shouted Rose, but Lark wouldn't go. She reached for her dagger attached to her belt, but the attacker hit her hand, and the blade went flying through the air. Then Lark bit the man in the arm and he shouted.

"Ow, you bitch! That hurt."

In the meantime, the second man threw Rose to the ground.

"Pull up your skirt, wench. I'm going to have my way with you."

Visions of what almost happened in the woods filled Rose's mind. It was a horrifying experience and this time Rook wasn't here to save her. The man lowered his trews and got atop Rose. He was heavy and though she fought him, she couldn't move.

Turning her head, she saw Lark's dagger within her reach. Rose was not going to let her time here at Horrabridge end this way.

She grabbed the dagger, her fingers wrapping tightly around the hilt. "You will not touch me, you filthy cur!" Without thinking about it, she raised the blade and plunged it into the man's heart. His eyes bugged out, and blood dripped from his mouth right before his lifeless body fell atop her, trapping her beneath him.

"God's eyes, what is going on?" she heard Rook as he entered the garden.

"Help me, Rook!" cried out Lark, still trying to fight off the other attacker.

From the corners of her eyes, Rose saw Rook raise his sword, stabbing the second attacker and throwing him to the ground.

"Lark, are you all right?" he asked.

"I am. Help Rose."

Rook spun around lifting his blade, then lowering it slowly when he realized the man was already dead.

"Rose," he said, pulling the man off of her and lifting her to a standing position. "God's eyes, are you all right?"

"I—I killed him," said Rose, her eyes going to the dead body at her feet. "I killed a man, Rook."

Rook held Rose tightly to his chest, never wanting to let her go. He could feel the rapid beating of her heart against him. Between that and the way her body trembled, he could tell how frightened she was.

"What's going on out here?" said Rook's father, as he, Adeline, and Adeline's father entered the pleasure garden.

"The girls were being attacked, but the men are dead now. Damn it, I should have killed these bastards the first time," grunted Rook.

"That man has a dagger in his chest, but you are holding your sword," said Lord Croiset. "Who killed that one?"

"It was the gardener girl," spat Adeline before anyone could answer. "She needs to be put to death for it. We can't allow commoners to kill people whenever they feel like it."

"What?" gasped Rose.

"I agree," said Lord Croiset. "Commoners killing anyone needs to be addressed or they'll try killing nobles if you don't stop this."

"She didn't kill anyone," said Rook, yanking the dagger from the man's chest. "I did it."

"You?" asked Lord Croiset. "How? Your dagger is still on your weapon belt."

"Aye, it was me," said Rook. "I saw Lark's dagger on the ground and used it."

"Yes. That's right," said Lark, wiping the dirt off her gown. "That is my dagger."

Rose didn't say a word.

"Oh, look," said Adeline, pointing to Rose. "There's the pouch of money she stole from my betrothed. She has the nerve to wear it right on her belt."

"Get it from her, Blake," said Adeline's father.

"Nay, this is mine," said Rose, her hand covering the pouch.

"Rose," said Rook softly. "Sally told us that you found it digging in the garden."

"Now is a fine time to finally remember her name," said Rose. "I swear, Rook, this pouch of coins and jewels was given to my father by the earl. It went missing, and Bandit dug it up in the garden. The dog must have stolen it in the first place."

Bandit ran into the garden, barking.

"Did the wench just call you Rook, not using your title?" asked Lord Croiset, looking horrified.

"She did. I heard her," said Adeline. "Rook, take back what is ours, and ban her from here. I never want to see her again."

Rook, once again, felt like he was between a hard place and a rock. He wanted to defend Rose, but he couldn't. By rights, he needed to take the money from her. She said the earl gave it to her father, but he had no proof.

"Rose, can you prove the earl gave that to your father?" asked Rook, praying somehow she could.

She was silent for a moment and then slowly shook her head.

"Nay. I cannot," she told him. "But if you trust me, then you'll know it is the truth."

"This is preposterous," snapped Adeline.

"Blake, say something to your son," Lord Croiset said to Corbett.

"This is my son's manor," Corbett told him. "The decision of how he handles it is up to him."

"Well, are you going to take the money away from the wench or not?" Adeline asked Rook.

"I am starting to doubt that you are capable of anything a nobleman of your status should do," Lord Croiset insulted him.

Rook looked back at Rose, who stared up at him with all the hope in the world in her eyes. He'd just saved her from going to the gallows by lying and saying he killed the attacker. He wanted to tell her to keep the money, but if he agreed to it with no proof it was hers, what kind of message would that give the rest of the servants or commoners? Not to mention the trouble it would cause with his betrothed and her family.

He was starting a new life now and needed to be respected by all. Unfortunately, that also included the woman to whom he'd soon be married. Damn, why was this decision so hard? If only Rose was a lady instead of a commoner, things could be so much different for him.

"Rook? Take it from her or I will do it myself," threatened Adeline.

"Rose," said Rook, his heart already breaking. "I'm sorry, but you found that money on my land. You'll have to hand it over."

"Really?" The surprise, as well as the hurt in her voice, made him wonder what she had really expected him to do. After all, he couldn't just let servants and commoners take whatever they wanted from his land and home. If he allowed that, he'd be broke in no time.

"I'll take it now," he told her, holding out his hand.

He could see Lark scowling at him from next to his father.

"I see," said Rose, yanking the bag of coins from her belt and slapping it into his palm. "I suppose you'll be wanting what your steward paid me for the gardening work back now, too?"

"Nay," said Rook, taking the pouch, feeling so choked he could barely speak. This didn't feel right at all, but it was what he was expected to do as a noble. "That is yours," he said softly.

"I'll be leaving now," said Rose as Bandit kept barking. "Were you serious when you told me to take Bandit, or was that a lie, too?"

"Nay. Take the dog. Please," said Rook, the barking making his head hurt like the devil.

"Come on, Bandit. We're going home," said Rose, heading for the entrance to the labyrinth. She stopped for a moment and turned back. "Goodbye, Lady Lark."

"I'll miss you, Rose," said Lark, raising her hand in the air.

"Thank you for hiring my father for the job, Lord Corbett," Rose continued. "I hope the work is to your liking."

"Aye. It's fine," said Corbett, seeming like he didn't know what to say.

"I don't agree that it's fine," snorted Adeline. "I mean, look at that old bench over there. That shouldn't be here. It is old and ugly. Burn the thing."

"Nay!" shouted Rook. "The bench stays."

When he looked back to where Rose was standing, she and the dog were both gone.

CHAPTER 19

A week later, Rose woke feeling as if she needed to make a change. Ever since being back home in Somerset, all she could do was think of Rook. He filled her every thought and distracted her from anything she tried to do. Then he entered her dreams as well. It was starting to become exhausting.

"Good morning," said Thomasina, stirring a pot of porridge over the fire.

Rose still shared the same small hovel with Thomasina, Phineas, and Georgiana. They were eating for now, but the money from the gardening job wasn't going to support them forever. That is why they had all gone back to work for Lord Morcant, having had no other choice. Rose and Georgina worked as kitchen maids at the castle, and Thomasina and Phineas worked in the fields. They were free tenants and shouldn't have to do this. Then again, there would be no more gardening job requests coming in since word got out that her father had died.

"Good Morning," said Rose with a yawn and a stretch, still lying on her pallet. She swore she could still smell Rook's manly scent in her bed. She'd been dreaming of Rook again last night, and that only made her heart hurt even worse.

Rook had sent a page with a missive early this week, saying he wanted to see her. She had sent the page back to tell him that she never wanted to see or speak to him ever again. After taking away her only means of support, she couldn't let him hurt her further. Nay, she decided, it was over between them and was never meant to be in the first place. They were from two different worlds and didn't belong together.

Bandit barked and licked her face, making her feel irritable. She got up and opened the door. "Out," she said, pointing her finger. The dog ran out, and she closed the door.

Georgiana opened all the shutters, letting in the sun. "It's a beautiful day for a–" She stopped in mid-sentence, but it didn't matter. Rose knew what she was going to say.

"For a wedding, right?" asked Rose, getting dressed to go work at the castle.

"Nay. That's not what I was going to say." Georgiana looked so guilty that Rose almost laughed aloud.

"It's all right, cousin. It doesn't bother me anymore. I know today is the day that Rook is getting married." Damn, it still hurt, but she didn't want anyone to know it. She needed to remain strong. Rose also felt that if she could ignore it or deny it, then mayhap someday she'd be able to get over Rook for good.

"I thought you had feelings for Lord Rook," said Thomasina, banging the wooden spoon against the edge of the pot to remove the porridge stuck on it.

"Yes, I have feelings of anger and hate, but nothing else," explained Rose.

"Really?" asked the older woman. "I could have sworn you two were in love."

"Lord Rook doesn't know what love is, just lust," said Rose, longing to have heard Rook say he loved her, but he never did. "I might have thought I loved him, but I don't anymore."

"Rose, how can you say that?" asked Georgiana.

"It's true," said Rose, trying to convince herself. "I don't have a care in the world for the man and wish I had never met him. Plus, I never want to see him again, as long as I live."

"Well, here's the porridge. Help yourself," said Thomasina with a shrug. "Phineas is waiting for me in the fields. I've got to get to work."

"I'm not hungry," said Rose. "Besides, we've got to get to the castle, Georgiana. Lord Morcant requested his meal early, before he goes to Rook's wedding."

"So, you're not going to the wedding then?" asked Thomasina, pausing at the door.

"Nay. Why would I?" asked Rose.

"I just figured you'd be making the flower arrangements for the wedding, like Lord Rook requested. After all, it is a paying job and we need the money."

"What in heaven's name are you talking about, Thomasina?" Rose had no idea what the woman meant.

"The missive," said Thomasina.

"What missive?" asked Rose.

"The one that arrived here two days ago. You were working, and I told the page to leave it on the table. He said it was a request for you and Georgiana to come to Horrabridge to make the flower arrangements for the wedding. I think he also said something about your presence at the wedding being mandatory."

"Nay, there was no missive. Did you see one, Georgiana?" asked Rose.

"I didn't."

"Oh, I should have mentioned it earlier," said Thomasina. "I'm sorry, but I've been so busy and so tired working in the fields that I totally forgot about it until you two mentioned the wedding just now."

"Thomasina, are you sure there was a missive that said that?" asked Rose once more.

Bandit barked outside the cottage and pawed at the door. Rose walked over and opened it. In the dog's mouth was a half chewed-up missive.

"Forget it. I think I found it," said Rose, taking the letter from the dog. She couldn't read much of it, and the bottom half with the signature was completely gone.

"Bandit, you are so much trouble." Rose let out a sigh.

"Are we going to the wedding, then?" asked Georgiana, sounding confused.

"Nay," said Rose. "I'm sure by now they've found someone else to do the job. Besides, how could Rook possibly think I would be willing to come and make his bride flower arrangements after the way she spoke to me? I'm not wanted there. None of us are. If we go, it'll only cause trouble."

"I'm going to work," said Thomasina, leaving the cottage.

"Rose, you can't turn down the request of a nobleman," said Georgiana.

"I surely can," she answered. "I'm not a serf, I am a free tenant."

"Still, you can't disobey a noble."

"I never read that missive, so I have an excuse," said Rose. "Besides, the last thing I want to do today is to watch the man I once loved marry another woman."

"Mayhap Rook loves you, too," said Georgiana.

"Nay, he doesn't. He might lust for me, but that is all. He never said he loved me, and if he really did, he would be marrying me today instead of that French dragon!

"Well, I think you should tell him how you really feel about him," said Georgiana.

"It's too late," said Rose. "Rook will be married today, and most likely never even think about me again. I need to live my life without him. He is a noble and I am a commoner. We don't belong together and we could never end up married, even if it was my dream for a while. It's over now. Now come on, we need to get to the castle before Lord Morcant fires us and we end up starving to death."

Rook woke up and once again wished he were dead. Today was his wedding, and he felt like he was going to the guillotine instead of the altar. Honestly, he almost wished it was the guillotine, because at least then, it would all be over. Now, his life was about to become one of torture, as soon as he married the wretched Lady Adeline.

There was a quick knock at the door, and his squire poked his head into the room. "My lord? Are you awake?" asked Harold. "Can we come in?"

"I am now. Yes, come in." Rook sat up and rubbed his aching head. He drank so much yesterday, trying to forget about Rose, that he felt as if he were still drunk.

"Cousin, you're still in bed?" Robin entered the room, followed by Rook's squire. They left the door wide open. Robin walked over and opened a shutter, letting in a stream of sunlight.

"Today is your wedding and the guests will be arriving at the church soon. You'd better get ready," said Robin.

"I don't want to go."

"Listen to yourself complain," said Robin. "You sound like a spoiled child who is pouting because he didn't get his way."

"Well, I didn't."

"You got land, a manor house, and even a bride with a

dowry so big you are set for life," said Robin. "What more could you possibly want?"

"He is in love with Rose that's why he's pouting. Right?" asked Harold, flashing a quick smile. "I mean, is that right, my lord?"

"I didn't say that," Rook answered. "And if my head didn't hurt so bad, squire, I'd reprimand you for talking to me that way." He yawned and started to dress.

"You are still smitten with the gardener girl, I agree," said Robin.

"The buzz around the kitchen is that you fell in love with a commoner, just like Lady Raven," Harold reported.

"By the way, Rook, Raven and your mother just arrived," Robin informed him.

"Great," said Rook, not wanting to see anyone today.

"Is what your squire says true?" asked Robin. "Are you really in love with the gardener? I mean, I knew you were smitten, but love? Really?"

"What does it matter?" asked Rook. He tied his trews and plopped down on a chair. The purple pouch with the coins and jewels was still there on the table. He'd never wanted to take it away from Rose, but he had been in a bind. He did it because it was what a man of his status was expected to do. It was also what his future wife demanded. Rook reached out and ran his fingers over the velvet. "Rose doesn't want me. I sent a page to her with a missive and she sent one back saying she never wanted to see or talk to me again."

"Don't feel bad about it, Rook," said Robin. "Remember, she tried to steal from you. You are better off without her."

"Oh, you mean that pouch of money?" Harold nodded at the pouch on the table.

"Yes. That's it," said Rook.

"Lady Lark told me that Rose said the earl gave it to her father and then it went missing," reported Harold.

"Yes, Lark told me that too," said Robin with a chuckle. "I don't think I could even make up such addled stories such as that."

"Rose did say that," mumbled Rook. "And as crazy as it sounds, in my heart I believe it to be true."

"Then why didn't you let her keep it?" asked Harold.

"He couldn't," said Robin. "She is only a commoner. Besides, there was no real proof."

"That's right," agreed Rook. "With no actual proof that was what really happened, I couldn't let her keep it."

"You did the right thing," said Robin. "There was nothing else you could do."

"Excuse me, my lord," said Godwin, knocking at the open door.

"What is it, Godwin?"

"Your betrothed decided she wanted the wedding here at the manor instead of at the church."

"What?" Rook's head popped up. "Weddings are required to take place at the church."

"Her father has already sent word to the priest. They are going to put a note on the door telling the guests to come here instead."

"I no longer care. We can have it in a gong-pit, it doesn't matter," said Rook, playing with the strings on the pouch, figuring it no longer mattered where he meet his doom.

"Oh, I see you found one of the earl's money bags," said Godwin, glancing down at the table.

Rook's heart jumped. "Come in, Godwin," he said, standing up with the pouch in his hand. "Are you saying this was the Earl Clive's?"

"Yes. Yes, I'm sure of it," said the steward, cocking his head to inspect it.

"You'd be willing to verify that in front of others?"

"Of course."

"You are not mistaken?"

"Nay, my lord. I am certain. Actually, most of the earl's money pouches were black or green. Except for the one he gave the master gardener, Oliver Ashdown. I remember that day distinctly. The earl made me hand sew that pouch out of the purple curtains that hang around his bed because he said that the gardener's young daughter told him she liked the color purple." The steward walked over to the bed, reaching down and pulling up the bottom of one of the bed curtains. "See? I added black velvet here to cover the hole. No one ever noticed." He showed them and dropped the bed curtain to the floor again.

"God's eyes, Rose was telling the truth," said Rook, staring at the pouch in his hand. "We have proof now. Godwin, tell me, did the pouch go missing?"

"Yes," said Godwin. "Actually, Oliver told me it had been stolen, but I had to promise never to tell the earl or even his daughter. I guess the money was Rose's future, and Oliver felt terrible about it. He had been careless and thought it was his fault it went missing. Plus, he didn't want to cause trouble by mentioning it to the earl."

"Bandit stole it!" Rook dropped the pouch to the table and jumped to his feet. "Rose was right. God's eyes, I've been such a fool," said Rook.

"Will there be anything else, my lord?" asked Godwin.

"Nay. Thank you."

Rook hurriedly dressed, a million thoughts swarming in his head. His entire life would be determined by what he did next.

"I know that look in your eyes," said Robin. "You are going to do something stupid, aren't you?"

"Not stupid," said Rook. "Just something that I should have done long ago."

"Did you want me to help you dress for your wedding, my lord?" asked Harold.

"Nay. I have somewhere to go first." He strapped on his weapon belt and tied the pouch with the coins onto it. "Harold, get my horse. I have no time to waste."

"Wait," said Robin. "Where are you going? You are expected to be here for your wedding that is starting soon, in case you've forgotten."

"I have to tell her I love her," said Rook.

"You love Lady Adeline?" asked Robin with a fake shiver.

"Nay. I'm talking about Rose. I have to tell her I'm sorry and so many other things. Now get out of my way. We need to ride for Somerset anon."

"What about the wedding?" asked Robin. "People will be arriving and you need to be here to greet them."

"If Rose really doesn't want me, then I'll return and marry the shrew, because then, nothing in life will even matter. Cover for me while I'm gone."

"Cover for you?" gasped Robin. "I can't tell your betrothed all that!"

"Then make something up. I don't care. I won't give up Rose before I've had the chance to tell her exactly how I feel about her. I am such a fool for not having already done so."

CHAPTER 20

Rook rode up to Rose's cottage with Harold right behind him. Bandit saw him and came running, wagging his tail like crazy.

"Hello, you troublemaker," said Rook, dismounting and patting the dog on the head. The dog seemed to accept him now. "Where is Rose?"

"Lord Rook?" Thomasina came waddling toward him with a big basket of vegetables in her hands. She bowed slightly. "Why are you here? Isn't today your wedding?"

"Thomasina, it's important that I see Rose right away. Is she in the house?"

"Nay," said Thomasina. "She and Georgiana work at the castle for Lord Morcant now. That's where they are."

"Really?" said Rook, looking over at the castle in the distance. A knot formed in his stomach. He didn't want Rose working for that man. She deserved so much better. "Where at the castle is she? I'm going to see her."

"Lord Rook, are you sure that is a good idea?" asked Thomasina.

"Why not?" asked Rook. "I want to tell her that I love her. I should have told her long ago. I need to know if she loves me, too."

"Oh," said Thomasina with a frown.

"What's the matter?" he asked. "You can speak freely."

"It's just that Rose told me this morning that she didn't have a care in the world for you. She said a few other things as well."

"Like what?" asked Rook.

Thomasina shook her head. "I'd rather not say, my lord."

"Thomasina, I need to know. Please, tell me everything. It is very important. I need to find out how she feels about me."

Thomasina let out a big sigh and then continued. "Rose said she no longer loved you and that you only knew lust and not love, my lord," said the woman. "She also said that she wished she'd never had met you and that she never wanted to see you again. She's moving on with her life now."

"Oh. I see." This wasn't what Rook expected, and not at all what he wanted to hear. He retrieved the pouch of coins, running his thumb over the velvet. "Well, thank you for letting me know."

"My lord, if we're going to get back to the manor in time for your wedding, we need to hurry," said Harold.

"Aye. Of course," said Rook in deep thought, wishing things could have been different, but he supposed this was the way it had to be. There was no sense in pestering Rose if she really felt this way about him. "Thomasina, please give this to Rose and tell her that I'm sorry I didn't believe her earlier, but that I know she was telling the truth." He held up the pouch of coins.

"Is there money in there?" asked Thomasina.

"Aye, plenty of it. Plus jewels. It's hers to live on."

"Oh, my lord, I would rather not have that responsibility,"

she told him. "I need to work in the fields, and I do not want to take it with me. I would have to leave it on the table in the cottage for her, but I'm not sure how safe that would be."

Bandit barked and jumped up and down, trying to get the pouch.

"On second thought, my squire will stay here until Rose returns. I don't want that damned dog to steal it again."

"Me?" asked Harold. "I'll miss your wedding, my lord." Harold dismounted.

"You won't be missing anything of importance, I promise," said Rook, slapping the pouch into Harold's hand. "Now, don't return until you give Rose that money personally."

"Aye, my lord," said Harold, not sounding happy at all.

"Do you like porridge?" asked Thomasina. "I have a pot of it on the hearth."

"I could go for a little something to eat," said Harold, making his way to the house while Rook rode back to Horrabridge for the wedding from hell.

Rose headed back to the village on foot, just after Lord Morcant left for Rook's wedding. Georgiana was with her.

"Rose, did you really have to sell the horse to Lord Morcant?" asked Georgiana.

"We still have the plow horse," Rose told her. "There was no need to keep it since we will only be going from the castle to the village and back from now on. Besides, we needed the money."

"I suppose you're right."

"I'm glad Lord Morcant gave us the rest of the day off, because I'm feeling sad," said Rose.

"This is about Lord Rook getting married, isn't it?"

"I wonder if I was wrong about him," said Rose.

"What do you mean?"

"Well, he did send a messenger, saying he wanted to speak to me. Then, he even sent a missive asking me to come to the manor to arrange flowers."

"Rose, you said you didn't care about him, so don't feel guilty for not going."

"I only said that because I was trying to convince myself that it's true, but we both know it's not. I still love him. Now I wish I had gone to the manor to arrange flowers because at least I'd be able to see him once more."

"Rose, let him go. You said yourself that he knows lust but not love. You could never be happy with someone like that."

"Mayhap you're right. But I still miss him."

Rose pushed open the door, and the girls entered the house. Rose stopped in her tracks when she saw Harold leaning back on her pallet, fast asleep and with a half-eaten bowl of porridge next to him. Bandit was lying down with his head on Harold's lap.

"Harold?" she asked, in surprise. "What are you doing here?"

Harold's eyes sprang open. "Rose!" He jumped up, and so did the dog. When he did, something fell to the floor. Rose looked down to see the purple pouch. Coins spilled out and rolled over the floor. "Oh, I'm sorry." Harold bent down at the same time as Rose to pick up the coins.

"My pouch of coins from the earl," said Rose, picking it up to inspect it. "What are you doing with it?"

"Lord Rook and I came by earlier to give it to you."

"Rook is here?" Her heartbeat quickened. Rose stood up, looking around the room for him, but he wasn't there. "Where?"

"Nay, he's no longer here," said the squire. "You see, he left to go get married." Harold scooped up the money, shoving it back into the pouch.

"Oh," she said. "Of course. After all, it is his wedding day." She sat down on the bench at the table.

"Wait a minute," said Georgiana. "I thought Lord Rook took that away from Rose. Why is he giving it back to her now?"

"Yes. Why is he?" asked Rose.

"All right, hold on. Let me think about this," said Harold, standing up holding the pouch. Bandit whined sadly from behind him. "Lord Rook said he is sorry he didn't believe you, but now he does. Yes, that's it," said Harold, placing the pouch in front of Rose on the table. "He wants you to have the money."

"Rose, that's great," said Georgina. "That is really going to help us survive and will provide a good future."

"Yes," said Rose, fingering the pouch. "What made him change his mind?"

"The steward told him it was true. Godwin knew all about the pouch of coins," said Harold.

"So, Rook didn't believe me until he had to hear the truth from someone else?" This didn't make Rose feel happy.

"Yes. I mean no," said Harold, holding up a finger. "Lord Rook said in his heart he always knew you were telling the truth, but he did what he had to do."

"Because he's a noble and I'm a commoner." Rose sighed and stood up. "Thank you for coming, Harold. You'd better leave now so you don't miss the wedding."

"Wait. There was something else I was supposed to tell you. What was it? Think, think."

"That Lord Rook was angry with me for not coming to the castle to arrange flowers for the wedding?" asked Rose.

"Huh?" asked Harold. "Nay. Why would you say that?"

"Because he sent a missive requesting me to do so."

"No, he didn't," said Harold. "Or if he did, I don't know about it, and I am sure he would have told me."

"Well, either way, thank you for coming, Harold." Rose walked the squire to the door. Bandit followed, wagging his tail. "I still don't know why Lord Rook wasted his time coming here on his wedding day just to return a pouch of coins."

"That it!" said Harold, spinning around. "I remember what that other thing was now."

"What?" asked Rose.

"Lord Rook came himself because he wanted to tell you how he felt about you before he got married," announced Harold, seeming happy that he remembered the message.

"What do you mean?" asked Rose, curious to know more now.

"He said he wanted to tell you that he loved you and that he should have told you long ago."

"H-he loves me?" asked Rose. "Harold, are you sure that's what he said?"

"Yes. He loves you," said Harold. "He has been miserable ever since you left."

"Why?" asked Rose. "He's about to be married."

"That's why," said Harold, making a face. "He cannot stand Lady Adeline, and he doesn't want to marry her."

"He doesn't?" asked Rose, this being music to her ears.

"Nay. He's only doing it because he feels he has to. Personally, I think he came here today because if you said you loved him too, he was going to do something to stop the wedding."

"But I do love him!" shouted Rose. "I love him with all my heart and soul."

"You do?" Harold jerked backward and shook his head.

"Nay, you don't. I mean, that's not what Thomasina told Lord Rook earlier."

"What do you mean?" asked Rose. "What did Thomasina say?"

"She told Lord Rook that you told her just this morning that you wished you'd never met him and that you never want to see him again." Harold pointed back and forth with his finger as he relayed the message.

"I only said that because I was trying to convince myself I don't have feelings for him," said Rose. "He's getting married and that hurts me so much. I am miserable without him."

"Then why did you tell Thomasina that Lord Rook only knows lust and will never know love?" asked Harold.

"Dammit, she told him that, too?" spat Rose.

"Uh huh," said Harold, nodding. "That's when Lord Rook left, saying he was going to marry Lady Adeline because you didn't want him."

"That's not true!" shouted Rose. "I love him and yes, I want him. I was only trying to forget him because I didn't think we could be together. He's a noble and I'm a commoner."

"True," said Harold. "But don't forget, Lady Raven married a commoner, so mayhap Lord Rook changed his mind."

"I have to tell him," said Rose, feeling as if nothing else in the world mattered. "I have to let Rook know I love him before he goes and marries Lady Adeline."

"It might already be too late," said Harold. "After all, by now the wedding has probably started."

"Nay!" she shouted, feeling frantic and more urgency than she had ever felt in her life. "I have no way of getting there," Rose told him. "I sold my horse to Lord Morcant this morning."

"I'm a pretty fast rider. I'll get you there in no time flat," said Harold. "Come on, you'll ride with me."

They ran out to the horse and took off for Horrabridge with

Bandit barking and running behind them, following. Rose could only pray that Harold would get them there in time. Even if Rook wouldn't marry her because of who she is, she had to take the chance and tell him she loved him before he said his vows and she lost him forever.

CHAPTER 21

R ook solemnly walked out into the garden where everyone, including his bride, was waiting for him. The priest stood with his prayer book in his hand, right in the center of the archway of flowers that Rose had made for his wedding.

It was a beautiful wooden arch with ivy and other climbing flowers reaching upward and winding around. Rose had placed hidden pots of planted flowers within the arch, since cut flowers never would have lasted this long. Now, fresh roses, pansies, bluebells and peonies, and something she had called snowdrops, were woven together with greenery and trailing vines, around the entire archway. It was magical, and much too nice for this wedding.

He couldn't stop thinking about how Rose said she made this arch because she always dreamed of having one at her wedding. Damn, why couldn't he be marrying her now instead of the French dragon?

Since the wedding had been planned so quickly, only the neighboring lords and ladies had been invited, and it was just a small crowd. Lord Morcant was there, even though Rook didn't want the man at the wedding. Rose had said he was a benevolent lord, but Rook still harbored anger toward him for thinking Rose was a whore.

Rook's parents, as well as his sister and Lark, were on one side of the arch and Lady Adeline's parents and entourage on the other. Robin stood close to the arch of flowers, holding a box that contained wedding rings, waiting to give it to Rook. Rook had asked him to find rings since he was too distraught about Rose to do it.

Dressed in his normal clothes, just covered by his long, red cloak, Rook stepped up to the arch of flowers, next to Lady Adeline. He hadn't had time to change after returning from Rose's cottage. Or mayhap he did have time, but didn't care enough to do so.

"That's what you're wearing to our wedding?" the shrew asked from the side of her mouth.

"Yes," he answered, not even bothering to look at her. The glimpse he had of her was more than enough. She wore the clothes of a noble, a cloak, gloves and even a full veil covering her face. Every bit of her body was hidden, and no skin showed anywhere. Hell, he might as well be marrying a nun.

The priest cleared his throat and started the ceremony. Thunder rumbled overhead, and the sun disappeared as the sky became dark and cloudy. A storm was moving in quickly. Rook wasn't surprised. It fit his mood right now, and also the way his life was heading.

"Hurry," Lady Adeline told the priest. "I don't want to get wet."

"Then you should have kept the wedding in the church where it belongs," Rook said from the side of his mouth now.

The priest started. "Do you, Lady Adeline..." Rain started to fall lightly.

"Make it short," spat the shrew. "I'm about to get wet!"

"Yes, of course, my lady," said the priest, shaken. He quickly flipped the pages in his book, searching for his spot with his finger.

"Just ask us to say, I do," complained Adeline. "There is no time for anything else."

"Yes. Yes, whatever you want, my lady," said the priest, looking up at the sky and back down, not even using the book now. "Do you, Lady Adeline Croiset take Lord Rook Blake for your husband?"

"I do," said Lady Adeline quickly. "Go on," she told the priest. "Now, ask my betrothed."

Lightning flashed a jagged bolt through the sky and a loud crash of thunder made them all jump. "Hurry!" screamed Adeline.

The priest looked up at the sky and then blessed himself and continued with the ceremony. "Lord Rook Blake, do you take Lady Adeline Croiset for your wife?"

Thunder boomed again, and the rain started to fall in big drops now. Rook laughed, thinking how fitting this all was that this would happen on such an important day.

"Stop laughing and say your vows," snapped Adeline. "Hurry, or we're going to get wet."

"I'm not afraid of a little rain, my lady. As a matter of fact, I like the water." He found himself thinking about making love in the river with Rose. That was something he would never forget and also never have the chance to do again.

"Move this inside. Quickly," called out Adeline's father.

"Nay!" shouted Rook, stopping anyone from leaving. "This is my wedding and no one will go anywhere until I say my vows and we finish this damned wedding. Understand?" He glared at Adeline when he said it.

Rook thought he heard Bandit barking and figured it was

just his memories becoming louder in his brain. He opened his mouth to say his vows, but before he could answer, he heard Rose's sweet voice.

"Rook! Wait."

This time it sounded as if she were really right here in the garden with them. He closed his mouth and turned to look, just to make sure.

"Wait, Rook. Wait," she called out.

Rook saw Rose atop a horse with Harold. They rode right up to the arch, everyone moving to the sides to let them through. The rain started to fall faster.

"Rose?" he asked. "What are you doing here?"

"I couldn't let you get married before I told you that I love you," she shouted, loud enough for everyone to hear.

"You do?" he asked. "But I thought–"

"Forget what you heard. All that matters is what I am saying to you right now. I love you, Rook, with all my heart and soul. I love you and wish I could marry you, because that is what I want more than anything in life."

"Me too," he whispered, his eyes fastened on the woman he loved, still sitting atop the horse with his squire. Everyone was silent, waiting to see how this would unfold. "Rose, I love you, and I'm sorry I didn't say it before."

"Father, make him finish our vows," Adeline told her father, breaking the silence.

"Blake, tell your son to act like a noble and stop this nonsense," shouted Lord Croiset. "Send that commoner away. She shouldn't be here. She's going to ruin everything."

"Rook? What's going on?" asked Corbett.

"Father, I'll tell you what's happening. I'll tell everyone," said Rook, no longer caring if he was acting proper or not. All that mattered to him was to stop pretending and start living the truth. "I am not marrying Lady Adelaide because I love Rose. She is the only woman I want for my bride," said Rook.

"Adeline, not Adelaide," screeched the shrew, right before she swooned. Her father caught her before she hit the ground.

"Blake, this wedding will happen or there will be a battle between us," called out the Frenchman. "We made an alliance, and you cannot break it."

"Rook? What are you doing?" asked Corbett, coming to Rook's side.

"I'm doing what I should have done all along," Rook told him. "I'm being true to my heart."

Rook heard his father groan.

"Father, to be fair about this, I married a commoner," said Raven, standing next to her husband. Jonathon gave her a smile.

"He loves Rose, and we all like her," said Lark. "Uncle, please let Rook marry whoever he wants."

"Corbett, you can see he is in love with Rose," Rook's mother pointed out.

"Mayhap so, but we can't break the alliance," said Corbett. "Rook is my eldest son and heir. He must marry someone of his status and not marry from below the salt."

"That's right," snapped the Frenchman, helping Adeline to stand. Her mother put her arm around her as well. "We came here from France and with a huge dowry to offer. You're going to let all that go?"

"Father," said Adeline in a weak voice. "I don't want to marry him either."

"Really?" asked Lord Croiset.

"Nay," she said, pulling her veil around her as the rain continued to fall. "I want a much richer man who has a castle instead of just a small manor house. I want someone better than Lord Rook."

"How about me?" Lord Morcant stepped forward, holding out his arms as if he were making an offering of himself.

"What are you doing, Morcant?" asked Rook.

"Marry me, Lady Adeline. I'm Lord Morcant of Somerset and I need a wife."

"Do you have a castle?" asked the haughty, greedy woman.

"I have a huge castle, and I'm very rich as well."

"I do," said Adeline too quickly.

"Lords Blake and Croiset, will you be willing to break your alliance and let me marry Lady Adeline instead of Lord Rook?" asked Morcant.

"Corbett?" asked Devon, looking up at her husband.

"God's eyes, why does this keep happening to me?" complained Corbett.

"Please, Lord Blake," said Rose, as Rook helped her dismount. "Your son and I are in love. I know I am only a commoner, but I promise to do whatever it takes to make you, and Rook, and everyone accept me."

"I accept ye now," said Lark.

"Me too," said Raven.

"I'm fine with it," said Devon.

"Father, I know this isn't what you want, but it is honestly what I want and need," said Rook.

"I'm not sure the king is going to like this once he hears about it," grumbled Corbett.

"Oh, but the king likes me," said Rose. "Of course, I haven't seen him in years now, but remember, he thought highly of my father."

"Yes, that's right," said Rook. "Father, I'm sure it will be all right. I am going to marry Rose. Will you please accept it?"

"Honey?" asked Devon, reaching out and holding Corbett's hand. "I want all our children to be in love with their spouses. Just like we are in love."

"Well... I suppose," said Corbett, just as thunder boomed overhead again.

"Say your vows, hurry," Adeline commanded Lord Morcant.

"Now, now, be patient, Lady Adeline, or you're not getting that castle you want, or anything else I have to offer."

"Sorry," said Adeline, her eyes flashing back to Rook. She smiled at Morcant. "Whenever you are ready."

The priest continued with the vows.

"I do," said Morcant, just as the sky opened up and the rain started to pelt down upon them.

"Everyone, get inside," shouted Lord Croiset.

"Wait!" yelled Rook. "Anyone who wants to stay for my wedding, stay put. The rest of you are free to go."

"Rook?" Rose looked up to him with those beautiful big earthy eyes. "Do you want to wait until it's better weather?"

"Nay," he said, taking her hand and walking up to the flower archway as everyone from the French side ran into the keep.

"Morcant, are you coming?" asked Lord Croiset.

"Not yet," said Morcant. "First, I need to apologize to both Lord Rook and Rose."

"Can't it wait?" asked the Frenchman.

"Not at all."

Croiset swore in French and ran inside with the others. Corbett's family stayed in the rain, waiting for him to marry Rose.

"I'm sorry, Rose, for ever insinuating you were a whore. I know you would never do that," said Morcant. "Please forgive me."

"It's all right," she told him. "I hold nothing against you, Lord Morcant."

"Lord Rook, I'd like to apologize to you, too." Morcant looked over at Rook next.

"No hard feelings," Rook answered. "And by the way, I'd like to thank you for taking Lady Adeline off my hands so I could marry Rose."

Morcant chuckled. "Yes, that woman is a little haughty, but I like a challenge. Congratulations, you two." He shook Rook's hand and went inside.

"Rook, we're still standing here in the rain waiting," called out Raven. "Can we move this along, please?"

Rook held Rose's hand. "Go ahead, Father," he told the priest. "Marry us."

They were married right there in the garden with all of Rook's family supporting them, not to mention dripping wet by the time they were finished.

CHAPTER 22

Rose walked hand-in-hand with Rook the next morning, having spent the most amazing wedding night with Rook. She was dressed as a lady today as they headed out to the courtyard, having said their goodbyes to Lord Morcant, his new wife, and the French entourage last night. Lord Morcant had been eager to return to Somerset with his new bride and her entourage.

"Rook, I'm sorry that I don't have anything to bring to this wedding, but mayhap this will help ease the pain of losing that big dowry to Lord Morcant." Rose lifted up the purple pouch of coins and handed it to him.

"Are you sure about this?" asked Rook. "Rose, this was meant for you and your future."

"I don't need it anymore, now that I have you."

He leaned in and kissed her, holding her tightly right there in the courtyard, in front of servants and nobles alike.

"I have a surprise for you," he said.

"What is it?" she asked. "I like surprises."

"Well, to start, I want you to know that I convinced Morcant to take Sally with him to Somerset. For good."

"Really?" asked Rose with a giggle. "So Sally will be his servant now?"

"She'll be his problem now, is more like it."

"Thank you, Rook. I must admit it was hard for me when she was around since I knew what you two did together."

"Well, no more of that, I swear. Now that we are married, you are the only woman for me." He hugged her and kissed her once again.

Bandit nipped at their heels, barking.

"What's the matter, Bandit?" asked Rose.

"He is trying to get you out in the garden," said Rook.

"Really?" Rose looked at him slyly. "Is something going on, Rook?"

"I told you, I have a surprise for you. Now, let's go to the pleasure garden, please."

"The pleasure garden?" she asked in a playful, flirting manner. "What kind of pleasure will you give me there?"

"You'll see. Come on." He took her hand and they ran to the center of the labyrinth, where she stopped in surprise to find Rook's family as well as Thomasina, Phineas, and Georgiana there waiting for them.

"Surprise!" shouted Georgiana.

"Rook? Why is everyone here?" asked Rose.

"They are here because I asked them to help us celebrate our wedding."

"We did that last night," said Rose.

"My cousin likes to repeat his mistakes," jested Robin, getting an elbow to his ribs from Raven.

"Oomph," said Robin, holding his stomach. "Just jesting," he squeaked out.

"Our wedding in the rain was done in a rush," Rook told

Rose. "It was only because I didn't want to take the chance of waiting and possibly losing you."

"More than likely what you mean is that you didn't want me to change my mind," said Corbett, still sounding sore about how things played out.

"So, we're getting married again?" asked Rose. "Really?"

"We are," said Rook, nodding to the old bench that she'd carved her name on as a child. The archway of flowers had been moved and stood right in front of the bench now. All around the pleasure garden were big urns of greens and colorful blooming flowers to add to those that Rose had previously planted. The statues of the Greek gods and goddesses were cleaned and placed at various spots in the garden atop small wooden platforms. The previously empty pond in the garden was now filled with water, fish, and even frogs. Rose laughed when she saw that! The garden looked magical and beautiful, and it made her heart soar.

"It smells so wonderful in here with all these flowers," said Rose.

"And the sun is shinin' brightly today, so we willna get wet," added Lark, walking up to Rose, holding a small lace veil and a gold circlet in her hands. Raven was next to her, carrying the biggest bouquet of flowers that Rose had ever seen.

"This is for ye, Rose." Lark helped her don the veil and put the golden circlet over it to hold the veil atop her head. It made Rose feel like a queen.

"These are the clothes and veil of a lady," said Rose, feeling lucky, happy, and a bit overwhelmed. Never in her life did she think she would be dressed like this.

"You are a lady now," Devon reminded her.

"It's a courtesy title only," Corbett spoke up. "Because you are the wife of my son."

"Thank you," said Rose. "I like it. Thank you, so much."

"Here, hold these flowers while you say your vows." Raven handed her the flowers.

"They are beautiful. Rook, I am sorry I didn't come when you sent the missive requesting me to make the flower arrangements for your wedding. That was wrong of me."

"Rose, I didn't send a missive asking you to do that. I would never have put you in that position," said Rook.

"Then who did?" asked Rose.

"I did," Lark answered. "I have to admit that I didna want my cousin to marry that Frenchwoman. I figured if ye thought he asked ye to do a job, ye'd come, so I sent the missive. I kent ye two were in love and I hoped that ye'd get married."

"Thank you, Lady Lark," said Rose. "I am the luckiest girl in the world to have married into such a wonderful family. This means everything to me."

Once again, Rook and Rose were wed by the priest, but this time they sat on the bench under the archway to say their vows. Bandit lay at their feet, wanting to be a part of it.

"You may kiss the bride," said the priest as the ceremony ended.

Rook kissed Rose passionately, leaning her back so far that Rose thought she was going to fall right off the bench.

"Get rid of these flowers. They're in the way," said Rook, taking the bouquet and tossing it. Lark caught it.

"Oh, Lark, you caught the flowers," said Raven. "That means you are next to marry."

"I dinna think so," said Lark, sniffing the flowers but sounding so sad. "No one would want me. Not anymore."

"Lark, dinna talk like that, because I willna hear of it. Ye need a husband for yer daughter," came a low male voice from the entrance of the labyrinth. A Highlander stood there dressed in a billowing-sleeved leine covered by a purple and green plaid. He had long blond hair with touches of silver speckling it, especially at the temples. Around his waist was a weapon belt with the biggest sword Rose had ever seen in her life.

"Och!" Lark's mouth dropped open and she gasped.

"Who is that man?" Rose whispered to Rook.

"That is the famous Highlander, Storm MacKeefe. He is also Lark's father. He is laird and chieftain of the clan, and also my uncle," said Rook.

"Are we too late for the weddin'?" Storm asked.

"Nay, not all. Come in and join us, Uncle," said Rook with a wave of his arm.

"Hold on," said Storm, looking over his shoulder. "I found them, Wren," he called out. "They're all hidin' in here, tryin' to avoid us."

A little girl ran out of the labyrinth to join them with a dark-haired woman chasing her.

"Florie, slow down or you'll fall," called out the woman.

"That's my Aunt Wren," Rook told Rose. "And Lark's daughter, Florie."

"Florie," cried Lark. She slapped the bouquet of flowers against Robin's chest. Robin, of course, didn't want to be seen holding flowers, and he handed them off quickly to Georgiana. Lark ran to greet her daughter, scooping up the little girl and giving her a big hug.

"Mother, I missed ye," said the girl, giving Lark a kiss.

"I missed ye, too, sweetie. I am so happy ye are here."

"What about us?" asked Storm, holding out his arms. "No hugs for yer parents?"

"Of course, Father." Lark carried Florie over to Storm and greeted her parents with hugs and kisses. "I've missed ye all."

"This garden is beautiful," said Wren, taking in her surroundings.

"Rose and her family are responsible for that," Rook told them, introducing Rose to Storm and Wren.

"Oh, is this your family, Rose?" asked Wren, looking over at the others. "I'd like to meet them."

"Well, Georgiana is my cousin, but Thomasina and Phineas are my friends from my home in Somerset," Rose told them.

Rook cleared his throat. "Rose, this is your home now," he reminded her.

"Oh, that's right." Rose giggled. Then she became sad. "I am going to miss you three."

"Nay, you won't," said Rook. "Because Georgiana, Thomasina, and Phineas are going to live here, too, from now on."

"They are?" asked Rose.

"Yes," said Rook. "I spoke to Lord Morcant last night. He said that since your father bought their freedom, they are free to go. I've already asked them to be my gardeners here at the manor."

"He did," said Georgiana happily. "Lord Rook is also giving us a room in the manor, instead of making us live in the village. Two rooms, actually. Rose, I'm going to have my own room for the first time in my life."

"I have an idea," said Devon. "I think Georgiana would make a fine handmaid for Rose, now that Rose is a lady."

"Me? A handmaid to a lady?" Georgiana looked so shocked that Rose wasn't sure she wouldn't swoon.

"Oh, Georgiana, this is perfect," said Rose. "That way, we can always be together."

"I agree," said Rook. "It sounds like a perfect plan to me."

"Oh, thank you, Lord Rook," said Rose, kissing him over and over again.

"Sweetheart, you can call me Rook now that we're married," Rook reminded her. "No title is needed since you are my wife."

Bandit barked and jumped up on them. "Can Bandit stay at the manor, too?" asked Rose.

"Of course, Bandit can stay," said Rook. "He's lived here longer than me, so he's already considered part of the family." Bandit ran over and grabbed at Robin's sleeve, tugging at it, not letting go.

"Leave me alone, you mangy mutt," spat Robin.

"He wants to play," said Storm. "I'll show ye how." Storm MacKeefe started chasing the dog around the pleasure garden. Bandit let go of Robin's sleeve and ran in circles, faster than Rose had seen the dog move in years. It was one of the funniest things Rose had ever seen. And when Bandit ripped Robin's sleeve and ran around with the torn part in his mouth, Robin chased the dog and everyone got involved, laughing and having a good time.

"Rook, I am so happy," said Rose. "I never thought I'd be your wife. This is a dream come true."

"It has made me the happiest man in the world," Rook told her. "I hope you have everything you ever wanted, Rose."

"I do. The only thing that could have made it better is if my father could have been here with me."

"Well, I think I can fix that as well," said Rook.

"Rook? What are you saying?" asked Rose. "What does that mean?"

"I mean, I have made arrangements to have your parents' caskets exhumed and brought here to Horrabridge. If you agree, I thought we'd have them buried right here at the far end of the pleasure garden."

"Really, Rook?" asked Rose, so happy she could barely contain her excitement. "You can do that?"

"I can and I will, my dear," he said, kissing her once again.

"My father's dying wish was to see this garden again. He

also told me with his last breath that you were a good man, Rook, and he was more than right."

"We'll even get headstones for your parents with their names engraved in them," Rook told her. "Now, you'll never have to feel alone again. You'll be able to visit your parents' graves every time you come to the garden."

"Yes, it is perfect," agreed Rose. "My father would have loved the idea of making Horrabridge Manor his final resting place."

"You mean, Rookrose Manor," Rook corrected her.

"What?" Rose asked with a giggle.

"I've wanted to rename the manor ever since I inherited it. So, it is now going to be called Rookrose Manor, after both of us."

"I like that," said Rose, kissing her new husband once again. "Rook, I have to admit that when I first met you I really didn't like you. However, as I got to know you and discovered what a wonderful man you really are, I fell in love with you."

"I have to admit I might not have been infatuated with you from the start either, my little Primrose, but like the flower, you grew on me, too."

"I'm so glad you decided to marry me, Rook. I know it's a big risk to take, being a noble and marrying someone from below the salt."

"It was the best decision I ever made, my beautiful wife. Because of you, I believe I've changed for the better."

"Oh, you did change, and I'd like to think that I changed too," said Rose. "I am going to continue to change even more, trying to be the best wife I can be."

"You don't need to change, Rose," Rook told her. "You are perfect just the way you are, and I think I knew that from the moment I met you, but was too stubborn to admit it to myself."

"Really?" she asked. "Rook, I'll never truly be a noble. Doesn't that bother you?"

"Nay, wife, it doesn't. Not anymore. You are special to me, just like I've told you before."

"Thank you, Rook, but I really don't know anything about being a noble."

"It doesn't matter, Rose. I don't want you to be anyone other than who you really are. You are a breath of fresh air in my life, and I like it. You are truly **A Rose Among the Thorns.**"

FROM THE AUTHOR

I hope you enjoyed Rook and Rose's story and will take a moment to leave a review for me.

The garden has always been a special place for me. As many of you know, I live in the suburbs of Chicago, but have a secret garden in my yard. In that garden, amongst other many wonderful plants and magical things, is my hammock. Or my writing hammock, as I call it. In the summertime this is my office. I lay in my hammock listening to the birds, feeling the breeze and sun on my face, and breathing in the sweet scent of lilacs and other beautiful flowers. The sound of the fountain makes a soothing background and allows me to slip away into the worlds, places, and times that make up my stories that I write to share with you.

That being said, I just had to make one of my characters a gardener in my new Below the Salt series, and so Rose filled that spot.

It was uncommon for any noble to marry below their status in the medieval times. They married for alliances, not for love. But since I like to push the envelope when I write, I decided to write about places or people outside the castle too. After all, love has no bounds, and anyone can fall in love.

Be sure to read Rook's cousin Lark's story, which is next in **Love Letters for Lady Lark**. She has made some mistakes and had a hard life so far, but don't worry. She's about to find her happily ever after as well. Let me tell you, they say the pen is mightier than the sword, and you'll see how strong words can be when a scribe falls in love with a lady.

This series follows the generations of the Blake family. If you'd like to read about Corbett Blake and his wife Devon, you can find their story in **Lord of the Blade**, book 1 of my **Legacy of the Blade Series**. Be sure to read the **Legacy of the Blade Prequel**, to find out what makes Lord Corbett Blake such a hardened man. The stories of his long-lost siblings can be found in **Lady Renegade, Lord of Illusion**, and **Lady of the Mist**. Orrick, the sorcerer's story from the Legacy of the Blade Series is the last book and one of my favorites, called **Keeper of the Flame**.

Stop by and visit my **Website**. You can follow me on Amazon, **Bookbub, Goodreads, Facebook** and **Twitter**. I also have a **Private Readers' Group** on Facebook that I invite you to join.

Thank you,
Elizabeth Rose

ABOUT ELIZABETH

Elizabeth Rose is an Amazon All-Star, and bestselling, award-winning author of nearly 100 books and counting! Her first book was published back in 2000, but she has been writing stories ever since high school. She is the author of fantasy/paranormal, medieval, small town contemporary, and western romance. You'll find sexy, alpha heroes and strong, independent heroines in her books. Sometimes her heroines can even swing a sword.

Her earlier fantasy romance novels started out with her **Greek Myth Series**, inspired by the TV shows *Legendary Journeys of Hercules* and *Xena: Warrior Princess*. One of the books, **The Oracle of Delphi** was featured on the History Channel during a documentary of the Oracle. Elizabeth joins Oliver Heber Books with her **Portals of Destiny Series** which brings back characters from some of her other fantasy series, making guest appearances.

She loves adding humor to her work, because everyone needs to laugh more in life. Her **Bad Boys of Sweetwater: Tarnished Saints Series,** focuses on 12 brothers, a bunch of kids, and lots of humor. This small-town romance series was inspired by people, places, and things in her own life. The location is the lake and small town of Michigan where she grew up visiting her grandparents.

Living in the suburbs of Chicago with her husband, Elizabeth has two grown sons and one granddog – so far. A lover of nature, she can be found in the summer swinging in her 'writing hammock' in her secret garden, creating her next novel. Her secret garden is what inspired her medieval series, **Secrets of the Heart**, which of course centers around a secret garden too!

Visit elizabethrosenovels.com where you will find book trailers, sneak peeks at upcoming covers, excerpts from her books, as well as original recipes of food that her characters eat in her stories. If you'd like to sign up for her newsletter, join her private readers' group, or follow her on social media, just copy and paste the following links.

Join Elizabeth's Newsletter
Join Elizabeth's Facebook Group

Also by Elizabeth Rose

Medieval Series:

Legendary Bastards of the Crown Series

Seasons of Fortitude Series

Secrets of the Heart Series

Legacy of the Blade Series

Daughters of the Dagger Series

MadMan MacKeefe Series

Barons of the Cinque Ports Series

Holiday Knights Series

Highland Chronicles Series

Pirate Lords Series

Highland Outcasts

Medieval/Paranormal Series:

Elemental Magick Series

Greek Myth Fantasy Series

Tangled Tales Series

Portals of Destiny

Contemporary Series:

Tarnished Saints Series

Working Man Series

Western Series:

<u>Cowboys of the Old West Series</u>

And More!

Please visit http://elizabethrosenovels.com